SHE TRIED TO REMEMBER THAT MISSING HALF HOUR.

Was she losing her mind? Developing Alzheimer's? Had she suffered a stroke? Been kidnapped by aliens? She had never experienced any memory loss before. At least she didn't think she had. But how was she to know? Feeling suddenly tense, she went into the bathroom and filled the tub, thinking a warm bath might help her relax.

Later, submerged to her shoulders in lavender-scented bubbles, she closed her eyes.

A tall man dressed all in black. Deep, dark eyes that captured hers. Strong arms holding her close. A faint prick in the side of her neck. A sudden sense of warmth that permeated her whole being. . . .

Callie bolted upright with a start, water sloshing over the sides of the tub as she glanced around the room, her heart pounding as the memory of what had happened that night flooded her mind.

The man had bitten her!

Other titles available by Amanda Ashley

Published by Kensington Publishing Corp.

ENCHANT
THE NIGHT

AMANDA
ASHLEY

ZEBRA BOOKS
KENSINGTON PUBLISHING CORP.
www.kensingtonbooks.com

ZEBRA BOOKS are published by

Kensington Publishing Corp.
119 West 40th Street
New York, NY 10018

All Kensington titles, imprints, and distributed lines are available at special quantity discounts for bulk purchases for sales promotion, premiums, fund-raising, educational, or institutional use.

Special book excerpts or customized printings can also be created to fit specific needs. For details, write or phone the office of the Kensington Sales Manager: Attn.: Sales Department. Kensington Publishing Corp., 119 West 40th Street, New York, NY 10018. Phone: 1-800-221-2647.

Zebra and the Z logo Reg. U.S. Pat. & TM Off.

First Printing: September 2020

ISBN-13: 978-1-4201-5159-6
ISBN-10: 1-4201-5159-2

ISBN-13: 978-1-4201-5160-2 (eBook)
ISBN-10: 1-4201-5160-6 (eBook)

10 9 8 7 6 5 4 3 2 1

Printed in the United States of America

To my children,
grandchildren,
and
great-grandchildren.
I know you love me

But I love you more!

Prologue

Chanting softly, twelve bearded men sat around a small fire in the middle of the Dark Wood. All had taken a solemn oath to destroy the last of the Hungarian vampires. These vampires, born rather than made, were capable of breeding with human females and reproducing more of their kind, and they were considered an affront to all that was holy.

The twelve rose when the Elder Knight appeared. On this night, they had gathered under the light of a full moon to initiate the newest member of their Order. Shrouded in long, black hooded cloaks and masks, they formed a circle around the initiate and the Elder Knight.

"This is a solemn occasion," the Elder Knight intoned, and though he did not shout, his voice rang in the darkness. "Do you understand the gravity of the Oath of Allegiance you are about to make?"

The initiate bowed his head and said, "Yes."

"From this night forward, you will be known as Ricardo 42. Our laws are simple. You will never reveal the names of those gathered here, nor will you ever reveal the location of our temple in the Dark Wood.

From this night forward, your sole purpose in life will be to protect humanity from any and all supernatural creatures, even at the cost of your own life. To betray these laws is punishable by death. Will you now swear on your life to obey these laws?"

"I so swear."

The Elder Knight reached into his long, black robe and withdrew a jeweled dagger. After piercing his own palm with the dagger, he did the same to each of the Knights, and to Ricardo 42 last of all. Then, one by one, each Knight pressed his bleeding palm to that of the initiate. When it was done, the cuts in their hands vanished.

"You are now one of us, Ricardo 42."

A Knight bearing a robe came forward and presented it to the initiate, then stood back as Ricardo put it on.

A rush of wind stirred the trees and a woman in a long, gray cloak appeared, the hood pulled down low to hide her face. She placed an intricately-carved, ivory medallion around his neck. "This will alert you to the presence of Hungarian vampires." Reaching into the pocket of her robe, she withdrew a small package. "This cloak of invisibility will hide you from their sight. Use it wisely." And with that bit of advice, she vanished.

One by the one, the Knights welcomed Ricardo 42 into their midst.

And then, one by one, they disbanded, each to their own territory to seek out and destroy the last of the Hungarian vampires.

Chapter 1

Quill strolled through the shifting shadows of the night, a tall, dark-haired man shrouded in a long, black coat, unnoticed by passersby. *Mortals*, he thought, *so oblivious to the world around them*. Not only its incredible beauty, but the danger that dwelled in their midst like a hungry lion among lambs.

Times changed. Centuries rolled on. The old myths and legends lost their power. He had seen the rise and fall of nations and kings. But he remained forever the same, a solitary creature with little hope of forgiveness either in this life or the next. He had traveled the world from one end to the other. Made love to many women— but loved none of them. They had provided fleeting moments of passion in a long line of conquests that satisfied his lust as their blood fed his hunger.

He had long ago accepted that he was forever damned. With that acceptance came a measure of peace. He had not chosen this life, but bemoaning what he was, what he had to do to survive, accomplished nothing.

His needs were few and easily met. Still, after the first few hundred years, there had been times when he had grown weary of his solitary existence. It didn't happen often, but when it did, he went to ground, seeking rest and relief.

The last time he had done so, he had risen to a new generation filled with inventions and technology he had never imagined. Computers and cell phones, jet planes and drones and satellites, and a hundred other amazing devices, some that would have been viewed as witchcraft or the works of the devil in the century when he'd been born.

It was a new age, and he reveled in it. Humanity no longer believed in his kind anymore. Hiding from the world was, in some ways, easier than ever. There were so many other monsters roaming the planet—remorseless gangs that preyed upon the weak, drug dealers who sold death in pretty pills to innocent children, politicians who betrayed their country for cash and power.

All thought of the past faded as his gaze settled on a young woman emerging from the shop in front of him. She was petite and comely. A cloud of golden wheat-colored hair fell over her shoulders and down her back in a riot of waves. She radiated youth and vitality as she hurried down the street, her stiletto heels clicking on the sidewalk.

Increasing his stride, he moved up beside her and caught her arm. A few quiet words calmed her fears as he led her into a shadowy alley between two large buildings. She stared at him blankly, eyes unblinking, lips slightly parted as he caressed her cheek.

He had intended to drink deeply, but something in the depths of her midnight-blue eyes changed his mind. Muttering an oath, he drew her into his embrace, bent his head to her neck, and satisfied his most basic need.

Chapter 2

Feeling as if she was wandering in a fog, Callie Hathaway walked to her car and drove home. Plagued by an overwhelming thirst, she hurried into the kitchen and filled a glass with water. When that didn't satisfy her, she gulped down a can of root beer. It helped but only a little. Tossing the empty container into the trash, she wondered why she was so thirsty. And why the side of her neck tingled. And why she couldn't remember what had happened between the time she'd left Sally's Boutique and the moment she'd slid behind the wheel of her hot-pink VW.

Brow furrowed, she padded into the living room and sank down on the sofa, a throw pillow clutched to her chest as she tried to remember that missing half hour. Was she losing her mind? Developing Alzheimer's? Had she suffered a stroke? Been kidnapped by aliens? She had never experienced any memory loss before. At least she didn't think she had. But how was she to know? Feeling suddenly tense, she went into the bathroom and filled the tub, thinking a warm bath might help her relax.

Later, submerged to her shoulders in lavender-scented bubbles, she closed her eyes.

A tall man dressed all in black. Deep, dark eyes that captured hers. Strong arms holding her close. A faint prick in the side of her neck. A sudden sense of warmth that permeated her whole being . . .

Callie bolted upright with a start, water sloshing over the sides of the tub as she glanced around the room, her heart pounding as the memory of what had happened that night flooded her mind.

The man had bitten her!

In his lair on the other side of the city, Quill's head snapped up as the woman he had preyed upon earlier woke to the realization of what had happened to her in the alley. How was that even possible? He had wiped the memory from her mind. He frowned into the darkness. No one had ever resisted his compulsion to forget. How had this female managed to do so?

Rising, he paced the floor of his lair as he considered his options. There were really only two. He could drain her dry or he could wipe the recollection from her mind again and hope this time the memory stayed submerged.

Killing her was the best solution. He hadn't existed this long by being careless. Not only would it solve his problem, but it would allow him to taste her again, something he had been desperately wanting to do since the first crimson drop had slid over his tongue.

It had been decades since he had taken a human life to preserve his own existence. But sometimes, like now, it was necessary.

Tomorrow night, he would seek her out and do what had to be done.

* * *

Quill rose with the setting of the sun, showered and dressed, then left his lair. Opening his preternatural senses, he pinpointed the scent of the woman and followed it to a small, single-story house on a narrow street. Lights shone behind the windows. A faint breeze stirred the wind chimes on the front porch.

Veiling himself in shadow, he settled down to wait.

Hours passed. Like all predators, he had the patience of Job.

Focusing his attention on the house, he heard the woman moving from room to room, smelled the fried chicken she cooked for dinner, heard the voice of a local news anchor as he reported the events of the day. At eight, she switched to a movie channel. At ten, she fixed a cup of hot chocolate.

Shortly thereafter, she bathed and went to bed.

Thwarted, Quill stared at the front door. He was the most powerful creature on earth, yet something as flimsy as a threshold had the power to repel him.

Cursing softly, he willed himself to the next town in search of prey.

The woman had been lucky tonight, he mused. But, sooner or later, she would leave the safety of her home. And when she did, he would be waiting.

Callie woke late on Sunday morning, unsettled by the fact that she had dreamed of the dark-haired man in the long, black coat again. He had invaded her dreams the night before, too, although that one had been more like a nightmare, filled with gruesome images of bodies drained of blood and hideous eyes as red as hellfire. And always the man in the long, black coat had been there, lurking just out of sight. Who was he? And what did her dreams mean?

Recalling what had happened Friday night had kept her in the house all day Saturday. Was she going to hide inside today, too? And what was she really hiding from? Some memory that couldn't possibly be real? A dream that made no sense? Nightmares couldn't hurt you.

She lifted a hand to her neck, felt an odd tingle in her fingertips. Had he really bitten her? Or had she imagined the whole incident?

Moving to the bedroom window, she parted the curtains and glanced outside. It was a beautiful morning, the sky a clear bright blue. A lovely day for a walk, she decided. And maybe lunch at her favorite hamburger stand and an early movie.

Callie had planned to be home well before dark. Not because she was afraid, she told herself, even though she knew, deep down, that it was a lie. She *was* afraid. However, like the best laid plans, hers didn't work out. She ran into her best friend, Vivian, at the movies and when it was over, Vivian insisted on going out to dinner at Tony's Italian Restaurant. If there was one thing Callie couldn't resist, it was Tony's pasta. He made the best spaghetti and meatballs in the city, not to mention the world's best garlic bread.

"So," Vivian said, after they'd ordered, "what's new and exciting?"

"I'm exhausted. I photographed a wedding last week.

It was the biggest job I've ever had. Ten bridesmaids and ten ushers. Not to mention the parents of the bride and groom and their combined siblings, which ranged in age from five to twenty-five. Oh, and the aunts and uncles and grandparents, of course. Naturally, the bride wanted a picture with her mom and dad and then with her whole family. And the groom needed pictures of his whole family. The worst of it was, they wanted the photos taken in the park across from the church, which just happened to have swings and slides. Trying to keep all those kids corralled was impossible!"

"I don't envy you, that's for sure."

"And then there was the reception and all the usual photos—first dance, cutting the cake, throwing the bouquet. Pictures of the guests and toasts to the bride and groom. Thankfully, I don't have anything else scheduled for a while." Callie didn't really need to work, but doing so gave her a sense of purpose. Most of the time, she loved what she did, and the fact that she set her own schedule was the icing on the cake. "How are you doing?"

"Same old, same old. I'm thinking of looking for a new job."

"Really? Why?"

"My old boss is retiring and his son is taking over." Vivian shook her head. "You don't need an assistant, do you?"

"Not at the moment, sorry. Are you really going to quit?"

"Probably not." Vivian worked for Dean and Shipman, an up-and-coming software company that offered good pay and excellent benefits.

They made small talk over dinner, reminiscing about old boyfriends and all the crazy things the two of them had done in college. They'd lost touch for a while, until Viv had moved back home.

"Are you dating anyone?" Vivian asked.

"Not since Bryan." Callie had met him at a friend's wedding earlier in the year. They had dated for a couple of months. He'd been nice enough, but they'd had little in common and even though he'd been easy to get along with, he'd been as dull as dishwater. She'd felt bad when she'd broken up with him, but there had been no real chemistry between them, no sparks. She had the feeling Bryan had felt the same and was relieved when she called it quits so he wouldn't have to. "How about you?"

"I met a new guy. We've only been out a few times, but he seems really nice," she said, grinning ear to ear. "I have high hopes for Greg."

"That's great. I hope it works out." Vivian rarely had trouble meeting men. She was tall and slim, with fiery red hair and bright green eyes.

"You're awfully quiet tonight," Vivian remarked as she helped herself to another slice of garlic bread. "Something on your mind?"

Callie ran her fingertips around the rim of her glass. "Can I ask you something?"

"Well, sure, hon. What is it?"

"I had a really weird experience on Friday night."

"Oh?" Folding her arms on the table, Vivian leaned forward expectantly.

"You'll probably think I'm crazy. I think so, too, but this guy took me into an alley—"

"What? Are you all right? Did you call the police?"

"I'm fine. The thing is, I'm just not sure if it really happened. It was like some bizarre nightmare. When I got home that night, I couldn't remember what happened from the time I left Sally's to when I got into my car. It was like those stories you hear about people who've been abducted by aliens and how they lose hours of time."

"You think you were abducted?"

"No, nothing like that, but it was equally creepy." Callie lifted a hand to her neck. "I think the guy bit me."

Vivian stared at her in disbelief.

"I know, it sounds crazy."

"For sure!"

"But the more I think about it, the more I'm convinced it really happened."

Vivian leaned back in her chair, arms crossed, brow furrowed. "So, you're saying this guy, whoever he was, took you into an alley and *bit* you?"

Callie nodded, wishing she had never mentioned it. Said out loud, it sounded preposterous.

"Maybe he was a vampire," Vivian said, stifling a grin.

"That's not funny! What if he was some crazy homeless guy and he had some horrible disease?"

Vivian leaned forward again, her gaze narrowing. "Did it leave a mark?"

"No. But it kind of tingled for a while afterwards." Callie took a deep breath and blew it out in a long sigh. She never should have said anything.

Callie was reaching for the check when the oddest sensation engulfed her. Almost as if drawn by some invisible hand, she turned toward the entrance, felt a sudden chill snake down her spine when she saw the tall, dark-haired man standing in the doorway. It was him! The man who had bitten her. She was sure of it. "Vivian! Look! Over there, by the entrance! It's him!"

"Where? I don't see anyone."

Callie frowned. "But . . . but he was there a second ago. I saw him! I know I did."

Quill melted into the shadows, shaken by the peculiar sense of awareness that had passed between him and the woman when their gazes had met. Had she felt it, too?

And what the hell did it mean?

Chapter 3

At home, Callie couldn't relax. She tried to watch a movie, only to turn it off and reach for a book, which she soon put aside. A cup of hot chocolate didn't help to calm her nerves. Neither did a warm bubble bath or a lavender-scented candle.

Clad in her favorite PJs, she paced the living room floor, unable to forget or understand the odd sensation that had thrummed through her when she'd met the stranger's eyes—some weird connection she couldn't explain or deny, almost as if his soul had touched hers.

She told herself that was ridiculous. She didn't believe in psychic soul mates or love at first sight, although what she felt was far from love. The man was stalking her, and that scared her to death. What if he wanted to bite her again?

What if, as Vivian had so flippantly suggested, he really was a vampire?

She dismissed that thought out of hand, but having once considered it, it kept sneaking back in. He certainly *looked* like a vampire. Long, dark hair. Long, black coat. Hypnotic eyes.

She shook her head. Nobody believed in vampires these days, not when there were so many other, scarier, things to be afraid of.

Mentally exhausted, she stretched out on the sofa. Unable to get comfortable, she shuffled into the bedroom, slid under the covers, and closed her eyes. . . .

And he was there. A tall, broad-shouldered man with mesmerizing deep-gray eyes and thick, brown hair so dark it was almost black. A jagged white scar started at the edge of his jaw, ran down his neck, and disappeared beneath his shirt collar.

She shivered as his gaze caught and held hers, stood frozen as he glided toward her.

Callie. He whispered her name, drawing it out like a caress.

The sound of his voice did funny things in the pit of her stomach. When he extended his hand toward her, she was helpless to do anything but go to him. She whimpered when he took her in his arms.

His gaze searched her face. *Who are you?* he asked, his voice filled with a note of wonder. *What are you?*

She stared up at him, not knowing what to say.

He trailed his knuckles along her cheek and down the length of her neck, then ran his fingertips over her lips. His touch, as light as butterfly wings, sent a frisson of desire racing through her.

Callie. Just her name. A single word filled with intense longing.

When he brushed her hair aside and lowered his head to her throat, she trembled from head to foot, whether from fear or anticipation, she couldn't say. His breath was hot against her skin.

She moaned softly when he bit her, surprised by the warmth that swept through her in wave after wave of sensual pleasure. He was a stranger, and yet it felt like the most natural thing in the world to be in his arms, to press her body to his. She felt bereft when he lifted his head, would have cried his name, had she known it. Would have begged him not to stop. Tears burned her eyes when he kissed her lightly, then vanished from sight. . . .

Callie woke abruptly, her cheeks damp with tears, her whole body quivering for his touch.

Lost in thought, Quill stood outside the woman's house. He had intended to call her to him and dispose of her, but when his mind touched hers, he had discovered she was dreaming about him. It had taken little effort to merge his thoughts with hers. He didn't know what had surprised him more, the fact that she was dreaming of him—or that he soon became as aroused as she. Dream or no dream, he had never felt such desire, such intense longing for any other woman.

Moving to the back of the house, he used his preternatural powers to open the bedroom window. Though the room was dark, he saw her clearly. She slept on her side, facing him, lips slightly parted, one hand beneath her cheek, the blankets bunched around her hips.

Callie.

She stirred but didn't wake.

We need to meet.

She nodded in her sleep.

I'll be waiting for you in Hunter Park tomorrow, just after sundown. Come to me.

Who are you?

Quill. Remember, Hunter Park. Tomorrow, after sundown.

She didn't answer, but a faint smile of anticipation curved her lips.

Callie woke slowly, only to lie in bed staring up at the ceiling and listening to the melody of the wind chimes outside her window. Grandma Ava had told her that wind chimes drove away evil spirits.

Turning on her side, she frowned. She'd had the most peculiar dream, by turns unsettling and erotic. Strangest of all was the feeling that she needed to go to the park near her house tonight after sundown, though she couldn't imagine why.

Shrugging it off, she slipped out of bed and wandered into the living room. It was Monday and she didn't have anything scheduled for the day.

The morning stretched before her. Ordinarily, she would have been happy to have the time off, but not today. Today, she needed something to keep her from dwelling on the bizarre happenings of the weekend.

Shuffling into the kitchen, she fixed tea and toast for breakfast, then sat at the table, her mind replaying the dream she'd had the night before. Was he real, that strange, sexy man in the long, black coat, or just a figment of her all-too-vivid imagination? And if he did exist, who the devil was he? Maybe the Devil himself, she thought, fighting down a burst of hysterical laughter.

"Quill." His name fell from her lips. How on earth did she know that?

The rest of the day passed in a blur. She vaguely remembered making her bed, talking to Vivian on the phone, thumbing through one of her photography magazines, eating lunch. But always in the back of her mind was the memory of her dream and the sound of a man's voice in her head, calling her name, telling her to meet him in the park after sundown.

She was becoming obsessed, she thought. Obsessed with a shadow man.

As the sun set, she pulled on a pair of jeans and a sweater, stepped into a pair of boots, and headed for Hunter Park. She told herself she must be crazy, going to meet a stranger in the park at night.

But it didn't keep her home.

Anticipation flowed through Quill as he watched the woman enter the park, a wary expression on her face as she strolled along the winding path that led to the fountain in the center. How long had it been since he had known this sense of excitement? A hundred years? Two? It pulsated through him, making him feel vital and alive again, as if he were a young man filled with the juices of life.

She was incredibly lovely, her figure slender and ripe, her skin glowing with good health.

She came to an abrupt halt when he stepped out of the shadows. Eyes wide and afraid, she stared up at him.

"Callie."

She swallowed hard, then nodded. It was him. She would recognize that deep, whiskey-smooth voice anywhere. He wasn't a figment of her imagination, after all. He was tall and broad-shouldered and exuded an air of strength and power that was frightening in its intensity. Why had she come here? Everything within her urged her to turn around and run from his presence just as fast as she could, but she seemed unable to move. She could only stand there, looking up at him, feeling small and helpless as his dark-gray eyes moved over her. Questions tumbled through her mind, but she couldn't find the courage or her voice to ask them.

A wry smile turned up one corner of his mouth. It sent a shiver of awareness down her spine as she remembered the feel of his lips on hers when he'd kissed her. It had only been a dream, she reminded herself, but it had felt so real.

She flinched when he reached for her, yet seemed incapable of resisting when he drew her into the circle of his arms. He held her lightly, his hand idly stroking up and down her back.

"You needn't be afraid," he murmured. "I won't hurt you."

At his words, all the tension drained out of her. She had no idea why she believed him, yet she was no longer frightened. Feeling as if she had come home after a long journey, she closed her eyes. A sigh escaped her lips when his tongue laved the skin beneath her ear. She clung to his shoulders when he bit her ever so gently.

He's drinking my blood.

The thought should have frightened her. Repulsed her. Instead, it filled her with a sense of peace and a familiar wave of sensual pleasure.

Her eyelids fluttered open when he lifted his head.

"Meet me here again tomorrow night, my sweet Callie," he whispered, his breath warm against her ear.

And then, between one heartbeat and the next, he was gone.

Callie glanced around the park, but there was no sign of him. How had he disappeared so quickly? She lifted a hand to her neck. If not for the faint tingling where he had bitten her, she would have sworn she'd imagined the whole thing.

Lost in thought, she turned and headed for home.

Curled up in the easy chair beside the small, brick fireplace, Callie tried to make sense of everything that had happened earlier, but to no avail. Feeling suddenly weary, she closed her eyes, felt her body go limp as long-forgotten memories of her childhood paraded through her mind.

Things like her paternal grandmother, Martha, telling six-year-old Callie that her parents had been killed in an auto accident and that she would be going to live with her maternal grandmother, Ava.

Grandfather Henry refusing to hold her or let her visit them because she was left-handed and he believed that was a sure sign of a changeling child. He claimed her presence in their house would cause some terrible catastrophe. Callie had never seen her paternal grand-parents again.

Her maternal grandmother, Ava Langley, making a mystical sign of some kind over Callie each night before she went to sleep. Ava and three of her cronies had performed strange rituals in the light of a full moon. Sometimes Callie had been included; sometimes she watched in secret from her bedroom window. She had vague memories of Ava whispering in her ear that she would understand everything when she was older.

Callie had grown up firmly believing that Grand-mother Ava was a witch, even though Ava had adamantly denied it. Callie continued to believe it until she went to high school and discovered boys were far more interest-ing than four old ladies behaving strangely whenever the moon was full. College courses had convinced her that there were no such things as witches or warlocks or magic spells and that everything could be explained logically and scientifically if one only took the time to think it through.

She had been eight or nine when she'd tried to per-form one of Ava's spells, but instead of turning water to hot chocolate, she had started a fire that had burned her grandmother's garage to the ground and scorched the backyard fence. That was the last time Callie had tried her hand at magic. Funny how she had forgotten about that until now.

Grandma Ava had passed away in her sleep at the ripe old age of a hundred and six. Callie had been on holiday in France at the time. When she'd returned home, she'd discovered that Ava had left her only heir a tidy nest egg and the house she had grown up in.

Yawning, Callie stretched her arms over her head,

wondering what had made her think of those things now. Too tired to care, she took a quick shower and went to bed.

She was on the verge of sleep when she heard Grandmother Ava's voice whisper in the back of her mind.

Be careful, Callie. You're on dangerous ground.

Chapter 4

Quill strolled through the park's winding paths long after Callie had gone home, his thoughts unsettled. Not all blood tasted the same. Most was warm and bland. Some people's blood was more satisfying than others'. Some was sweet, some bitter. And then there was Callie's blood—hot and rich and oddly familiar. Though he couldn't say why. Perhaps he had fed on one of her kinfolk. There was usually a strong similarity in taste among close relatives.

He was still puzzling over it when he realized he was being followed. Coming to an abrupt halt, he whirled around to confront his stalker but saw no one. And still the feeling persisted. Lifting his head, he opened his preternatural senses, searching the night for the source of his discontent.

He was about to continue on his way when a slight movement caught his eye. As he turned toward it, three men materialized from beneath a cloak of invisibility and rushed toward him brandishing wooden stakes and wicked-looking blades.

Before he could vanish, the Knights were on him. He let out a roar of pain and anger as a sharp stake drove deep into his chest, barely missing his heart. His attacker withdrew it and struck again—and again missed the mark. And all the while, the other two were slicing and stabbing.

The scent of blood—his and theirs—filled the night air.

Quill managed to break the neck of the man with the stake, but the other two were unrelenting. His injuries usually healed immediately but wounds inflicted by pure silver took longer to stop bleeding and longer to heal, and left nasty scars.

One of his attackers let out a holler, and two more Knights emerged from another cloak and joined the fray.

Weakened by the loss of so much blood and in agony from the cuts inflicted by their blades, Quill felt his strength fading. It took all his remaining energy to break the neck of one of the men holding him down.

"His head!" cried one of the Knights. "We have to take his head!"

Quill bucked violently as one of them produced a wicked-looking cleaver. The Knight was about to deliver the killing blow when a deep voice shouted, "Here now! What the hell's going on?"

The Knights attacking Quill ducked under their invisibility cloaks and were lost from sight.

The jogger stared wide-eyed at the place where the three men had been. Stared at the bodies sprawled on the ground near Quill, then turned on his heel and bolted toward one of the park exits.

Needing blood and needing it quick, Quill tried to go after him, but the pain was too severe. Dragging himself into the shadows, he closed his eyes, and found his link to Callie.

Come to the park. I need you.

* * *

On the brink of sleep, Callie jackknifed into a sitting position when she heard Quill's voice in her mind.

Come to the park. I need you.

Rising, she pulled a pair of jeans and a bulky sweater over her PJs, grabbed her keys, and ran barefooted out of the house to the garage. It was late, the sky dark and cloudy, the streets deserted. She drove like one possessed, ignoring traffic signals and stop signs, tires screeching as she pulled into the parking lot.

Not bothering to shut off the engine, she ran across the grass. She didn't stop to wonder how she knew where to go as she reached one of the winding paths.

She found Quill lying on the grass in a pool of dark red blood. His shirt and pants were in shreds. Blood leaked from numerous wounds on his arms, shoulders, chest, and legs. He was so pale, so still, she was sure he was dead.

As were the two men lying nearby, their heads at odd angles.

"Blood, Callie," Quill gasped, his voice little more than a whisper. "I need your blood."

As if it was the most natural thing in the world, she knelt beside him, pushed the sleeve of her sweater up to her elbow, and offered him her arm.

She flinched when his fangs pierced her skin. He seemed to drink forever, but, in reality she knew it was only a minute or so. He still looked like death warmed over when he finished, even though his skin had regained a little color and his wounds had stopped bleeding.

Releasing her arm, he said, "Help me up."

It was no easy task. He was a big man, but eventually she got him to his feet. He leaned heavily on her as they made their way toward her car.

When she opened the door for him, he practically fell into the passenger seat.

After sliding behind the wheel, she stared at him a moment. She couldn't deny it any longer. Vivian had been right. Quill *was* a vampire. Was that why he had such power over her? And why he was still alive when any other man would have bled to death from the numerous injuries he had sustained? Had he killed those two men in the park while defending himself? The answer seemed obvious.

So many questions, she thought, as she turned the car around and headed toward home. If he survived, would he give her the answers?

Callie had no idea how she got him into the house and down the hall into the guest room. With a great deal of effort, she managed to strip off the bedspread before he fell back on the mattress like a dead man, leaving her to wonder how she would explain his body in her house if he really should die. She had no idea where he lived, didn't know anything about him except his name, didn't know if Quill was his given name or his surname.

She considered trying to undress him and decided against it. If he died, she really didn't want to explain why he was in her house in his underwear, covered in dried blood from head to foot.

Maybe he *was* dead. He didn't seem to be breathing. Moving cautiously, she pressed her fingertips to the pulse in his throat, let out a squeal when his hand closed on hers in an iron grip.

He looked up at her through narrowed eyes shot with red. Recognition flickered in their depths, and he released her hand. His eyelids fluttered closed.

She darted away from the edge of the bed, turned and left the room. If he lived, she would deal with him in the morning.

And if he died . . . ? She didn't even want to think about that.

In her bedroom, she pulled off her jeans and sweater and crawled under the covers, only to lie there, staring up at the ceiling while a multitude of questions chased themselves around and around like hamsters on a wheel.

Callie was on the brink of sleep when she remembered her grandmother's words from the night before. *Be careful, Callie. You're on dangerous ground.*

Had Ava been warning her against Quill himself, or the danger that surrounded him?

With a shake of her head, she flopped onto her stomach and closed her eyes. There was no way in the world Ava could have known Callie would ever meet someone like Quill.

No way at all.

Callie's eyes felt gritty from lack of sleep when she woke in the morning. Her first thought was for the stranger in the guest room. Tiptoeing down the hall, she opened the door a crack and peeked inside. From what she could see, he hadn't moved a muscle since last night.

Heart pounding with trepidation, she crept into the

room. She started to reach out to touch him when she remembered how he had reacted the night before. Taking a deep breath, she placed her fingertips on the pulse in his neck.

He didn't grab her this time. Instead, he turned his head to look up at her, his eyes dark with pain.

"You killed those two men, didn't you?"

He nodded.

"Did you know them?"

"No." But he had known who they were.

Callie worried her lower lip. Why had those men attacked him? And what had they used to inflict so much damage? She couldn't shake the feeling that any other man would have died from his injuries. "Can I get you anything?" she asked.

His gaze slammed into hers.

Callie swallowed hard, afraid she knew exactly what he wanted.

He smiled faintly as he reached for her arm.

She turned away as he bit into her wrist. It had hurt last night. But today the feeling was oddly sensual when it should have been painful and repellant. He drank from her as if it were the most natural thing in the world.

And she let him.

After taking only a few swallows, he closed his eyes and released her arm.

Callie stared down at him a moment, then hurried out of the room. After quietly closing the door behind her, she returned to her own room. Feeling a sudden need to get out of the house, she changed out of her night-gown and into a pair of jeans and a sweater, grabbed her wallet and her keys and left the house.

After getting into her car, she drove aimlessly up one

street and down the other. Seeing a market ahead, she stopped and bought a quart of milk, a loaf of bread, and a bunch of bananas. It felt odd to be doing something so normal.

When she pulled out of the parking lot twenty minutes later, the realization of what she was doing sizzled through her like a bolt of lightning.

She was hiding a vampire in her house.

And he was feeding on her.

Later that afternoon, Callie spent several hours going over the photographs she had taken at the Nelson wedding before putting together a set of digital proofs. She felt a wave of pride when she finished. It had been a long shoot. She had photographed the bride while she got ready, the bride and her bridesmaids, the groom and his ushers. The wedding itself, of course. Then the family at the park. And, lastly, the reception. Counting the engagement photos and the ones taken at the reception, she had taken close to three hundred pictures.

After uploading the proofs to a password-protected website, she emailed the password to the bride.

Rising, she stretched her back and shoulders, and went through the clutter on her desk, tossing old store receipts and out-of-date coupons. She made sure her cameras were in working order before putting them away, then wandered around the room. She was stalling, she thought, reluctant to enter the guest room again, even as she wondered how her guest was doing.

Her guest. Hah. Some guest. The man was a vampire.

A vampire! How was that even possible in this day

and age? Or in any age? Should she call someone? Ghostbusters? An exorcist? The police? Who would believe her? Still, if they could see him lying there, unmoving and covered in blood, how could there be any doubt about what he was?

Gathering her courage, she tiptoed down the hall and peered into the room. She watched him for a few moments, then quietly closed the door.

In the kitchen, she made a turkey sandwich and carried it into the living room, then turned on the TV. She was flipping through the channels when one of the stations broke in with the news that two dead bodies had been found in Hunter Park, accompanied by a warning to avoid the area until further notice.

It was the top story on the news that night, as well.

And none of it seemed real.

The next two days didn't seem real, either. The vampire remained on his back in bed, unmoving. It was totally bizarre, knowing he was in her guest room. She wasn't afraid of him, exactly. After all, he had never hurt her and he didn't seem particularly menacing while he was just lying there like a . . . a dead man. She couldn't even tell if he was breathing. What would happen if and when he woke up was something she didn't even want to think about.

There was a strange aura hovering over her house. She noticed that the birds who usually visited the feeder in the backyard stayed away. Her neighbor's Siamese cat stopped using her flowerbed as his outhouse. Except for the mailman, everyone who passed by walked on the other side of the street. It was almost as if her house was invisible. Sometimes she felt like Sleeping Beauty, living in limbo while she waited for the prince to free her.

And late each night, her guest drank a little of her blood.

Thursday morning, Callie woke early. She dressed quickly, wolfed down her breakfast, and left the house, certain that if she didn't get out and see other people, she would lose her mind. She drove to the mall, thinking there was no other place where she would be surrounded by so many people. After leaving her car in the parking garage, she took the escalator up to the food court, where she ordered a hazelnut latte, then found a vacant table and sat down. It felt good to be in the midst of so many normal people doing ordinary things when her life was anything but normal.

What would happen if she told Vivian that she'd been right, that the man who had bitten her really *was* a vampire? Would her friend laugh again and tell Callie she was crazy? Insist she call the police? Or demand to see him herself? None of those options sounded appealing.

What if he got better and refused to leave? Who did you call to evict a vampire?

After finishing her latte, Callie strolled through the mall. She paused at a bookstore, then went inside, searching the shelves for books on vampires. Other than what she had seen in movies, she had little knowledge of the creatures. She found a remarkable number of books in the Mythology and Folklore department. Taking one from the shelf, she carried it to a chair in the corner and began to read.

According to the book, vampires were sexually appealing. Callie frowned. She couldn't argue with that. Scary as he might be, Quill was sexy as hell. They had very sharp fangs. They slept by day. Coffins seemed to be the preferred resting place. Some believed they had to sleep on their native soil.

Callie grunted softly as she remembered the vampire in *Dracula* shipping containers of his native earth to England when he left Transylvania.

It was believed the reason they couldn't be seen in mirrors was because they had no soul. They were said to be repelled by holy objects and garlic. They were hard to kill, with a stake through the heart or beheading being the preferred methods of destruction. Fire was also effective. They were virtually immortal. The Undead were also a popular character in horror movies, although they were frequently cast as romantic figures and occasionally appeared in comedies.

Callie snorted as she returned the book to the shelf. She didn't see anything remotely funny about being a vampire.

Or associating with one.

Leaving the bookstore, she returned to the food court for lunch. Later, she had her nails done, then went shopping at her favorite boutique, where she bought a blue sweater and a pair of overpriced jeans before finally, reluctantly, returning home.

"Please," she prayed as she pulled into her driveway and killed the VW's engine. "Please let him be gone."

But when she peeked into the guest room, he was still there.

Quill sat up when Callie opened the door. He sensed her distress at seeing him. No doubt she had hoped that he'd died in her absence or at least left the house. But, at the moment, this was the safest place for him. He had warded her home against any and all intruders. His wards, plus the inherent power of the threshold, would repel any unwanted visitors. Although he wasn't sure if it would repel the Knights of the Dark Wood.

She stared at him from the doorway, her expression wary.

The rapid beat of her heart, the scent of her blood, called to him. He didn't want to hurt her or frighten her. She had saved his life and for that he would be forever in her debt. He was a little surprised she hadn't called the police, although he was grateful for her restraint. It would not have ended well for the officers.

Lifting one hand, he beckoned her.

Powerless to resist, she walked slowly toward him, her whole body trembling.

"I'm not going to hurt you, Callie," he said quietly. "Please don't be afraid of me."

She recoiled when he reached for her arm.

"I'm sorry, but I need your blood."

She nodded, resigned, as he took hold of her arm and bent his head to the vein in her wrist.

As usual, he took only a little. Releasing her arm, he looked up at her. "You have questions?"

She nodded again.

"Ask them."

"What . . . what are you? Who were those men? Why did they attack you?"

"You know what I am."

"That's impossible."

A faint smile quirked his lips. "How can it be, when I'm here?"

"Maybe I'm dreaming."

He shook his head. "I come from a long line of beings. . . ."

"Beings?" Maybe he wasn't a vampire, after all. "What does that mean? Like aliens from another planet?" Even that would be preferable to what he was, she thought.

"We are a type of vampire, but we are different from most." He patted the bed beside him. "Why don't you sit down?"

Instead of doing as he suggested, she pulled a small chair from the desk in the corner and perched on the edge. He didn't miss the fact that she sat far enough away that he couldn't reach her.

"As I was saying, we are different from other vampires in that we are born this way and they are turned by others of their kind. We both must have blood to survive, but my kind can also consume human food if we wish. We both spend most of our waking hours in the dark. And although my kind can function during the day, we prefer the night."

"So that's why those men tried to kill you? Because you're a vampire?"

He nodded. "They are descendants of an ancient league of mystical knights who have dedicated their lives to destroying my kind."

"Just *your* kind?" she asked, frowning. "What about the other ones?"

"There are those who hunt them, as well."

"Are any of the other kind here?"

"Yes, a few. Most of them tend to stay in the mountains of Transylvania."

Well, that was a relief. "Are there very many of them?"

"Enough."

She looked thoughtful a moment. "Are there many like you?"

"No."

"Oh." Callie blinked at him as she tried to absorb everything he had told her.

After a moment, he said, "There is another major difference between the two types of vampires. Those who are made are inclined to kill their prey. Mine are not." Although it did happen from time to time, but he saw no need to tell her that. Nor did he mention that he had intended to kill her to silence her. His reluctance had something to do with the familiarity of her blood, though he didn't yet understand its significance.

Callie clasped her hands in her lap. She found it somewhat reassuring that he wasn't a murderer, but couldn't help asking, "If you don't kill people, then I don't understand why those knights wanted to kill you."

His gaze moved over her, lingering on the pulse throbbing in the hollow of her throat, the swell of her breasts. "Because, unlike other vampires, we can breed with mortal females. Our offspring are always male. The Knights perceive our ability to reproduce as a threat to the future of humanity."

Vampires fathering babies. Who'd have thought? A rush of heat flooded Callie's cheeks, followed by a sharp stab of alarm. Good heavens, was that why he was here? Was he looking for a woman to have his child?

And then she frowned. "Wait a minute. If your kind comes from mating with a human female, doesn't that make *you* half-human?"

"Only for a short time."

"What does that mean?"

"We are human for the first few years of our lives. Gradually, as we approach puberty, usually around the age of thirteen, our innate vampire nature takes over. Our necessity for food lessens and our need for blood grows stronger. By the time we reach our late teens, the change is complete. When we reach thirty, we stop aging physically."

She mulled that over before asking, "How old are you?"

"Thirty."

She lifted one brow. "How long have you been thirty?"

"A little over six hundred years."

Six hundred years. It was beyond her comprehension. Her grandmother had been over a hundred when she'd passed away, but that seemed young compared to Quill. Head cocked to the side, Callie looked at him as if seeing him for the first time. He was a tall, handsome, virile male who exuded sensuality and strength, something the female within her found incredibly attractive. How many women had he loved in the six centuries of his existence? How many children had he fathered?

Quill laughed softly as he read Callie's mind. He

had survived a very long time, made love to countless women, but he had never met one he wanted to spend a lifetime with. Until now. Looking at Callie, he found himself wondering for the first time what it would be like to settle down in one place, with one woman.

Chapter 5

Callie shivered under the intensity of Quill's scrutiny, her heart pounding so loudly she was sure he could hear it. What if he wanted *her* to bear his child? Lordy, the very thought stole her breath away. He was tall and dark and dangerous, his eyes hot as his gaze moved over her, lingering on her throat, her breasts, her hips.

She glanced at the door, wondering if she could outrun him, and even as the thought crossed her mind, the door closed, seemingly of its own accord. Feeling like a mouse trapped by a mountain lion, her hands gripped the arms of her chair.

"Ah, Callie," he murmured. "I do want something from you. Not what you're thinking," he assured her, amusement evident in the depths of his eyes.

"What am I thinking?"

"You're wondering how many children I've sired, and if I've chosen you to be the mother of the next one."

Callie pressed her hands to her heated cheeks as she blushed from the soles of her feet to the crown of her head. How could he possibly know that?

"To answer your question, I've never fathered a

child. But make no mistake, I would love to have one with you."

Callie swallowed hard, felt her heart skip a beat at the thought of being in his arms, in his bed, of giving birth to a vampire baby. She shook her head imperceptibly. This couldn't be happening.

He pushed off the edge of the mattress to tower over her. "Put your mind at ease, sweet Callie. All I want is a hot bath and a change of clothes."

Relief swept through her, leaving her feeling totally drained. "A . . . a bath?"

He glanced down at his blood-stained shirt and trousers. "Don't you think I need one?"

Nodding, she sprang to her feet. "I'll fill the tub right now," she said, eager to put some distance between them.

"I don't suppose you'd want to wash my back?"

A fresh wave of heat climbed up her neck and flooded her cheeks. Uttering a wordless cry, she flung open the door and made her escape. The deep, throaty sound of his laughter followed her down the hall.

Quill stared after her, his expression thoughtful. What would it be like, to make a baby with Callie? To hold her beautiful, slim body close to his and plant his seed within her? To taste and tease those sweet lips all night long, run his hands through the golden silk of her hair and over her soft, smooth flesh, to bury himself deep inside her sweetness and never let her go?

Callie paced the living room floor, trying not to imagine Quill lying naked in her bathtub. Wash his back indeed! How dare he even suggest such a thing! It was . . . was . . .

She blew out a sigh as she admitted that a small part of her found the idea very tempting.

What was wrong with her? The man was a vampire, for goodness' sake. Why wasn't she more afraid of him? Why was she still here? She could have run away any time in the last three days while he'd been recovering. So why hadn't she?

She paused as an unwanted thought crept into her mind. Was he using some kind of vampire hypnosis to keep her here against her will? Was that why she wasn't afraid of him? And if he was exerting some kind of supernatural influence on her, how was she to know? But he couldn't be keeping her here, she thought, not when she'd gone out to the mall that very day.

Needing some fresh air, she walked out the front door and stood on the porch. The night was cool and clear, the air fragrant with the scent of her neighbor's night-blooming jasmine. Feeling suddenly carefree, Callie walked down the stairs to the end of the narrow path that led to the sidewalk.

Turning left, she continued on her way. If she decided not to go back home, she could always spend a few days with Vivian. Except she'd have to go back home to get her purse and a change of clothes. And her car. And her phone.

And he would be there.

Pausing on the corner, Callie chewed on the edge of her thumbnail. She didn't have to go home. She didn't need her handbag or anything else. And Vivian would be more than happy to lend her something to wear and drive her wherever she wanted to go.

* * *

Quill reclined in the tub, arms resting on the sides, his eyes closed. The air was moist, fragrant with the scent of Callie's lavender-scented bubble bath. He smiled inwardly, amused by the turn of her thoughts. She worried that he was controlling her actions. Control was not quite the right word, he mused, though he had planted suggestions in her mind, like telling her to meet him in Hunter Park and calling her to him after the Knights attacked him. He wondered if she would decide to spend the next few days with her friend.

And if he would let her.

Callie was a block away from Vivian's house when there was a shimmer in the air and Quill appeared on the sidewalk, fully clothed, in front of her. Startled, she reeled back and would have fallen if he hadn't grabbed her arm to steady her.

"What . . . what are you doing here?" she exclaimed. "How . . . ?"

"It isn't safe for you to be out walking alone at night."

"I'm fine!" she snapped, jerking her arm from his grasp.

"Come home, Callie." His voice caressed her like dark silk. Lost in the depths of his eyes, she didn't resist when he captured her hand with his.

When he turned toward home, she fell into step beside him. They walked in silence for several blocks. Callie glanced at him surreptitiously from time to time, thinking he looked devastatingly handsome in a pair of black jeans and a pullover sweater the same shade of dark gray as his eyes. And then she frowned. "Where did you get those clothes?"

"I made a quick trip to my lair."

"Your *lair?*" Animals had lairs. People had homes.

"Where I take my rest."

"And where might that be?"

"I'm afraid that's something I never share."

"Is it nearby?"

His gaze assessed hers. "Why do you want to know?"

"You know where I live," she said with a shrug. "Turnabout is fair play, don't you think?"

"Ordinarily, yes. But in this case, it's better for both of us if that remains a mystery."

Callie mulled that over. Surely he wasn't afraid of *her?* Maybe he was worried that she might betray him if she knew. She wanted to believe that was something she would never do, but in reality, she feared that, under certain circumstances, she might tell his enemies anything they wanted to know.

Quill smiled as he followed her train of thought. The longer he knew her, the better he liked her.

"How long are you planning to stay at my house?" she asked as they turned onto her street.

"Would you like me to leave?"

She started to say yes, but the words died, unspoken. The truth was, she liked having him there. Until she met Quill, her life had been dull and predictable. Save for Vivian, she had few close friends. Most of the girls she had known in college had married or moved away.

When they reached home, Quill held the door for her, then followed her inside.

Callie went into the kitchen for a can of soda. When she returned to the living room, he was sitting on the sofa, his long legs stretched out in front of him, one arm resting along the back of the couch. His gaze met hers, a question in his eyes.

She hesitated for the space of a heartbeat, then went to sit beside him. A million butterflies took wing in the pit of her stomach when he slipped his arm around her shoulders. She looked up at him, suddenly breathless as he took the soda from her hand, placed it on the coffee table, and drew her into his embrace.

For a time, he simply held her. Not so tightly that she felt trapped. She met his gaze, wondering what secrets lay hidden in the depths of his eyes. Anticipation thrummed through every fiber of her being as he lowered his head. She had expected him to bite her, felt an unexpected thrill of excitement when his mouth claimed hers.

His lips were firm and cool, his tongue hot as it swept over her lower lip. Leaning into him, she moaned softly as he deepened the kiss. She clung to him as the world spun out of focus and there was only the two of them, mouths fused together, bodies straining to be closer as his tongue tangled with hers. When he lifted his head, she whimpered softly.

"Callie."

It took a moment for his voice, husky with longing, to penetrate the fog of desire that engulfed her.

Extricating himself from her grasp, he muttered, "Callie, we need to stop."

She looked up at him, a rush of embarrassment flooding her cheeks. Never in all her life had she behaved so wantonly with a man, let alone one who was pretty much a stranger. And certainly strange, she thought with a faint grin.

His knuckles brushed her cheek. "You are the most desirable woman I've ever known."

Did he honestly expect her to believe that? The man had lived for six centuries. He must have known literally hundreds of women. Made love to hundreds of women more beautiful and certainly more experienced than she.

Taking her hand in his, he said, "I'm a man, not a monk, sweet Callie. But I've never met anyone like you. Never wanted a woman as desperately as I want you. But passion and love are not the same thing, and I want your heart and soul before I take you to my bed."

Rising, he bowed over her hand and kissed it. "I have to go out for a while. Keep your doors locked."

"Where are you going?"

He hesitated a moment before saying, "I need to feed."

She frowned. "But . . ."

"I would rather drink from you, my sweet girl." He trailed his fingertips along the side of her neck. "But I don't want you to think of yourself as prey, because you mean so much more to me than that. Do you understand?"

She nodded, though she couldn't help feeling a twinge of jealousy at the thought of him drinking from someone else. And how sick was that?

He was still holding her hand. Heat suffused her when he turned it over and ran his tongue over her palm. "I won't be gone long," he murmured, and vanished from her sight.

He wanted her love, Callie mused as she kicked off her shoes, then padded into her bedroom. His declaration had come as a complete surprise. Just thinking about it made her smile. Slipping into her pajamas, she had to admit that falling in love with Quill wouldn't be hard at all.

Returning to the living room, Callie picked up her soda and sipped it slowly while she recalled their conversation. He was six hundred years old. He hadn't said as much, but it didn't sound like he had ever married. He'd said he had never fathered a child. She found that odd, somehow. Surely, in six hundred years he would have impregnated at least one of the many women he'd seduced, whether on purpose or by accident.

She wondered if his lair was nearby. And what it looked like. Was it dark and dreary like in the movie *Dracula*? Did it have dusty, winding staircases, and lacy cobwebs in every corner? A Renfield lurking in the shadows? A coffin filled with earth in the basement?

Had he meant it when he'd said he had never wanted another woman the way he wanted her? She still found that hard to believe. She wasn't a raving beauty, didn't possess any rare or unusual talents. She was just Callie Hathaway, she thought dryly. Vampire magnet.

The thought made her laugh so hard she almost choked on her soda.

Quill fed quickly. It was remarkably satisfying, but all the while, he wished it was Callie in his arms, Callie's sweet blood warming him. He had known her only a few days and yet, for reasons he did not understand, she had become the most important thing in his life. Her lack of fear baffled him. He knew she was afraid of what he was, but it wasn't the instinctive terror most people experienced. And he wondered again what there was about her blood that set her apart and why he couldn't recall where he had tasted something similar before.

He was on his way back to her house when he sensed the presence of one of the Knights of the Dark Wood. From what little he had learned about their secret society through the years, he knew there were always thirteen of them. With two dead, he had expected the rest to return home and initiate two more.

Apparently, he had been mistaken.

Chapter 6

The Knight known as Trey 95 paused in the shadowy darkness, one hand reaching for the silver-bladed knife at his side when the ivory medallion at his throat began to hum. Every Knight wore a similar pendant. Each one had been enchanted by a Dark Witch to alert the Knights to the presence of one or more of the Hungarian vampires.

Hatred burned like acid in his gut as he rushed forward, eager to destroy the beast who had killed two of his companions.

He had been ordered back to the Dark Wood to approve the initiation of two new Knights, but he had refused to obey. His twin brother had been one of the men the vampire had killed. He would not return to the Dark Wood until he had separated the vampire's head from his body and burned the remains. Only then would his thirst for vengeance be satisfied.

He swore a vile oath as the medallion went silent, indicating the vampire had fled the area.

"I found you once," he hissed, fingering the magical pendant at his throat. "I will not rest until I find you again. I swear it on my brother's blood."

Chapter 7

Callie lay awake long after she'd gone to bed, starting at every noise, every creak, as she replayed her conversation with Quill. He was six hundred years old. He could impregnate a human female. There were two kinds of vampires—his kind and the bloodthirsty ones who killed those they fed on. In spite of the aura of power that clung to him, he didn't seem menacing—at least not to her. She wasn't sure why he wanted to stay in her house when he had a lair of his own. Nor did she understand why she wasn't more afraid of him, of what he was. So, he didn't kill his prey. That didn't mean he wasn't capable of violence. She had seen ample proof of that in Hunter Park.

If not a child, what did he really want from her? And how was she to know if any of what he'd said was even true? For all she knew, maybe there was only one kind of vampire and he had invented the story of "his" kind in hopes of gaining her trust.

She tossed and turned all that night, and when sleep finally claimed her, she dreamed she was being chased by vampires—hideous bat-like creatures with inch-long fangs and hell-red eyes who pursued her through a dark, winding tunnel that had no end.

In the morning, Callie's first thought was for Quill. She hadn't heard him come in last night. Had he decided to return to his lair, wherever that might be? But when she tiptoed down the hall and peeked into the guest room, he was there.

Oh, Lordy, was he there! She gasped when she saw him. He was naked to the waist, the sheet covering his long legs. She couldn't help staring at him, her gaze moving over the width of his shoulders, traveling down his broad chest to a firm belly ridged with muscle. It wasn't so much the beauty of his physique that had her staring as the numerous thin white scars that crisscrossed his arms, chest, and belly. Were they *all* souvenirs of the night he had been attacked? If so, how had he ever survived?

Her gaze moved to his face. His brow was unlined, his cheekbones high and prominent, his nose a straight slash, his lips . . . she knew their contours, their taste. Even at rest, she could feel the aura of power that surrounded him.

Hoping to escape unnoticed, she took a step back, but it was too late. His gaze trapped hers, bringing a flush of heat to her cheeks and a flutter of excitement in the pit of her stomach.

He didn't say anything, and neither did she. Silence stretched between them, so thick it was almost palpable.

Heart pounding so fast she thought she might faint,

Callie moved into the room. One step. Two. And then she hesitated, waiting for some sign from Quill.

Sitting up, he swung his legs over the edge of the mattress. She was relieved to see that he had slept in his jeans.

With his gaze still on hers, he held out his arms.

It was all the invitation she needed. He gathered her close, his hand stroking her back while he rained feather-light kisses on her brow, her cheeks, the tip of her nose, before claiming her lips with his.

She stood nestled between his thighs, one hand resting over his heart, the other delving into the hair at his nape as he kissed her again and yet again. Time ceased to exist as he fell back on the mattress, drawing her down on top of him, her legs straddling his.

Holding her close, he rolled over and tucked her beneath him. She gasped as she felt the evidence of his desire, felt a rush of apprehension when she dared look at him. His gaze burned into hers, so hot she was surprised it didn't set her hair on fire. She was acutely aware of the weight of his body pressing down on hers. His musky scent enveloped her, arousing her still more.

She bit down on her lower lip, afraid to move. Afraid to breathe for fear he might read it as an invitation. *Vampire.*

He went suddenly still.

She didn't know if that was a good sign or not. She wondered again why she wasn't more afraid of him, why she was so drawn to him. Sometimes she felt as if she had been waiting for this man, this moment, her whole life.

"I should have warned you," he said, his voice gruff. "My hunger and my desire are closely entwined." His fingertips settled on the pulse throbbing rapidly in the hollow of her throat.

Now he tells me, she thought—and wondered which he wanted more, her virtue or her blood.

"I'll leave that up to you."

She swallowed hard. Then, moving ever so slowly, she offered him her arm.

"Not this time," he growled.

Before she could decide what he meant, he lowered his head to her neck. Fear shot through her, followed by a wave of intense sensual pleasure. She closed her eyes, her fingers tangling in his hair to hold him close.

He was drinking from her. It was far more sensual than having him drink from her wrist. She was floating, drifting on a crimson sea, weightless as a feather.

When she came back to earth, he was gone.

Callie sat up slowly, a little confused as to what had just happened between them. She had never expected things to get so hot and heavy, or to escalate so fast.

She lifted a hand that was none too steady to her throat. He had never taken so much before. Had she been in danger? She remembered Quill saying his kind didn't kill their prey. But there was a first time for everything, and she couldn't help feeling that she was lucky to be alive.

Quill stormed through the city's back streets, striking anything that got in his way—trees, block walls, trash cans, stop signs.

He could have killed her. The knowledge—the fear—burned through him like holy water against preternatural flesh. He had been so close to taking it all, to sheathing himself in her sweet flesh as he buried his fangs in her throat.

In his six hundred years, he had never felt such an overwhelming desire for any other woman. Why Callie? And why did her blood taste so damnably familiar?

Witch blood, he thought. It reminded him of witch blood.

Frowning, he slowed to a walk, hands shoved into his pockets.

In his long existence, he had only taken blood from one witch, and that had been over a hundred years ago. She had been a pretty young woman. He thought her to be in her mid-twenties. Later, he had learned that she was older. Much older. The sexual attraction between them had been instantaneous. They had made love that very night. He had hoped for a long-term affair but after that first encounter, she had refused to bed him again. When he'd asked why, all she'd said was that it wasn't meant to be. They had continued to spend time together for several months before he'd moved on. Funny that he remembered her so clearly when he barely remembered any of the other women he'd known.

Muttering an oath, he came to an abrupt halt. He even remembered her name. Eva something. No, not Eva. Ava. Ava, who'd had the same honey-gold hair as Callie, the same incredibly deep blue eyes.

* * *

Callie spent the morning shopping online for the best price on a camera she had seen in a magazine. After making her choice, she added a case and a couple of new lenses. When that was done, she went out to lunch. And all the while, she found herself wondering about Quill. Where was he? He tended to sleep during the day, she mused, then remembered he kept a lair somewhere. No doubt he had gone there.

She should be relieved he was out of the house, but she couldn't help wondering if she would ever see him again.

Later, needing to get her mind off Quill, she called Vivian and asked if she was in the mood to see a movie. They made plans to meet at the theater.

It felt good to get out of the house, to spend time with her best friend, and yet Quill was there, in the back of her mind, all the while.

When Callie climbed into bed later that night, she blinked back her tears, refusing to acknowledge that she missed him.

The next morning, Callie told herself she was relieved that the bed in the guest room was empty. Muttering, "Good riddance," she closed the door with an air of finality. She was well rid of him, she thought. Who needed a vampire in their house? Sure, he was sexy as hell and his kisses were more intoxicating than the finest wine, but being with him was also dangerous to her health. In the bright light of a new day, what had almost happened the day before seemed even more frightening. She had the unshakeable feeling that, had Quill possessed less self-control, he would have drained her dry. He might have regretted it when it was done, but that wouldn't have made much difference, at least not to her. She would have been just as dead.

She immersed herself in housework—stripping the sheets from the bed in the guest room as well as her own, dusting, vacuuming. When that was done, she cleaned out a cupboard and then the linen closet, refusing to admit how empty the house seemed without him, telling herself again and again that she was glad he was gone.

By sundown, her house was spotless, she had caught up on a week's worth of laundry, there were clean sheets on the beds, the windows sparkled.

She was in the kitchen, looking over her choices for dinner, when her phone rang.

Hoping it was Vivian wanting to go out for the night, she answered on the second ring. "Hello?"

"Callie."

His whiskey-smooth voice went through her like liquid fire. Feeling suddenly weak, she sank down on one of the kitchen chairs, her mouth dry, her heart pounding.

"Callie? Are you there?"

"Uh-huh."

"I'm sorry for yesterday. I almost lost control, but you can hardly blame me. You're a beautiful, desirable woman."

Callie frowned. "Are you blaming *me* for what almost happened?"

"You can't deny the attraction between us. It's not all on my side."

That was true. She hadn't made much of an effort to rebuff his advances.

"I was hoping I could take you out to dinner and apologize in person."

After what had happened the day before, she had no intention of ever seeing him again. Sexy or not, she had to remember that he was a vampire. Just being with him was dangerous in more ways than one. She opened her mouth, intending to give him a polite "No, thank you," and hang up. Instead, she heard herself saying, "I'd like that."

"What time shall I pick you up?"

"Eight?"

"See you then."

Callie stared at the phone. What on earth had possessed her to accept?

Two hours later, Callie stood in front of the full-length mirror in her bedroom. She had showered, washed and blow-dried her hair, and then tried on every dress in her closet, finally settling on a turquoise-blue sheath with a slit up the side and a pair of beige heels. She had just applied her favorite lipstick when the doorbell rang.

Taking a deep breath, she counted to ten, hoping she wouldn't live to regret her decision to see him again.

Quill whistled softly when Callie opened the door. The dress she wore outlined every delectable curve. "You look fantastic. Are you ready?"

"Just let me grab a jacket and my purse."

She didn't invite him in. He took the hint and waited outside.

"Where would you like to go?" he asked when she stepped out on the porch and closed the door behind her.

"Have you ever been to Tony's?" she asked, and then blushed, remembering who she was talking to.

"No." He grinned at her discomfort. "But I like Italian food. Shall we?"

Callie followed him down the stairs to the curb where his car—a silver Jaguar—waited. He opened the door for her, waited until she was settled before closing it. She loved her VW, but this . . . she ran her hands over the leather. It was buttery soft.

Sliding behind the wheel, he smiled at her before starting the car.

Callie searched her mind for something to say. "I've never ridden in a Jaguar before."

"It's a nice car."

Nice! The engine purred like a contented cat and ran so smoothly, she didn't even feel the bumps in the road.

At the restaurant, he pulled up in front of the valet parking sign. The valet opened her door for her. Then Quill was there, reaching for her hand. A shiver of awareness slid down her spine as his fingers closed over hers.

As they entered the restaurant, she didn't miss the fact that every female in the place turned to look at Quill with wide-eyed admiration. The waitress seated them immediately, ignoring several other couples who were ahead of them. As she handed Callie a menu, the woman leaned close to her ear, whispering, "Honey, you are one lucky lady," before sending a radiant smile in Quill's direction.

Callie looked at him, one brow raised in astonishment. "Does that happen often?"

He shrugged.

"What did you do to her?"

"Nothing."

"Is she a friend of yours? Is that why she let us go ahead of all those other people?"

"I never saw her before tonight."

Callie glanced at the tables closest to theirs. Every woman, regardless of age, was looking at Quill, some surreptitiously, others with blatant interest. "So, do females just naturally fall all over themselves around you?"

He shrugged one shoulder. "What can I say?"

Eyes narrowed, she stared at him. Was she like those other women? There was no denying that even knowing what he was, she'd been attracted to Quill almost from the beginning.

Before she could ask any more questions, the waitress returned. She placed a large basket of breadsticks on the table, then took their orders. Callie decided on her usual, spaghetti and meatballs. Quill opted for lasagna and asked for a bottle of red wine.

With a wink and a smile, the waitress left to turn in their order.

"You look upset," Quill remarked. "Is something wrong?"

"Are you using whatever it is that's attracting the attention of all these other women on me?"

"What?"

"You know what I mean," she hissed. "You're a . . .

you know. Are you using some kind of supernatural aphrodisiac to make me care for you?"

Quill scrubbed a hand over his jaw, amazed that she'd even thought such a thing. Not that he didn't have the power to control human thoughts. When he fed, he always erased the memory from his prey's mind. He had wiped the incident from Callie's memory, too, for all the good it had done. He still didn't understand why it hadn't worked. But he'd never tried to use his preternatural power to make a woman care for him.

"Is that what's bothering you? You think I've used some kind of love spell on you?" He shook his head. "Believe me, Callie, if you have any feelings for me, they're all your own."

She reached for a breadstick, her brow furrowed thoughtfully. Maybe he wasn't doing anything. He was, after all, a remarkably handsome man. If she thought so, it seemed only natural that other women would think so, too. Glancing at some of the men the other women were with, Callie couldn't blame them for staring at Quill. He was easily the best-looking guy in the place.

"Callie?"

She looked up at him, feeling foolish.

"Do you believe me?"

"I guess so."

They made small talk over dinner. It wasn't until they were in the car again that Quill brought up the subject that had been nagging at him. "Tell me about your family."

Startled, Callie stared at him. "My family? Why?"

"I'm just curious about you," he said with a negligent shrug. "About your past."

"Oh. Well . . . my parents died when I was six and I

went to live with my Grandma Ava. She's really the only family I had."

"What about your other grandparents? Didn't you ever see them?"

"No." She shifted uncomfortably, remembering how hurt she'd been when they cut her out of their life. "My Grandpa Henry thought I was a changeling because I'm left-handed. He was always looking at me strangely, as if he was waiting for me to put a curse on him or turn into some kind of . . . I don't know what. It got to be an obsession with him. After my parents died, he refused to have anything to do with me and wouldn't let Grandma Martha visit me, either. She sent me money in birthday cards and Christmas cards for a few years, and then they stopped." Callie blinked rapidly to stay her tears. "I guess she passed away."

"But you were close to your other grandparents."

Callie smiled. "Grandma Ava's husband passed away before I was born. But I loved living with her. She was so good to me, although I have to say she was a little eccentric. When I was a little girl, I was sure she was a witch."

Ava. Quill frowned. Was it a coincidence that her grandmother's name was the same as that of the witch he had known so long ago? He shot her a quick glance. "What made you think that?"

"Oh, she and her friends used to dance in the backyard on nights when the moon was full. Sometimes I watched them from my window and I could hear them chanting, though I couldn't understand the words. She used to sing and make weird signs over me at night when I went to bed. She said it would protect me, but she didn't say from what. I asked her a couple of times, but all she said was that someday I'd understand." Stifling a grin, Callie glanced at Quill. "Maybe she was protecting me from vampires."

"Maybe she was." There was no humor in his tone. Or his expression.

Callie stared at him. She had spoken the words in jest, but suddenly they didn't seem so funny.

There was an abrupt shift in the atmosphere when Quill said, "I think she *was* a witch."

An icy shiver skated down Callie's spine. "Why would you say that?"

"You said she cast a spell of protection on you."

"Yes."

"It worked."

"What do you mean?"

"That first night when I bit you, I wiped the memory from your mind. And still you remembered. There's no one living, except for my own kind and the Knights of the Dark Wood, who know of my existence. I had intended to silence you. Permanently."

Callie's eyes widened in disbelief. "You were going to . . . to *kill* me."

He didn't deny it. "But I couldn't. Now I know why. Whatever protective spell your grandmother cast on you all those years ago very likely saved your life."

She shook her head. "It isn't possible. None of this is possible."

"Whether you believe it or not, I know witches exist. I've met a few." And he was more certain now than ever that Callie's grandmother was the witch he had known decades ago. They looked the same. They tasted the same.

"Why didn't she tell me? Maybe not when I was little for fear I might tell someone else. But why she didn't she tell me later, when I was old enough to understand?"

Quill shook his head as he pulled up in front of her house. "I have no idea."

Callie stared at him. If vampires were real, then why not witches? It was all too much to take in. Vampires. Witches. Knights of the Dark Wood. What next? Were-wolves? Zombies? Little green men from Mars?

"I've got to go," Callie said, anxious to be alone with her thoughts.

"We aren't finished, you and I," he said as she opened the car door.

Heart pounding, she grabbed her handbag, stepped out of the Jaguar, and ran up the porch steps. Key in hand, she tried to unlock the door, but she was shaking so badly, she couldn't fit the key into the lock.

And then Quill was standing behind her, taking the key from her hand.

She felt his breath against her cheek as he leaned past her to open the door, the brush of his fingers against hers as he handed her the key. When she stepped over the threshold, he closed the door behind her.

She stood there a moment, his last words whispering in the back of her mind.

We aren't finished, you and I.

Suddenly weak in the knees, Callie sank down on the sofa, wondering if those last words had been a threat or a promise.

* * *

Brow furrowed, Quill left his car parked in front of Callie's house and strolled down the street. He could understand her confusion and dismay as she tried to come to terms with the fact that her grandmother had been a witch. He had met Ava over a hundred years ago. He had known when he drank from her that she was a witch. It had added a certain spice to their friendship. He had met the members of her coven, as well. Betty, Hilda, and Maxine. Being a vampire had its own kind of magic and the five of them had spent many an evening trying to out-magic each other, but Ava had clearly out-classed all of them.

What he hadn't realized until now was just how power-ful Ava had been. She had apparently known that her granddaughter would meet one of his kind. To that end, she had cast a protection spell on Callie, he mused, per-haps even before Callie had been born.

Ava had not only been a powerful witch, but she had possessed the Sight. Quill frowned. When he had made love to Ava all those years ago, had she somehow fore-seen that one day in the future, Callie would meet *him?* If so, it would explain why Ava had refused to bed him again after that first time.

Either way, he *had* met Callie—and Ava's incantation had done its job and protected her vulnerable grand-daughter from the big, bad vampire.

Or had it? Sure, he had been certain the only way to ensure that Callie kept his secret was to take her life, but once he had talked to her, found out a little about her, all he'd wanted to do was get to know her better. She was enchanting, vibrant, and beautiful. And she had a kind and generous heart. What man wouldn't want her?

For the first time since he'd met Ava, he had met a woman who intrigued him, one who had captured his heart and soul. One who knew him for what he was and hadn't run screaming from his presence.

He wasn't about to let her go without a fight.

Chapter 8

Callie met Vivian for drinks the next night. Now, sitting at a table by the back window of their favorite nightclub, she said, "I'm so glad you called." She had spent the day by turns missing Quill and grateful that she hadn't heard from him. "I really needed to get out of the house. Although I was surprised to hear from you. I thought you'd have a date with Greg, it being Sunday night and all."

"Don't mention that man to me!"

"What happened? I thought you had high hopes for him."

"I did. Until I found out he's married with two kids and one on the way!"

"Oh, Viv, I'm so sorry."

"Me, too. I really liked him." Sniffling, she reached for a napkin and wiped her eyes. "I don't know why I'm crying. He's not worth it, the lousy two-timing cheat. So, how are you?"

"Fine."

Vivian wadded up the napkin and put it aside. "What is it, hon?"

"Nothing."

"You can't fool me. I know that tone. It always means man trouble of one kind or another. So, who is it and what did he do?"

Callie shook her head. "You wouldn't believe me if I told you."

"After what I learned about Greg, I'll believe anything."

"You can't repeat a word of what I'm about to tell you. Promise me, Viv. Not a word to a soul. Not your mother. Not your priest."

"I promise."

Callie bit down on her lower lip. She hoped she wasn't putting Vivian in danger, but she had to talk to someone. "What if I told you that you were right about Quill, that he is a . . ." Callie glanced around, then leaned forward and lowered her voice. ". . . a vampire."

"Callie, really? You can't be serious."

"But I am."

"I was kidding when I suggested that."

"I know. But it's true! Not only that, but there are people hunting him. They almost killed him the other night."

"How do you know that? Good Lord!" Vivian exclaimed. "Were you there?"

"No, but he called me for help."

Looking skeptical, Vivian said, "In the movies, the vampires always heal instantly."

"Shh!" Callie glanced around again, relieved to see that no one was paying them any attention. "He told me it takes longer for them to heal when they're wounded with silver."

Vivian shook her head. "You're really buying into all this, aren't you?"

"I know how it sounds, and if the shoe were on the other foot, I probably wouldn't believe you, either. But I've been with him for the last week or so, and believe me, it's true."

Vivian looked intrigued and mortified. "Did he bite you again?"

Callie nodded, hardly aware of reaching up to touch her neck where Quill had bitten her.

The move wasn't lost on Vivian. "I don't know what to think, hon. Either you're crazy or you're telling the truth. So, where is he now?"

"I don't know. I haven't seen him today."

"That's probably for the best."

"I guess so." Callie took a deep breath. "But that's not all."

"There's more?"

"Remember in college when we were reminiscing about the crazy things we believed when we were kids?"

"You mean like angels and fairies and invisible friends?"

Callie nodded. "Do you remember when I told you I used to think my grandmother was a witch?"

Vivian laughed. "How could I forget that? You almost had me convinced."

"I think it might have been true." Quill had seemed certain of it.

Vivian looked up as a waitress paused at their table, pad in hand. "I think I'm going to need another one of these," she said, holding up her empty glass.

"And you, miss?" the waitress asked.

Callie nodded.

"So, what's he like, this vampire of yours?" Vivian whispered when the waitress left.

"See for yourself," Callie said, gesturing toward the man striding toward them. "He's here."

Startled, Vivian looked up, mouth agape, when Quill stopped beside their table.

"Good evening, Callie."

She stared at him, fear settling in the pit of her stomach. Did he know what she'd told Vivian? Had she just signed her own death warrant and put Vivian's life in danger by betraying his secret?

"We need to talk," he said, reaching for Callie's hand. "I'm sure your friend will excuse you."

Vivian nodded, her eyes wide, her face suddenly pale.

Callie knew a moment of terror as Quill's hand closed over hers. Thinking she might faint, she stumbled to her feet, murmured, "Bye, Viv," as Quill's hand tightened on hers.

Feeling like a condemned prisoner being led to the gallows, she followed him out of the club, into the darkness beyond.

"You told her, didn't you?" Quill asked, his voice tight with anger.

Mouth dry, Callie nodded.

"Why?" His dark gaze burned into hers with all the intensity of a forest fire.

Too frightened to speak, she stared at him, wishing she could call back every word. But it was too late. Would he kill her and Vivian to silence them forever?

Forcing the words past her dry throat, she begged, "Please don't hurt Vivian."

"Why, Callie?" he asked again, his voice filled with hurt at her betrayal. "Why would you tell her about me?"

"I'm sorry, but I had to talk to someone. I just couldn't keep it all bottled up inside any longer. You don't understand." Tears burned her eyes and dripped, unheeded, down her cheeks. "I don't know what to believe anymore. Not about you, not about me, or my grandmother. Sometimes I think I'm trapped in a horrible nightmare or lying in some hospital lost in a coma. Either way, I wish I could wake up."

Quill swore under his breath as he pulled her gently into his arms. Murmuring her name, he held her close. "It's all right, love. Don't worry about your friend. I won't hurt her. But I will wipe tonight's conversation from her memory." *I just hope her mind isn't as strong as yours.*

Callie looked up at him. "You promise?"

"I promise. If you need to talk about all this, talk to me. No one understands better than I do." *Or loves you more.*

"I've just been so confused."

He nodded again as he brushed his thumbs over her cheeks, wiping away her tears. "Let's get your car," he said, "and I'll take you home."

Callie couldn't help thinking he looked out of place behind the wheel of her VW. Long-legged and broad-shouldered, he reminded her of a giant driving a toy car. His presence, his nearness, brought all her senses to life.

She grew tense as he pulled out of the parking lot. He had promised not to hurt Vivian, and for that, she was grateful beyond words. If anything had happened to her friend, she never would have forgiven herself. *But what is he going to do to me?* That was the question pounding in her head as he pulled into her driveway, killed the engine, then focused all his attention on her.

She shrank back against the seat, her breath coming in hard gasps.

"Relax, Callie," he said. "I'm not going to hurt you or try to wipe your memory again."

"Why not?" she blurted, then clapped her hand to her mouth.

He laughed softly as he took her hand in his. It sent a shiver of awareness racing down her spine. His gaze moved over her face. "You must know how I feel about you."

She nodded warily.

"I've never met anyone like you. I know we got off to a bad beginning, but is there any chance we could start over and you could forget what I am and pretend I'm just a guy who wants to get to know you better?"

"I don't know."

"Will you try?"

Callie bit down on her lower lip, her gaze sliding away from his. What *did* she want? A life without him? Or a chance to get to know him better? Yes, he was a vampire, but if she put that aside, he was just a remarkably handsome man who treated her with kindness and respect. On the other hand, they couldn't have much of a future together. And the more she got to know him, the harder it would be to let him go when it was over.

She stared at his hand holding hers, felt the tension building in him as he waited for her answer.

"I'll try. I can't promise anything. But I'll try." She felt the tension drain out of him as he leaned forward and kissed her cheek.

"Are you busy tomorrow night?" he asked.

"No."

"May I call on you?"

She nodded. "What time?"

"As soon as the sun goes down. What would you like to do?"

"Dinner and dancing?"

"Nothing I would like better than a chance to hold you in my arms." He kissed her palm, sending little frissons of delight spiraling to the core of her being.

Exiting the car, he went around to open her door. He slipped his arm around her shoulders as he walked her to the porch. "May I kiss you good-night?"

Callie nodded, excitement fluttering in the pit of her stomach as his lips claimed hers in a long, slow kiss she wished would never end.

Murmuring, "Until tomorrow," he kissed her once more, lightly, then descended the stairs and disappeared into the darkness.

Callie smiled faintly, thinking there was no way to pretend Quill was just an ordinary man. But she was more than willing to try.

* * *

Quill arrived at sundown the next night looking splendid in a pair of black slacks, a gray shirt, and a thigh-length black leather jacket. He whistled when he saw her.

"Like it?" she asked, twirling around in front of him. She had spent the better part of the afternoon looking for just the right thing to wear for the evening.

"What's not to like?" Her dress was pale-blue silk with a fitted bodice and a short skirt that outlined her figure to perfection. She wore a pair of matching high heels and a sapphire bracelet. Her honey-gold hair fell in glorious waves around her shoulders. A deep breath carried the scent of her perfume and her own warm, womanly fragrance. "Ready?"

Nodding, she grabbed a long, white sweater from the back of a chair, collected her handbag, and followed him out the door. She blinked in surprise when she saw the car in the driveway. "What happened to the Jag?" she asked as he opened the door to a fire-engine-red Corvette.

"It's a clear night. I thought we'd take the convertible for a change."

"How many cars do you have?"

"Three."

"Must be nice," she muttered as he closed her door. Of course, she could buy a luxury car if she was of a mind to, but Ava had bought the pink VW as a high school graduation present for Callie. Driving it was fun and made her feel closer to her grandmother. "Where are we going?"

"The Chalet. Have you ever been there?"

"No."

"Me, either." He smiled at her. "A first for both of us."

Callie nodded, thinking she had experienced a lot of "firsts" since she'd met Quill.

The Chalet was a small, intimate restaurant. The lighting was dim, the music low.

Callie ordered shrimp and rice; Quill chose steak, very rare, a baked potato, and a bottle of cabernet.

Spreading her napkin in her lap, Callie said, "Can I ask you something?"

"Anything you want."

"How did you get that scar on your neck?"

"Oh, that." He ran the back of his forefinger over the jagged scar. "Souvenir of a nasty fight with one of the Knights of the Dark Wood."

"You told me all your injuries healed."

"They do. But wounds made with pure silver don't only hurt like hell, they tend to leave a mark," he said with a rueful grin. "I'm afraid that attack the other night left me with a few more."

More than a few, she thought.

"Anything else you'd like to know?"

"Your parents . . . are they still alive?"

"As far as I know."

"Are they both vampires?"

"Only my father."

"And your mother's still alive? How is that possible? Vampires might live for hundreds of years, but ordinary people don't."

"Perhaps one day I'll tell you."

She lifted one brow. "But not now?"

"No."

"Do they live here, in the States?"

He shook his head. "Last I heard, they were living in Australia. Sydney, I think."

"Do you see them often?"

"Often enough so that they don't forget who I am," he said, grinning.

"Were you born here?"

"No. In Savaria, Hungary. Most of our kind still live there."

"Why did your parents leave?"

"My father's got an itchy foot and doesn't like staying in any one place too long. They move every fifty years or so."

Callie mulled that over until their dinner arrived. She grimaced when she saw Quill's filet mignon. He had asked for rare, but she couldn't help thinking if the steak had been cooked a minute less, it might have stood up and walked away.

Her meal, however, was excellent, the wine a rare vintage that lingered on the tongue. They made small talk during the meal. While waiting for dessert—a rich chocolate mousse Callie had been unable to resist—she asked about Vivian.

"She's fine."

"Did you . . . ?"

"Yes. Last night, after I took you home."

"Will she remember that we were together Sunday night, or did you erase that, too?"

"She'll remember that you met and had a good time together. That's all." Seeing her frown, he said, "You don't approve?"

"No," she said flatly. "It seems wrong, messing with people's minds. You tried to make me forget what you are. What else have you made me forget?"

"Nothing, love. That was the one and only time."

She wanted to believe him, but how was she to know if he was telling her the truth?

"Trust me, Callie. Please."

It was the *please* that did it.

"Do you want a bite?" she asked, when the waitress brought her dessert.

He slid a glance at her throat.

"That's *not* what I'm offering."

"I know. More's the pity. But in answer to your question, no, thank you." He smiled as she took a taste, wondering if she wore the same look of exquisite pleasure during lovemaking. He rather enjoyed watching her. "Do you want another?" he asked when she'd licked the last trace of chocolate from the spoon.

"I'd love one, but no. Too many calories."

"Maybe we can shed a pound or two," he suggested, nodding toward the dance floor in the adjoining room.

"Good idea."

Taking her hand, he led her into the other room. The lighting was soft, the music slow. Callie felt a rush of excitement when Quill drew her into his embrace, so close she had no trouble following his lead. It was heaven, being in his arms. He was incredibly light on his feet for such a big man.

There was something magical about being in his arms. To Callie, it seemed as if they were floating over the floor. Her heart skipped a beat when she looked up to find him gazing down at her, his eyes smoky with desire.

The first song blended seamlessly into another ballad. Drawing her closer, he brushed a kiss across her lips.

Callie closed her eyes when he kissed her again, longer

this time. She leaned into him, her insides quivering at his touch.

The room fell away, the music faded, and there was only Quill, his mouth moving over hers, trailing fire. She felt the warmth of his tongue against her neck. *He's biting me,* she thought, but it didn't matter, not when it felt so good to be in his arms.

When the song ended, he took her hand and they returned to their table.

"Callie?"

"Hmm?"

"Are you all right?"

She nodded.

"I'm sorry," he murmured. He had asked if they could start over, if she could pretend he was just an ordinary man, but how was she to do that if he couldn't resist tasting her?

"Don't be." She might regret it later, she thought, but not now, when she could still feel the pleasure of his bite.

He took her home a short time later.

Callie felt a flutter of excitement as she unlocked her door. Would he kiss her good-night? Should she invite him in? Would he misinterpret it if she did?

He solved the dilemma for her. "Thank you for this evening," he murmured. His kiss, when it came, made her toes curl. "I'll call you tomorrow."

Callie nodded, then stood there, watching him stride down the stairs and slide behind the wheel of the Corvette.

She could try to pretend Quill was just an ordinary guy, she thought as he backed the convertible out of the driveway. But nothing about him was the least bit ordinary. She ran her fingertips over her lips. Least of all, his kisses.

Smiling, she went inside to get ready for bed. If she was lucky, Callie thought as she crawled under the covers, she just might dream about her shadow man again.

Chapter 9

That night, Callie's dreams were oddly disjointed. Sometimes Grandma Ava was there, looking as young and pretty as she had when Callie was a child, her long golden hair whipping in the wind, her calico skirt swirling around her ankles as she danced outside under a full moon, an ebony wand in her hand. At other times, Ava was locked in Quill's embrace as he bent over her neck, his fangs extended, eyes as red as blood.

In one instance, Ava's gaze met Callie's and she distinctly heard her grandmother's voice, again admonishing her that she was in danger. And then, in a bizarre twist, Callie and her grandmother became one.

Just before she woke up, Quill came to her, his presence so vital, his touch so intoxicating, she was certain he was really there, in her bed, holding her close, his hands learning the contours of her body while he rained kisses over her brow, her cheeks, the curve of her throat.

She woke with a start when he bit her.

Heart pounding, she glanced around the room. Had he really been there? Perhaps it had been a mistake to invite him into her home. The websites she had visited said you could uninvite a vampire merely by saying his name and revoking his invitation. Did that work on Hungarian vampires, as well? Should she try it? Would it make him angry if he found out? How would she explain her decision to do so?

A glance at the bedside clock showed it was a little after 7 AM. Snuggling back under the covers, she closed her eyes, but sleep eluded her. Sitting up, she propped a pillow behind her head.

Quill was convinced Grandma Ava had been a witch. If he was right, it explained a lot of peculiar goings-on that Callie had accepted without question as a child— like the fact that Ava had always appeared to be much younger than she was, and that meals had, on occasion, appeared on the table seemingly out of thin air. There had been times when a murmured word from Ava had warmed the water in the teakettle, even when it wasn't on the stove. She remembered that she had always had clean clothes even though she didn't remember ever seeing Ava use the washer or dryer.

Perhaps the strangest memory of all was Ava telling Callie that she must never, ever tell anyone her full name. When she'd asked why, Ava had whispered that giving someone your full name gave them power over you. What kind of power, Callie had no idea. As a little girl, she hadn't given any thought to these bizarre incidences, but had merely assumed that everyone's grandmother could do the same things.

Closing her eyes, Callie remembered how she had tried to turn water from the hose into chocolate milk and unleashed a ball of fire that had burned down Ava's wooden wishing well. At least Callie thought she had done it. The memory was hazy. She had vague memories of other incidents, like the time she'd wished really hard that one of the boys in third grade would trip and fall into a snowbank, and he had. When she'd mentioned that and other odd happenings to Ava, her grandmother had blithely explained them all away.

Funny, Callie thought, how, as she had gotten older, she had forgotten all those queer events. Why had she remembered them now? If Grandmother Ava was in fact a witch, why had she kept the knowledge from Callie?

She felt a chill as a new thought crossed her mind. Was being a witch inherited, like hair color and blood type? If so, was she, herself, a witch?

Suddenly restless, Callie slipped out of bed and headed for the kitchen, where she filled a teapot with cold water and set it on the counter. Focusing on the kettle, she whispered the words her grandmother had used, then shook her head. What was she doing? She wasn't a witch.

Callie turned toward the door, intending to go back to bed, when a shrill whistle made the hairs on her arms stand up. Whirling around, she saw a cloud of steam rising from the spout. Still doubting, she touched the side of the kettle, let out a yelp of pain when it burned her fingers.

Murmuring, "Oh, Lord, maybe I *am* a witch," she dropped into one of the kitchen chairs.

Why hadn't her grandmother told her the truth?

Callie mulled it over as she prepared breakfast, but she couldn't think of a single good reason why Ava had hidden the truth from her. Sure, it might have been hard to explain about witches and witchcraft when Callie was a child, but Ava could have let her in on the secret later, when Callie was old enough to understand. Why hadn't she?

The question niggled at the back of her mind while she ate, and later, while she was making her bed. And in the shower. She had just finished dressing when, from out of the blue, she had a sudden urge to explore her grandmother's room, certain that she would find the answers inside.

Heart pounding with trepidation, she padded barefoot down the hall to Ava's bedroom. Except for dusting and vacuuming, she had rarely gone inside. Even as a child, she hadn't ventured in there. It had been her grandmother's sanctuary, the way Callie's bedroom had been hers.

She hesitated, her hand on the knob, then took a deep breath and opened the door.

The room was furnished with antiques—a four-poster bed covered with a crocheted spread, a round oak table topped by a white linen cloth and a black bowl, a narrow shelf with an assortment of implements Callie had no name for. There were no mirrors in here, not on the wall or above the dresser. She had always thought that odd.

Two antique bookcases stood side by side against one wall. Callie had come in here once looking for something to read, but none of the titles made for light reading—they were mostly thick volumes about ancient history, many written in foreign languages, their pages yellowed and faded with time.

Feeling suddenly melancholy, she ran her fingertips over the spines—blinked and blinked again when the title of the book beneath her hand wavered, the title changing from *The Architecture of Ancient Rome* to *Practical Magic for Young Witches*. In a ripple effect, all the titles transformed as she ran her gaze over the shelf, changing from historical treatises to *The Herbal*

Alchemist, Wicca for Beginners, Wiccapedia. She ran her hand over the spine of one of the books on the second shelf and discovered not tomes on ancient civilizations, but books on incense and spells, volumes on magic, black and white.

She lifted a thick, leather-bound volume entitled *Rivers of the Ancient World*. At her touch, the title vanished. Sitting on the edge of the mattress, she opened the book. Perusing the pages, she realized it was a grimoire filled with magical spells and pictures. She was amazed at how many of the enchantments seemed familiar, particularly the protection spell Ava had chanted over her every night.

There were charms to influence thoughts or the weather, to heal warts or a broken heart, and other, more sinister spells, like those used to summon demons to do a witch's bidding. Many of the pages had notes in the margins, written in her grandmother's lacy script, noting changes Ava had made to one spell or another.

Names held power. Blood had power. Circles infused with a witch's will had power. They could be used for keeping something in, or shutting something out.

Reading on, she noted that several pages included instructions for making candles and using them to summon a lover to your side, or to bring you luck, or wealth.

She thumbed through the pages, then stopped when she came to an incantation to make people forget. Perhaps Ava had cast more than one spell on her granddaughter.

She read until her vision blurred and her stomach growled, and then she went into the kitchen for a late lunch. Sitting at the table, she tried to make sense of all she had learned about her grandmother and herself in the last eight hours.

And then she frowned. What if she really *was* a witch? What would that mean in her day-to-day life? Would she suddenly find herself practicing magic, casting spells, dancing under the full moon?

How would being a witch—if, indeed she was one—affect her life?

And how would it affect her burgeoning relationship with Quill?

Callie's tumultuous thoughts roused Quill from his rest. Sitting up, he let his mind link with hers. So, he thought, she had learned the truth about Ava—and about herself—at last. Since he'd put two and two together, he had wondered how long it would take Callie to discover the secret Ava had kept hidden, and how it would affect her. He had attempted on several occasions to breach the walls Ava had erected around her mind once she discovered what he was, but to no avail. Ava had been a strong, stubborn woman, and he suspected Callie had inherited those traits, as well.

Like Callie, he, too, wondered what changes her new-found knowledge would make in her life.

And how it might change their relationship.

Rising, he showered and dressed, then headed for the next town in search of prey. Anxious to see Callie, he mesmerized the first lone woman he saw, fed quickly, wiped the memory from her mind, and willed himself to Callie's front door.

He stood there a long moment before ringing the bell.

* * *

Callie looked up from the grimoire when she heard the doorbell. It was Quill. She knew it without a doubt. Excitement and trepidation warred within her as she wondered whether or not to tell him what she had discovered. Laying the book aside, she went to let him in, only to find herself strangely tongue-tied as he followed her into the living room.

"You okay?" he asked.

"I don't know." She sat on the sofa.

He took the chair across from her, eyes narrowed as his mind brushed hers. *Fear. Confusion. Weariness. Mental exhaustion. Unanswered questions.* "Do you want me to leave?"

"No! No. I can't stop wondering why my grandmother didn't tell me she was a witch. It's been preying on my mind all day."

"I'm sure she must have had a good reason." Though he couldn't imagine what it was.

"I keep telling myself that, but . . ." She shrugged. Bit down on her lower lip. Then blurted, "I think maybe I'm a witch, too."

He lifted one brow.

"I warmed a kettle of water using the words she had used. And I found her grimoire. I know it's hers because she made notes in the margins about spells she'd tried and those she'd changed. And I remember some of them, like the protection spell she wove around me every night."

"It might be hard for you to accept, but I know you're a witch, Callie. I tasted it in your blood. As for how powerful you might be, that's something you'll have to learn for yourself. You can either experiment with witchcraft and see if you can summon it and control it, or you can just ignore it."

She nodded slowly.

"Would you like to go out tonight? Take your mind off it?"

"That sounds great. Where are we going?"

"Wherever you like. Dinner. Dancing. A movie. A walk in the park?"

"Not the park," she said emphatically, remembering all too well what had happened the last time she had gone there. "What about the county fair over in Chester?"

"Sure, if that's what you want."

"Just let me change my shoes and grab a sweater."

The fair was in full swing when they arrived. Being there reminded Callie of all the times she had gone to similar events with her grandmother. Ava had loved all the carnival rides, loved having her fortune told, loved stumping the kids whose job it was to guess her age, which they failed to do time after time. Ava had never looked her age. Her face had remained unlined, her hair had never turned gray, her eyes had been as bright and clear at one hundred and six as they had been when Callie was a little girl. Was that part of being a witch?

She shook off thoughts of her grandmother as they climbed into one of the cars on the Ferris wheel. When Quill put his arm around her, she snuggled closer to his side, felt her stomach lurch as the car swung into motion. When it stopped at the top, Quill cupped her cheek in his palm and kissed her. Her lips were still tingling when the ride ended.

Hand in hand, they walked to the Fun Zone, where he proceeded to win half a dozen stuffed animals of varying sizes.

"Are you just a really good shot?" she asked. "Or did you use some of your vampire magic to knock over those milk bottles?"

"It was all me," he said, his grin a trifle smug. "You forget, I've had years and years to practice."

"True." She glanced down at the armload of stuffed animals. "What am I going to do with all these?"

Plucking a gray dolphin from her arms, he paused by a little girl who was crying because her daddy hadn't won her anything. "Here you go," he said, handing her the toy.

The girl stared up at him, brown eyes wide as she hugged the furry little thing to her chest.

"I . . . thank you," her father stammered. "That's really nice of you."

Quill waved away the man's thanks.

Following his lead, Callie gave away the rest of the stuffed animals—all except a brown-and-white puppy with big ears and sad eyes that was small enough to fit into her sweater's oversized pocket.

"Are you hungry?" Quill asked as they left the Fun Zone behind.

"I'd love some cotton candy."

"Wouldn't be a fair without it," he said with a knowing smile.

She took pink, he opted for blue.

Callie couldn't help it. She laughed out loud as he popped a healthy portion into his mouth.

"What's so funny?"

"It just struck me as odd, watching a vampire eat

cotton candy. I mean, seriously, who'd have thought you'd have such a sweet tooth?"

He glowered at her, and then grinned. At least she wasn't brooding about her grandmother. He felt a sudden stirring of desire as Callie licked a bit of pink fluff from her lips. Her tongue was as pink as the candy.

Looking up, Callie caught him staring. And the world seemed to stop.

Quill took the paper cone from her hand and dropped it, along with his, in a trash can. Without a word being said, she followed him into the darkness beyond the noise and the bright lights. She went into his arms gladly, her eyelids fluttering down as his mouth covered hers in a searing kiss that sent heat rushing to every nerve and cell in her body. Standing on her tiptoes, she clung to him, desperate to hold him close and never let him go. His tongue dueled with hers in a mating dance as old as time.

She was breathless when he lifted his head. His eyes glowed with a need that sent a shiver of awareness down her spine.

"Callie?"

She knew what he wanted, what he needed. It never occurred to her to refuse. No doubt Vivian would think it was gross that he drank from her, but it had created a bond between them, one Callie didn't want to end.

At her nod, he gently brushed her hair away from her neck, leaned forward and bit her.

Head tilted to the side, she leaned into him, eyes closed as warmth and pleasure flowed through her.

He took only a little.

Lost in a haze of sensual pleasure, she moaned softly as he ran his tongue over the tiny wounds, sealing them.

He rested his forehead against hers, grateful for her generosity, ashamed of his weakness. He had told her he didn't want her to think of herself as nothing but prey, but how could she think otherwise when he couldn't resist the siren call of her blood?

"Quill?" She laid her hand against his cheek. "It's all right. I understand."

"Do you?" he asked, his voice a low growl.

"You need it and I'm happy to give it to you. After all, I enjoy it, too. Maybe more than you do."

He lifted his head, his gaze burning into hers. She meant what she'd said. The truth was there, in the depths of her eyes. Sighing, he held her close, determined that she would never have cause to regret her generosity.

Later, at home, he walked her to the porch, then took her in his arms again, humbled by her trust, her kindness. "See you tomorrow?"

"You'd better."

Smiling, he kissed her one more time, then waited on the porch while she went inside and locked the door.

He wanted to buy her something, he thought as he slid behind the wheel of the Jag. Something to show his appreciation for her willingness to ease his hunger. He ran his hands over the steering wheel, then smiled.

He knew exactly what to give her.

Chapter 10

Trey 95 walked the length and breadth of the city as he did several times each day between sundown and sunrise—always searching for some sign of the vampire who had killed his brother. He knew the creature was in the city. All he had to do was locate him. Sadly, that was no easy task. The vampire was old and wise and merciless. Trey was still amazed that they had taken Quill by surprise in the park. Who knew when they'd find him again?

He had taken off with the other Knights after being interrupted by a jogger's untimely appearance. Trey had returned alone a short time later, fully intending to destroy the vampire, only to be thwarted yet again when a woman had come to his aid.

Trey would gladly have dispatched the woman save for this fear of facing the Elder Knight's wrath. It was an unwritten law of the Brotherhood that killing was never to be done in the presence of mortal witnesses.

Trey frowned. The woman. Who was she? Did she know what kind of loathsome creature Quill was? Had the vampire mesmerized her to do his bidding?

The woman. Perhaps she was the answer to his dilemma.

Find the woman, find the vampire.

Chapter 11

Callie woke late the next morning. Not surprisingly, her first thought was *I'm a witch.* And hard on the heels of that revelation came the realization that she had a lot to learn. Again, she wondered why her grandmother had kept the truth from her, and why Ava hadn't instructed her in the magical arts.

Scuffing into the kitchen, Callie fixed scrambled eggs, toast, and orange juice for breakfast. Sitting at the table, she checked her calendar. She had a shoot scheduled for the end of next month. Sipping her juice, she wondered if she should cancel it. The more she considered the idea, the better she liked it. She didn't need the work. It was a small job, after all. She could return Mrs. Steffan's advance and recommend another photographer, then take some time off and discover the extent of her magical abilities, as large—or as small— as they might be.

For all she knew, being able to say a few words to heat a kettle of water might be the beginning and end of her power. Quill had said practicing her magic or not was entirely up to her. But she couldn't help thinking it might be fun to explore her powers and learn if she could do more than just heat a pot of water. What if she could be like the Sorcerer's Apprentice and command her broom and her mop to clean the floors, order the bed to make itself. How cool would it be if she could scour the toilets with a wave of her hand? Maybe she could open a little shop and sell love potions, she mused with a giggle, or sell charms to angry young women who wanted to get even with boyfriends who had broken their hearts.

After breakfast, Callie called Mrs. Steffan and apologized for canceling, then recommended someone she had occasionally worked with when a client wanted a second photographer.

Relieved that the conversation had ended on a good note, Callie went into the living room and picked up her grandmother's grimoire. She was looking for an easy spell she might try when she heard Ava's voice in the back of her mind.

The key is in the bottom of my jewelry box.

Key? Callie frowned. *To what?*

Putting the heavy book aside, she went into her grandmother's room and opened the bottom drawer of Ava's very large jewelry box. She found a large brass key under a tangle of silver bracelets. When she picked it up, it felt warm in her hand.

"So, what am I supposed to with it?" Callie wondered. It was far too big to be the key to a safe deposit box. And too old-fashioned to fit any of the locks in the house.

Without knowing why, she opened the door to the closet. She had been meaning for a while now to donate Ava's clothes to the Salvation Army, but she'd kept putting it off, reluctant to part with anything that had been her grandmother's.

Pushing the dresses out of the way, she saw a metal box on a shelf. Picking it up, she carried it to the bed and sat down. The box was large and square, with an ancient padlock.

She looked at it for several minutes. Took a deep breath. And inserted the key in the lock. She hesitated a moment before lifting the lid. It opened with an eerie, creaking noise, revealing a leather-bound journal inside. A black owl with piercing yellow eyes adorned the cover.

Callie ran her fingers over the bird's outline, recalling Ava's affinity for owls. The birds had nested in the trees in the backyard. In the evenings, they had perched on the kitchen windowsill or on the front porch railing. Funny, she hadn't seen any since her grandmother had passed away.

After taking another deep breath, Callie lifted the book onto her lap. It was heavy, the paper yellow with age. Curious, she opened it to the first page.

My dear Callie ~ I have much to tell you, but where to start? Perhaps by now you've realized that I kept much from you while you were growing up. Before I married your grandfather, I was married to someone else. . . .

Callie gasped. Good grief! How many secrets had her grandmother kept hidden from her?

My first husband was a wonderful man. His name was John Edward Morris. He was tall and blond, with beautiful green eyes and a smile that could make angels weep. He was a Knight of the Dark Wood.

Callie read that line twice, remembering that Quill had told her it had been knights who had attacked him in Hunter Park. Had he meant those Knights? She shook her head as she resumed reading.

These Knights of the Dark Wood belong to a secret organization sworn to protect humankind. They are forbidden to marry unless they leave the brotherhood. I knew how much being a Knight meant to John and could not ask him to forsake his vows. And he knew that I could not renounce my magic.

We were very young and very much in love and we married in secret, certain no one except his father would ever know. I swore never to reveal his secret or betray the brotherhood, and he vowed never to tell anyone that I was a witch. In those days, it was not safe to be a witch or a warlock. I rather doubt that has changed, as mere mortals have always tended to view those who are different from themselves with suspicion and fear.

John and I were married almost ten years— exciting years filled with danger and adventure. When he was killed by a vampire, I thought my life was over. And then I met your grandfather. Will, too, was a wonderful man. Sadly, he passed away shortly before you were born. I never told him that I was a witch. He was a solid, down-to-earth person and would never have approved or understood. Your dear mother never knew, either, although I think she suspected, since she knew her grandmother also had the Gift. It seems to

*skip a generation and is bestowed only on the
women of our family.*

*I know I should have told you the truth about
myself when you were old enough to understand.
I had hopes that my magic had passed on to you
when you tried to turn water into chocolate milk,
and again when you tried to turn water into hot
cocoa. But, after that, you never displayed any
magical abilities, or indicated you had any
interest in the Arts. And even though I knew you
suspected what I was, you never asked any
questions or seemed interested and I thought it
best to wait. Sometimes the Gift comes late in
life. If it has come to you, I would caution you to
use it wisely.*

*I have protected you against evil as best I can.
The Knights of the Dark Wood are still active,
still sworn to protect humankind from any and all
supernatural creatures. And although they never
actively hunted witches, they have been known to
destroy them if one crosses their path.*

*If you choose to explore your magical talent,
you will find my grimoire helpful. Use it to
freshen the wards around our home. It is a simple
spell, on page 407. I'm sure the wards I originally
erected have faded with time.*

*I would also warn you against vampires—yes,
I know from personal experience that they exist—
both Transylvanian and Hungarian. The first will
steal your life, the second your soul.*

*Always trust your heart, my dearest child. Rely
on your faith. And know that I am always with you.*

Callie thumbed through the rest of the pages, but they were blank. It seemed odd, she thought, that her grandmother would have chosen such a large book for such a brief entry. Had she intended to write more? If so, why hadn't she?

Callie closed the journal, then sat there, staring into the distance as she tried to process all she had read. After sliding the book under one of the bed pillows, she stood and stretched her back and shoulders.

She had a lot to think about.

Callie was still in her PJs when the doorbell rang. A little thrill of excitement ran through her as she hurried to open the door. She knew it was Quill, yet after reading her grandmother's journal, she paused, her hand on the latch. With Knights and vampires at large, it paid to be careful.

Peering through the peephole, she saw that, as she'd suspected, it was Quill.

Smiling, she opened the door, eager to tell him what she'd found, when she saw the dark sapphire-blue convertible adorned with a large red bow sitting in her driveway. "Don't tell me you bought another Jaguar?" she exclaimed. Although she couldn't blame him. It was gorgeous.

"I did, indeed. Do you like it?"

"Well, the bow's a bit much, but it's beautiful."

"It's yours."

"What?"

He shrugged. "I wanted to buy you something."

"But . . . why?"

"It's a gift, Callie. You don't question it. You just accept it."

She shook her head. "I can't take that. It must have cost a fortune."

"It isn't polite to ask the price, or to refuse a gift freely given."

"Really, Quill, I don't feel right about keeping it."

"Please accept it, Callie. Consider it a heartfelt thank-you for saving my life and easing my thirst."

How could she refuse when he put it like that? "Can I ask you something that's kind of rude and none of my business?"

"I didn't steal it, if that's what you're thinking," he said with a wry grin.

She made a face at him. "How can you afford it?"

"Ah. I've made several rather good investments through the years. Believe me, my sweet Callie, this won't even put a dent in my savings."

"I don't know what to say."

"Say, 'Thank you, Quill. I love it,' and kiss me."

Going up on her tiptoes, she said, "Thank you, Quill. I love it." And she kissed him—until someone let out a wolf whistle. Stepping away from Quill, she saw one of her neighbors standing at the end of the driveway. He winked at her, then moved on.

Quill glanced at her pajamas. Lifting one brow, he said, "Isn't it a little early for bed?"

"I've been too busy to get dressed." She took another look at the car. "Can we take it for a drive later?"

"It's yours. We can do whatever you want."

"Well, come on in."

Callie felt an odd tremor in the air as he crossed the threshold. Funny, she had never noticed that before.

After closing the door, she followed him into the living room. Gesturing for him to sit down, she took the place beside him.

"You look troubled. What's wrong?" he asked.

"You mean aside from learning that my grandmother really was a witch and that I might be one, too? I found a journal that's mostly blank except for a letter from my grandmother. It explained a lot although I still have a ton of questions. Wait a minute and I'll get it."

She returned moments later with a large, leather-bound book. Resuming her seat, she handed it to him.

Quill ran his fingers over the cover. Even after all these years, Ava's scent clung to the leather. He glanced at Callie, wondering if Ava had written anything about him.

He read the letter quickly, until he came to one paragraph.

> *I would also warn you against vampires—yes, I know from personal experience that they exist— both Transylvanian and Hungarian. The first will steal your life, the second your soul.*

He read it three times, relieved that Ava hadn't mentioned him by name. He wasn't sure how Callie would react if she discovered the brief, intimate details of his association with her grandmother. Ava had been a free spirit, eager to explore all of life's mysteries. And he had been eager to share them with her. "How old was your grandmother when she passed away?"

"A hundred and six."

Quill nodded. Of course, Ava would lie about her age. In reality, she had been closer to a hundred and fifty. Even that was young, for a witch. They often lived to be over two hundred. In spite of the popular stereotype of old crones with big noses and warts, thanks to heredity and their ability to alter their appearance, they rarely appeared old or ugly.

"They told me she passed away quietly in her sleep."

He looked at her sharply. "You weren't there?"

"No, I was in Paris. She must have known she was going to die because she left instructions with her lawyer, saying that she didn't want her death to ruin my vacation and she wanted to spare me the necessity of arranging her funeral. When I got home, it was all over. Why would she do that?"

"You just told me. She wanted to spare you."

"I should have *been* there."

After setting the journal on the coffee table, Quill put his arm around Callie's shoulders. "There's nothing you could have done if you were here, love."

"I know, but it isn't right! She was the only family I had. I would have liked a chance to say good-bye."

"The lawyer had to obey her wishes."

"I know. But sometimes . . ."

"What?"

"Like I said, I never got to say good-bye. And I know this is going to sound a little weird, morbid even, but sometimes I feel like she's not really dead."

Quill nodded. Oddly enough, he'd been having the same feeling. Hoping to cheer her, he said, "Come on, let's take that new car of yours for a spin."

It was late when Quill left Callie's house. They had taken the Jag for a long drive, then returned home and sat in front of the fire for an hour, content to hold each other close.

After kissing Callie good-night, he went in search of prey. Due to the late hour, his choices were few—an old drunk passed out in an alley, or an addict high on the latest drug. Grimacing, he decided to go hungry.

Leaving the seedier part of town behind, he opened his preternatural senses, searching for the blood link that bound him to Callie's grandmother. He wasn't surprised when he couldn't find it. More than a hundred years had passed since he had last seen Ava. It would have been a miracle if the link had survived that long. But he couldn't shake the feeling that, for her own protection or that of her granddaughter, Ava had faked her death and gone into hiding. Unfortunately, the chances of finding her were slim if she didn't want to be found. Like vampires, witches and warlocks were remarkably creative in their efforts to hide from the world.

And Knights were equally adept at hiding from vampires.

That thought was brought home when Quill suddenly sensed he was being followed. He glanced over his shoulder just in time to see one of the Knights lower his cloak of invisibility. Lips pulled back in a feral grin, the Knight sprang forward, the dagger in his hand raised to strike.

Quill twisted out of the way as the blade descended and the knife, meant for his heart, sank to the hilt in his right shoulder. With a wild cry of pain and fury that echoed off the sides of the buildings, he grabbed the Knight and hurled him across the street just as a car came careening around the corner. There was an angry screech of tires and the scent of burnt rubber as the driver hit the brakes, but it was too late. The Knight let out a startled scream as he was thrown into the air and over the top of the car.

Quill didn't wait around to find out if his assailant lived or died. Jerking the dagger from his shoulder, he disappeared into the darkness.

Callie woke to the sound of someone knocking on the front door. A glance at the clock showed it was a little after 3 AM. She didn't know anyone who would come calling so late, she thought, frowning.

Except Quill.

And he wouldn't come this late unless something was wrong.

Jumping out of bed, she grabbed her robe, ran to the door, and looked through the peephole. As she'd feared, it was Quill. And he was bleeding again. After opening the door, she stepped aside.

"Sorry," he said, following her into the living room.

"For what?" she asked, turning on the lights.

"I need a favor."

She looked at his torn and bloody shirt and the ugly laceration in his shoulder. "You need blood," she guessed.

He nodded. "Only because I wasn't able to find any . . ."

Callie pressed her fingertips to his lips. "No need to explain." She held out her arm, frowned when he didn't take it. "What's wrong?"

His gaze moved to her throat and lingered there.

"Oh."

He started to reach for her, then paused. After removing his shirt, he wiped the blood from his shoulder, then wadded his shirt into a ball and tossed it into the fireplace before pulling her down on the sofa and taking her in his arms.

It was much more intimate—and pleasurable—to be held in his embrace when he drank from her. With a little shiver of anticipation, she pushed her hair out of the way and closed her eyes.

As always, he took only a little. When he was done, he ran his tongue over the tiny punctures, then kissed her cheek.

Callie smiled, and then frowned as a faint movement drew her gaze to his shoulder. She let out a gasp of amazement as she watched the ragged ends of the wound knit together.

"That's . . . that's . . . I've never seen anything like that."

"If I'd fed earlier, I wouldn't have needed to come here. Fresh blood always makes injuries hurt less and heal faster."

"Glad to be of service," she said with a wry grin.

"Ah, Callie, what a treasure you are."

"Did a Knight do that?"

He nodded.

"Is he . . . ?"

"I don't know. He was hit by a car during the struggle. I didn't wait around to see if he survived."

Callie stared at the faint white scars that marred Quill's arms, chest, and belly. She couldn't imagine what it must be like to be hunted, to be constantly on the alert, never knowing when or where you might be attacked.

Or killed.

"It's late," he said, rising. "You should get some sleep."

"Since you're here, why don't you spend the night? In the guest room," she added.

"You're sure you don't mind?" The wards he'd erected the last time he had stayed here were still in place. It should be safe enough.

"I wouldn't have asked if I did."

"Then I accept your offer, love. Thank you."

"Good night, then. Just make yourself at home."

Nodding, he watched her leave the room, heard the sound of her bedroom door close, the rustle of sheets as she got into bed.

For a moment, he stood there, wishing he had the right to slide in beside her, take her in his arms, and make love to her all through the night.

Sighing, he waved a hand to turn off the lights, then made his way to the guest room's lonely bed.

One of these days, he thought. One of these days, he would make her his.

Chapter 12

A harsh cry roused Quill from the Dark Sleep. All his senses alert, he threw back the covers and ran down the hall to Callie's bedroom. A second scream and he pushed the door open, ready to do battle, only to see her thrashing on the mattress as she fought off a terror only she could see.

Placing one hand on her shoulder, he whispered, "Callie. Callie, wake up."

Shouting, "Let me go!" she lashed out, her nails raking his cheek hard enough to draw blood.

"Callie! Wake up."

She woke with a start, her gaze darting right and left. "Quill?"

"It's me." A flick of his hand turned on the light beside her bed.

"You're bleeding! Did I do that?"

Plucking a couple of tissues from the box on the nightstand, he wiped the blood from his cheek and her fingertips. "You were having a nightmare and I got in the way," he said with a lopsided grin. "Do you want to talk about it?"

Callie blew out a shaky breath as she sat up. "I was a

little girl again, watching my grandmother dance under a full moon. Her friends were with her. One by one, they transformed into monsters. Betty turned into a ravening werewolf. Hilda became a hideous troll. Maxine's body shifted into a zombie, and they all turned on me, growling and hissing as they came toward me. And then my grandmother changed into . . ."

"Into what?"

"A vampire with glowing red eyes. She killed them all and then she was looking at me, her . . . her fangs dripping with blood."

"That was some hellacious nightmare."

"There's more." Callie clutched the blankets to her chest. "Another vampire materialized from out of nowhere and they fell to the ground and made love in the middle of all the dead bodies and . . ." She drew a deep, shuddering breath.

Quill knew a sudden sense of foreboding as he waited for her to go on.

"You were the other vampire."

"It was just a dream," he said. "I can assure you that I never made love to your grandmother surrounded by a bunch of dead monsters."

"Logically, I know that," Callie said. "I mean, how could you? But it was so horrible. So real! Why would I even dream of something so bizarre?"

"It's not too surprising. You're hanging out with a vampire who sleeps down the hall from time to time. And since I exist, your subconscious must have decided there might be other monsters in the world besides me."

"I guess that's as good an explanation as any." She yawned behind her hand. "And you're not a monster."

Not bothering to argue, he bent down and kissed her

cheek. It was soft and smooth, and his lips naturally gravitated to hers. He had meant only to give her a brief good-night kiss, but it quickly turned into something deeper and more meaningful. Sitting on the edge of the bed, he gathered her into his arms and kissed her again as his hand slid under her sleep shirt to explore the warm, smooth skin beneath.

Callie moaned softly as his tongue danced with hers, sending frissons of heat spiraling through her. Thinking turnabout was fair play, she ran her hand over his chest. His skin was cool, his stomach ridged with muscle. Her fingertips traced the scars on his chest and belly.

Desire turned to trepidation when he lowered her onto the bed, his body covering hers. "Quill. Quill, stop!"

He lifted his head, his eyes hot with desire.

She hadn't been this afraid of him since the night he bit her for the first time. But she was afraid now.

Afraid he wouldn't stop.

Afraid he would.

He drew in a ragged breath and let it out in a long, slow sigh. "I'd better go."

She nodded.

Rising, he left the room, quietly closing the door behind him.

Callie stared after him, not knowing whether to be sorry or relieved.

Quill stood at the front window in the living room, staring out into the darkness beyond and thinking how close he had come to making love to her. Had she waited another few minutes to slam on the brakes, he didn't think he would have been able to stop.

Reluctant to travel down that road, he thought how odd it was that he and Ava had been players in Callie's nightmare. And even more extraordinary that she had imagined him making love to her grandmother under a full moon, something that had actually happened more than a hundred years before Callie was born. Was it just some bizarre coincidence that made her subconscious bring him and her grandmother together? Because he was pretty sure that Ava hadn't confided the details of her love life to her granddaughter.

With a shake of his head, he padded back to the guest room and stretched out on the bed, only to lie there wishing Callie hadn't said no. Not that he could blame her. She didn't seem like the type to indulge in a casual affair, especially with one of his kind. No doubt she wanted the whole nine yards—husband, children, security, a lifetime commitment. He doubted she wanted to share her future with a vampire being hunted by the Knights of the Dark Wood, or give birth to a child who would one day become a vampire.

But he could hope.

In the morning, before she did anything else, Callie tiptoed down the hall to the guest room. As she peeked inside to see if Quill was still there, she was reminded of all the other mornings when she had done the same thing, usually hoping he'd be gone. But today she was glad he was still there. It seemed right, somehow.

After closing the door, she scuffed into the kitchen. It was there again, she noticed as she poured a cup of coffee and carried it into the living room, that peculiar aura that surrounded the house whenever Quill was here. It made her feel safe, protected.

Sipping her coffee, she thought about last night and how close she had come to letting Quill make love to her. She had no doubt he would be a wonderful lover. After all, he'd likely had centuries of experience. But she just wasn't ready. For one thing, she had only known him a short time. For another, he was a vampire. And although he seemed like a normal guy much of the time, there was no forgetting what he was. Power clung to him—a tangible presence.

He could speak to her mind—and read it, as well—which was disconcerting, to say the least.

He was a hunted man. It was probably dangerous to even be with him, and yet if he couldn't protect her, no one could.

He had killed the men in the park to save his own life. She couldn't fault him for that, but for all she knew, he might have slain countless others.

She was falling in love with him. She knew he wanted her, as she wanted him. But was he *in* love with her? Were vampires even capable of love?

With a sigh, she carried her cup to the kitchen and rinsed it out, then went into her room to get dressed. She had a lot of thinking to do. And she didn't want to do it alone. Grabbing her cell phone, she called Vivian.

Callie met Viv in their favorite coffee shop twenty minutes later.

"You sounded upset on the phone," Vivian said, stirring

sugar and cream into her coffee. "What's wrong? Did someone die?"

Callie almost choked on her orange juice. "No. I just needed someone to talk to."

"Well, I'm glad you called. I was beginning to worry about you. In fact, I almost called you last night, but it was kind of late when I thought of it."

Callie paused to glance around the café. "You remember that guy I told you about?"

"What guy?"

Callie's shoulders slumped as she recalled that Quill had wiped his memory from Vivian's mind.

"Callie?"

"I'm just having some man trouble, that's all."

"Did you meet someone new? Well, it's about time. Tell me about him. Is he tall, dark, and handsome?"

"You could definitely say that."

"So, what's the problem?"

"Our lifestyles and our backgrounds are totally different. I'm not sure we'd be compatible over the long haul, you know?"

"Oh, sure. Sometimes our hearts don't listen to our heads."

Callie nodded.

"How long have you been seeing him?"

"Not long. And yet, in some ways, I feel like I've known him my whole life."

"It sounds to me like you're falling in love with him."

"I am. I can't help it. He's gorgeous and sexy and . . . and he needs me."

"Being needed can be a turn-on sometimes."

"I guess. You won't believe what he gave me the other day."

"What?"

"A new Jaguar."

Vivian blinked at her, mouth agape. "He. Gave. You. A *Jaguar?*"

Callie nodded. "Wait until you see it."

"Is it here?"

"No. I haven't had time to get it insured, so I left it in the garage. But it's blue and beautiful."

"Girl, you've hit the jackpot this time. Sexy *and* generous. I'm dark green with envy. So, tell me, when do I get to meet this fabulous man?"

"How about right now?" Callie said, her heart skipping a beat when she saw Quill striding toward them. Oh, Lord, had he come looking for her because he knew she was talking about him again?

"What?" Vivian followed Callie's gaze. "Oh, my, he is a handsome one, isn't he?!"

Quill stopped beside their table, looking utterly gorgeous in a pair of black jeans and a dark blue shirt. "Callie, aren't you going to introduce me?"

After swallowing several times, she said, "Vivian, this is Quill."

"Delighted to meet you, Vivian," he said.

Vivian smiled at him, obviously smitten.

"Mind if I join you?" he asked.

"Please do," Viv said.

Quill pulled a chair from the unoccupied table beside them and sat down. "I hope I haven't interrupted anything important."

"No, nothing," Callie said. "We were just chatting."

"Girl talk?" His dark gaze bored into hers, a silent warning.

"Just the usual," Callie said.

He lifted one brow. "Indeed?" He glanced at Vivian, then back at Callie, the unspoken warning plain.

Callie was relieved when their orders arrived.

"Would you like a menu, sir?" the waitress asked.

"No need. I'd like a steak sandwich, rare, no onions."

"And to drink?"

"Nothing, thank you."

The waitress lingered a moment. Then, with a flirty smile and hips swaying, she went to turn in his order.

Callie followed Quill out of the coffee shop shortly after Vivian excused herself and left the café.

Callie unlocked the VW and slid behind the wheel. She waited until Quill climbed in beside her before asking, "Why did you follow me?"

"You know why."

"I wasn't going to say anything about you." She looked left and right before pulling out of the parking lot into the street. "I just needed someone to talk to."

"About what?"

She flushed under his knowing gaze. "Okay. About you. But I wasn't going to tell her what you are."

"No?"

"No. Do you think I want you messing around with her mind again? You might cause permanent brain damage."

"So, what kind of advice were you looking for?"

"On the wisdom of falling in love with someone who lives a completely different lifestyle than mine!" She blurted the words and immediately wished she could recall them.

Stunned by her revelation, Quill stared at her. "You're falling in love? With me?"

Callie's knuckles went white as she gripped the VW's steering wheel. Why had she said that? And what was she going to say now?

"Callie?" His voice low and whiskey-smooth, was tinged with hope.

"I said it, didn't I?" she snapped.

"But did you mean it?"

In a much softer voice, she repeated, "I said it, didn't I?"

Reaching across her lap, Quill grabbed the wheel and steered the car onto a side road heavily screened by trees and brush. Shutting off the ignition, he put his arm around her shoulders and drew her closer as he leaned in toward her.

Callie's heart skipped a beat as his mouth covered hers in a long, searing kiss. Her eyelids fluttered down as he kissed her again and yet again, each kiss deeper and more intimate than the last. She wished she had a bigger car, one from the fifties with a bench seat and no gear shift in the middle so she could climb onto his lap and wrap her arms around him.

Her pulse was racing when his head snapped up. Before she could ask what was wrong, her door flew open and a pair of strong hands dragged her out of the VW. She tried to fight the man off, kicking and scratching for all she was worth, but he held her easily, her back to his front, one meaty arm wrapped around her waist, seemingly impervious to her struggles. Helpless, she could only watch as three other men swarmed over Quill like hungry ants on chocolate.

Knights! she thought, her heart pounding with fear as she watched the life-and-death battle being waged only a few feet from where she stood. Knives flashed. Drops of blood—and not all of it Quill's—sparkled like rubies in the sunlight.

Quill fought like one possessed. He snapped the neck of one of the Knights, broke the arm of another.

The third man hollered, "Let's get the hell out of here!" when Quill reached for him.

Callie stumbled forward as the man who had been holding her pushed her out of the way and ran after his friends. One of them pulled what looked like a cloak from out of nowhere. Eyes wide with astonishment, she watched him spread the cloth over himself and his companions and disappear from sight.

With a shake of her head, Callie ran toward Quill. "Are you all right?" she asked anxiously. There was no way to tell how much of the blood was his.

"Don't worry about me. I'll be okay. Did he hurt you?"

"No, I'm fine." She pressed her lips together as she glanced at the dead man. "Shouldn't we do something about him?"

"No. Let's go."

"But . . ."

"Let's go."

There was no arguing with that tone. When he slid behind the wheel of the VW, she didn't protest, merely went around to the passenger side, got in, and shut the door. "They never give up, do they?"

"No," he said, curtly. "Never."

* * *

When the VW was out of sight, Trey 95 removed the invisibility cloak.

"What are you doing?" Thomas 63 asked. "We need to get Alan 12 to a doctor. From what I can see, it looks like his arm's badly broken."

Trey 95 shook his head. "You two go ahead."

"What are you going to do?"

"Don't worry about me."

"You're already in trouble with the Elder Knight for disobeying his orders to return to the Dark Wood," Thomas 63 reminded him.

Trey shrugged. The vampire had killed his twin brother. He wouldn't rest until Frank 95's blood had been avenged.

"Suit yourself," Thomas muttered. "It's your neck."

"That's right," Trey snapped. "So, get the hell out of here."

With a last, worried glance at Trey 95, Thomas struck out for the side of the road where they had left their van. Face pale, Alan 12 trailed behind him, his broken arm cradled against his chest.

Trey nodded to himself as he started walking toward town. He had memorized the license plate of the VW. All he had to do was look it up to find her address. And through her, the vampire. A piece of cake.

"I have you now, you dirty, bloodsucking freak," he muttered. "Next time, you won't get away."

"This is getting to be a habit," Callie remarked as she washed the blood from several deep gashes on Quill's arms and chest—and what a nice chest, it was, she thought. His six-pack abs weren't bad, either. She glanced at the tattered shirt on the floor. "You must spend a small fortune replacing your wardrobe."

He grunted softly. "Are you done yet?"

"I guess so." She dropped the bloody washcloth in the sink, then ran her fingertips over his broad shoulders, amazed yet again at how quickly he healed. All but the deepest cuts had disappeared before they got home.

"Careful," he growled as her fingers played in the dark hair on his chest. "You're on dangerous ground."

"In more ways than one," she muttered.

"I'm sorry about this afternoon," he said, drawing her into his arms. "I might have sensed them before it was too late but for your unexpected declaration."

"Oh, that." Feeling herself blush, she lowered her head, embarrassed because she'd confessed her feelings for him and he hadn't said anything. Of course, he really hadn't had time.

"Yes, that." Putting his finger under her chin, he tipped her head up. "You must know I feel the same way about you." He grinned at her. "It's not just your sweet blood that draws me back night after night, lovely Callie. Although that is a nice plus."

"Flatterer," she said, dryly.

"You know what I mean."

Feeling lighthearted, she nodded.

"As much as I'd like to show you just how much I care, I need to rest."

Callie nodded. It was the middle of the afternoon when the sun was at its hottest. And he'd been wounded. Rest would help him regain his strength.

"Okay if I bed down in your guest room again?"

"Consider it yours."

"I may take you up on that." He kissed her, ever so gently. "I'll see you at sundown."

"I'll be here."

He winked at her, then left the room.

Callie stared after him. She was madly, deeply, in love. With a vampire.

Chapter 13

Trey 95 stood in the shadows outside the woman's house. It had taken only moments to obtain her address. His medallion told him the vampire was with her. He had already broken two of the cardinal Rules of the Knights by refusing to return to the Dark Wood when summoned and attacking a vampire when there was a human present. If he interacted with the woman, he would be breaking a third.

But he didn't give a damn.

Thus far, confronting the vampire hadn't been successful. In the meantime, his brother's death went unavenged.

Attempting to destroy the vampire while he was in the woman's house was a bad idea on several levels, the least of which was breaking another Rule.

Kidnapping the woman and forcing the vampire to come to him seemed like a better alternative. Although that option, too, would be yet another blatant violation of the Rules. Still, it would allow him the opportunity to choose where and when to confront the monster. Plus, it would give him time to prepare an effective attack, one with minimum risk to himself and, hopefully, the woman.

And if she didn't survive? He shrugged. When one chose to hang out with vampires, one had to be ready to take the risks inherent in such a despicable association.

After leaving the woman's house, he hitched a ride back to his quarters. He had a lot of planning to do.

Chapter 14

An hour before sunset, Quill left Callie's house. After satisfying his thirst, he returned home for a change of clothes. He made his lair in the attic of an old two-story house he had bought when he'd first come to town. It was a grand old place, solidly built. The floors were hardwood, the furnishings sparse but of good quality, the colors the green and tan of a forest. He had lived there for the last ten years, but after the last two attacks by the Knights, he was beginning to think it was time to seek a new placc.

While dressing, he wondered how Callie would feel about moving. No doubt she would be reluctant to leave her grandmother's home, but it would only be for a while, until the Knights realized he had left town and they returned to the Dark Wood.

A number of his kind had left Hungary decades ago and taken up residence in a small town high in the hills of Northern California. The only humans who lived there were married to vampires. Occasionally, a tourist or two would pass through on their way to Oregon or

Washington, but they were few and far between because the town didn't show up on any maps.

He nodded inwardly. He would suggest it to Callie tonight.

"You want us to move to California?" Callie asked, frowning. "Why?"

"For your safety. And for mine," Quill added with a wry grin. "The Knights know I'm in town. You and I have been seen together." He draped his arm along the back of the sofa. "The Knights are sworn not to bring harm to humanity, but I can't help worrying that you might get caught in the cross fire."

From her place on the sofa, Callie glanced around the living room. This house was the only home she had ever known. She couldn't imagine living anywhere else. Everything she saw held a memory—sitting in her grandmother's rocker reminded her of all the times Ava had told her stories or rocked her to sleep in front of the fire. When she used the cast-iron pots and pans in the kitchen, it reminded her of learning to cook at her grandmother's side and made her feel closer to Ava. Sometimes she felt as if Ava were actually there with her while she baked the chocolate chip cookies, which had been Ava's favorite. She would miss all that.

"Why California?" she asked.

"Some of my kind reside there, in a small town. It's a beautiful place." He had stayed there for a few years before moving here. "I think you'll like it. The only people who live there are vampires and their human mates."

Callie frowned as she tried to imagine that. And failed.

"It's just like a regular town," Quill assured her. "There are shops and a movie theater run mostly by humans— and a few vampires."

Callie grinned at the thought of vampires holding down ordinary jobs.

"Except for the necessity of blood, my people and yours aren't so different. We need something to occupy our time, a way to feel useful."

"California. I don't know, Quill. It's so far away."

"It would just be for a few months. Will you at least think about it?"

"How soon did you want to go?"

He made a vague gesture with his hand. "Monday?"

Callie chewed on the corner of her lip. It wouldn't be forever. And she had always wanted to see the Pacific Ocean. And Disneyland. She didn't have any work scheduled, so there was nothing to keep her here. And if it meant putting some distance between Quill and the Knights . . . "It might be fun," she decided. "I haven't had a vacation lately."

"That's my girl!"

"Is that what I am?" she asked with a playful grin. "Your girl?"

He waggled his eyebrows and then winked at her. "Only if you want to be."

"What do you think?"

Suddenly serious, he said, "I'm not sure you want to know."

"Why not?"

His gaze caressed her from head to foot, the heat in his eyes so hot she swore she could feel it warming her skin.

"If we're going to live together, we need to set a few ground rules," she said.

"I can guess what they are," he muttered, his voice faintly amused.

"I'm not ready for us to . . . to consummate our relationship."

"I understand."

"You don't mind?"

"Oh, I mind." His fingers caressed her nape. "You don't know how badly I'd like to carry you to bed and make love to you all night long."

After the other night, she had a pretty good idea.

"I know you're not ready, sweetheart." His fingers delved into her hair. "But I'm a very patient man." Tilting her chin up, he kissed her lightly. "And I always get what I want."

And I always get what I want. Quill's words echoed in Callie's mind as she got ready for bed that night. On one hand, it had thrilled the primal cavewoman deep within her. On the other hand, it made the contemporary side of her a little uneasy. She told herself she'd read too many books, listened to too many news stories lately about sexual abuse. Quill had never forced himself on her. When she had felt things were going too far the other night, he had stopped.

But she couldn't help thinking that, with his preternatural powers, he probably did always get what he wanted.

One way or another.

It was a sobering thought.

* * *

In the morning, after a leisurely breakfast, Callie went down to her workshop. She added some recent pictures to her business website, Facebook, and Instagram. She studied the ad copy she'd written for one of the bridal magazines, but decided to hang on to it for a while. No sense advertising for new business while she was away.

She dusted the shelves, then put her cameras in their cases. She was about to go upstairs when she turned back and grabbed her favorite Nikon. If she was going to California, she wanted pictures of the trip.

With nothing pressing on her schedule, she took the time to mop and vacuum, then cancelled the newspaper and put a hold on her mail. She would see about having it forwarded when she learned her new address in Northern California, or maybe she'd ask Vivian to pick it up for her.

When that was done, she sorted through her old magazines and tossed the ones she no longer wanted.

She was thinking about going out to lunch when the phone rang. She smiled when she looked at her caller ID and saw Vivian's name. "Hey, Viv."

"Hi. I've got the day off and I was thinking, if you're not busy, maybe we could get together for lunch."

"You must have been reading my mind. Where shall we go? Jerri's Joint or Tony's?"

"Silly question," Viv said, a smile in her voice. "Tony's!"

"Okay. See you there at noon."

After taking a quick shower, Callie brushed her teeth and applied a bit of makeup. She dressed in a pair of jeans and a sweater, then pulled her hair back into a ponytail. A last look in the mirror and she was ready to go.

When she arrived at Tony's, Viv was already there. They ordered a ham-and-pineapple pizza and salad, then found a table near the front window.

"You look happy," Vivian said. "I take it you're still seeing Mr. Tall, Dark, and Handsome."

Callie nodded. "As a matter of fact, we're going away together for a while."

"Really? Where?"

"Up to Northern California. Some of his, uh . . . his family lives there and we're going for a visit." It was partly the truth.

Vivian frowned. "Are you sure going off with him is a good idea? I mean, you just met."

Callie took a sip of her soda. She couldn't very well tell Vivian that Quill feared her life might be in danger. And if the truth be told, she couldn't help being a little nervous about going away with him. Like Vivian said, she hadn't known Quill very long.

"Callie?"

"I know it's sudden, but I feel like I've been waiting for him my whole life. It's as if we're . . . we're . . ."

"Soul mates?"

"Something like that."

The pizza arrived, and they ate in silence for a moment. Callie wished she could confide in Vivian. It would be so nice to tell someone the truth.

"So, how long will you be gone?" Vivian asked.

"He didn't say."

"Do you want me to house-sit while you're away?"

"Sure, if you don't mind." She hadn't given a thought to who would water her plants while she was gone.

"You'd be doing me a favor. I've been wanting a break from my roommate. Dana's a great gal and fun to be with, but the girl's like a whirling dervish on steroids. I could use some peace and quiet. What about your business?"

"I don't have anything scheduled for a couple of months. Things are kind of slow right now, anyway."

Vivian finished her last slice of pizza. "I'd love to stay and chat, but I promised my mom I'd meet her at the Rug Emporium at two and help her pick out some new carpet. She's decided to redecorate the living room. Again. So, when are you leaving for California?"

"Monday."

"Okay. Keep in touch. And don't worry about a thing while you're gone."

"Thanks, Viv. I'll leave my key under the potted fern in the corner of the front porch."

After leaving the pizza place, Callie went shopping for a new pair of boots. She also picked up two pairs of jeans, a couple of long-sleeved shirts, and a warm jacket.

Back at home, she went through her wardrobe, deciding what to take with her. She emptied the dirty clothes hamper and put in a load of wash, then went looking for a suitcase.

She finally found one in Ava's closet. Pulling it down from the top shelf, she carried it into her room and dropped it on the bed. She pulled several pairs of jeans and shirts from her closet and dumped them beside the suitcase with her new clothes, then added underwear and socks and a pair of gloves. She rifled through the dresser drawers, looking for her favorite sweater, only then remembering it was in the wash.

Lifting the lid on the suitcase, she was surprised to find a notebook inside. Another journal? Picking it up, she thumbed through pages and pages of handwritten spells and incantations. Sitting on the edge of the mattress, she went back to the beginning, where she found a letter from Ava that she'd missed.

> *My dear Callie ~ These are the first spells my grandmother taught me when my magic manifested itself. They are simple and easy to master, meant to give you confidence as your magic grows stronger. They gradually grow more difficult. Remember, the power is within you. You must focus and concentrate to make it work. Many witches use wands to help direct their spells, but they aren't necessary. You will find a few of my things in the toolshed in a box marked Old Photos.*
>
> *Know that I love you and that, wherever I am, I miss you. Always remember to trust your heart.*
> *Your loving grandmother. Xoxoxo*

Callie read the letter again. She hadn't given much thought to exploring her powers in the last couple of days, but then, she'd been distracted, what with Quill being attacked again and his unexpected suggestion to move to California.

Putting the notebook aside, she went into the backyard and unlocked the toolshed. She found the box between a large, navy-blue suitcase and an old trunk.

Feeling a surge of excitement, she carried the box inside and set it on the kitchen table. After cutting away the twine that held it closed, she lifted the lid. There was a witches' treasure trove inside—a dull, black cauldron for brewing potions, a wrought-iron candelabra, a jeweled dagger wrapped in a silk cloth. A wand made of polished ebony wood. A smaller box inside the suitcase held a variety of interesting bottles.

Callie shook her head as she read a few of the labels: EYE OF NEWT, ST. JOHN'S WORT, OIL OF PEPPERMINT, a shaker filled with salt. A small glass jar held bat wings, another container was labeled DRAGONSBLOOD. A third had no label. And when she removed the lid, no odor. Puzzled, she replaced the cap and put it aside.

A small wooden box held a silver pentacle on a lovely chain. A black velvet bag contained an exquisite golden chalice etched with mystical symbols and runes.

When Callie ran her fingers over the pentacle, she was overcome by the feeling that her grandmother was standing behind her, that the air held a whiff of Ava's favorite perfume. Holding her breath, Callie glanced over her shoulder, let out a shaky laugh when there was no one there.

"What's all this?"

Callie whirled around, one hand at her throat at the sound of Quill's voice. "Oh, my gosh! You scared me half to death!"

He lifted one brow. "You look as pale as if you'd seen a ghost instead of an ordinary, run-of-the-mill vampire."

She shrugged one shoulder, feeling suddenly foolish. "You're going to think it's silly, but when I touched my grandmother's pentacle, I felt as if she was standing behind me. I'd swear I could smell her perfume."

Quill nodded. As he recalled, Ava had always worn lily of the valley. It had clung to her hair, her skin, her clothes. Even now, he caught a faint scent of it emanating from the black velvet bag on the table. "It's not silly at all. You're a witch, Callie. If you open your senses, you'll be able to detect things others can't."

She blinked up at him. "But she wasn't really here."

"No. But this was her home. These things connected her to her magic, which you inherited from her. It's a powerful bond, sweet Callie. I've no doubt your abilities are as strong as hers, if not stronger."

She thought that over a moment and then frowned. "How do you know so much about my grandmother?"

Damn. Was now the time to tell her the truth?

"Quill?"

"I just know a lot about witches," he said. Which was partly true. He knew a lot about one particular witch. "I can sense the magic lying dormant within you. For it to be so strong, your grandmother must have been a powerful witch. And from the number of books she left you, it's obvious she studied her craft."

Callie nodded slowly.

"Why don't you pack these things and whatever else you'll need and bring them with you? There's a lot of empty space where we're going. A perfect place to practice your magic without hurting anyone."

She smiled at him. "That's a good idea." Suddenly excited at the prospect of being able to experiment with her powers, she said, "Why don't we leave tomorrow instead of Monday? I'll call Vivian and let her know we're leaving early."

"Sounds good to me." Drawing her into his arms, he

kissed her. "I'm going back to my place to pack. I won't be back until after dark."

"Why so long?"

His gaze drifted to her throat. "I need to feed."

"What's it like?" she asked. "Feeding on people?"

Releasing her, he dragged his hand over his jaw. What *was* it like? "I don't know how to explain it. It comes naturally to me."

"Does it hurt the people you prey on?"

"Does it hurt when I drink from you?"

"No. It feels wonderful." She looked up at him, eyes sparkling with curiosity. "Does it feel that way for everyone?"

He stroked her cheek with his knuckles. "If I choose to make it so."

"Do you?"

He smiled at her. "Yes."

She was glad he didn't hurt anyone. At the same time, she felt a sharp stab of jealousy knowing other women felt the same way she did. "Do you feed on men, too?"

"Occasionally."

"Do they feel the same sensual pleasure I do?"

Quill chuckled, amused by her questions. "No."

She cocked her head to the side, her expression thoughtful. "Does all blood taste the same?"

"No, my curious one. Yours is the sweetest of all." Pulling her into his arms again, he brushed a kiss across her lips, her cheek, the tip of her nose. "Don't forget to lock the door after me."

While packing her grandmother's things, Callie tried to imagine what it would be like to be a vampire, to go out into the night and prey on unsuspecting men and women. To drink their blood. Try as she might, she just couldn't imagine it. It seemed so bizarre, so primal.

She tossed the last of the things she had decided to take with her into the navy-blue suitcase, then called Vivian to let her know they were leaving tomorrow night instead of Monday.

"No problem," Vivian assured her. "I guess you just can't wait to get away with him. Not that I blame you. The guy is drop-dead gorgeous."

Drop-dead gorgeous, Callie mused after saying good-bye. Viv had no idea how close to the truth she was.

Her life had certainly changed since she met Quill, she thought as she prepared an early dinner. She loved him more every day, and now she was going away with him.

Feeling suddenly daring, she added her one sexy nightgown to her bag. Because a girl never knew when she might need something a little more provocative than a pair of Minnie Mouse pajamas.

Chapter 15

Lurking beneath his invisibility cloak, Trey 95 stalked the vampire while the vampire stalked his prey—a young couple heading for the parking lot behind the movie theater.

He had to admire the vampire's stealth as he trailed after him.

The man was opening the car door for the woman when the vampire made his move. First, the creature mesmerized the couple; then he took the woman in his arms. A morbid part of Trey 95 wondered what the vampire's prey experienced while the monster fed.

When the vampire sank his fangs into the woman's throat, Trey 95 shrugged off his cloak and sprang forward, intending to stake the vampire in the back.

He let out a wordless cry of horror when the vampire vanished and the stake, intended to pierce the creature's heart, sank into the woman's chest.

She let out a shriek Trey 95 knew he would carry to the grave as the life went out of her eyes.

Sobbing, "I'm sorry, I'm sorry," he caught her in his arms as her body went limp.

The sound of the woman's cry shattered the vampire's

spell on the man. He stared at Trey, his eyes wide with shock. "What have you done?"

Sworn to secrecy, unable to tell the man the truth, Trey 95 pushed the woman into the man's arms, grabbed his cloak, and fled the scene.

"Damn you, vampire!" he swore. "That woman's blood is on your hands."

Trey 95 was in his room later that night when four of his brother Knights came calling.

At the sight of them, he fought down the urge to bolt, knowing they had been sent by the Elder Knight of the Brotherhood.

One of the Knights nodded. "You know why we're here, Trey 95. Let's go."

Resigned, he followed them to meet his fate.

The Elder Knight of the Dark Wood was an austere man, tall and lean, with little mercy for those who broke the sacred laws of the Brotherhood. And the First Law was to do no harm to humanity.

Trey 95 stood before him, shoulders back, his head held high, even though he was trembling inside.

"You know why I have called you here," the Elder Knight said, his voices as sharp as a double-edged blade.

Trey 95 nodded.

"You defied my order to come home for the initiation of two of your Brothers. You attacked a vampire in the presence of a mortal. And now I learn that you have been responsible for the death of a human woman. Do you deny these charges?"

Hands clenched at his sides, Trey 95 said, "No."

"Do you wish to offer any explanation for your behavior?"

He shook his head.

"I understand that the vampire you are pursuing killed your twin brother. That is unfortunate, but you must not indulge your need for vengeance over your duty. Is that clear?"

"Yes, sir."

"The punishment for disobedience is ten lashes, to be carried out immediately in front of the Brotherhood." The Elder Knight nodded to the two men attired in red robes standing beside him.

They stepped forward, one on each side of Trey 95, and escorted him into the courtyard.

A tall tree stood in the center. His brother Knights, all shrouded in dark cloaks, surrounded it, their faces solemn.

Trey 95 was visibly shaking as he removed his shirt. A fine sheen of sweat dotted his brow as they bound his hands to the tree.

One of the men clad in red shook out a whip. He cracked it in the air once. Twice. Three times.

Trey 95 flinched each time, fought down the urge to scream when the lash bit deep into his flesh.

The assembled Knights counted each stroke out loud.

"One. Two. Three . . ."

Blackness swam before Trey's eyes as they intoned, "Four. Five. Six . . ."

Feeling as though he had been standing there for eternity, he sagged in his bonds, his back on fire.

"Seven. Eight. Nine . . ."

Blood flowed down his back, and with it, a renewed hatred for the vampire who had brought him to this place. "Ten."

Merciful darkness enfolded him, carrying him away from the pain and humiliation.

Chapter 16

Callie looked up from the book she was reading when Quill materialized in the living room. Troubled by the harsh expression on his face, she asked, "What's happened? You were gone so long, I was starting to worry."

Shaking his head, he paced the floor in front of the fireplace.

"Quill, you're scaring me."

He stopped in front of her, hands fisted at his side. "That damn Knight tracked me while I was feeding," he said, his voice taut with anger. "When he came at me, I instinctively got out of the way. And . . ."

Callie sat forward, her hands gripping the edges of the book as she waited for him to go on.

"The stake meant for me killed the woman."

"Oh, no!" Callie stood, the book falling, unnoticed, to the floor as she went to Quill and wrapped her arms around his waist. "It wasn't your fault."

"Isn't it?" he asked, harshly. "An innocent woman is dead because of me."

Unable to think of anything to say, she hugged him.

His body was so tense, it was like hugging a rock. He relaxed gradually.

Taking her in his arms, he rested his forehead against hers. "She was so young," he murmured, his voice thick with anguish. "She had her whole life ahead of her, and now she's dead for no good reason and I'm to blame."

Tears stung Callie's eyes—shed for the young woman who had died needlessly, for Quill's anguish. She wished she could think of something profound to say that would comfort him, but nothing came to mind. Vampire or not, he was a good, decent man, she thought. Otherwise, he wouldn't be feeling such guilt over what had happened.

Taking his hand, she tugged him toward the sofa and pulled him down beside her. His gaze met hers, his dark eyes haunted.

Murmuring, "Oh, Quill," she laid her head against his chest.

Clinging to her hand, he murmured, "I love you, Callie. Thank you for not judging me. Or hating me."

"I could never hate you." She looked up, her gaze meeting his. A thrill ran through her when he pulled her into his arms and held her close. His kiss, when it came, was achingly tender. She felt his sorrow as if it were her own—his regret, his need for comfort. Cupping his cheek in her palm, she kissed him.

Growling her name, Quill's arms tightened around her as he fell back on the sofa, carrying her with him, so that they lay side by side, her legs tangled with his. He kissed her with a kind of quiet desperation, as if he could bury his guilt in her caress.

She felt the press of his desire against her belly,

tasted the need in his kisses, in the touch of his hands as he restlessly stroked her back and thighs.

His tongue traveled the length of her neck like a flame against her skin. When he groaned her name, she pushed her hair out of the way, giving him access to her throat.

His bite was gentle, followed by a familiar wave of pleasure that warmed her from the inside out.

She knew a rush of panic when he didn't stop after a moment or two as he usually did. Then, as if suddenly realizing what he was doing, he pulled away. Sitting up, he lifted her onto his lap, his arm around her waist. "I'm sorry," he murmured, his voice husky.

"For what?"

He shook his head. "I was about to take advantage of you."

"Oh?"

He trailed his knuckles along her cheek. "When we make love, I want it to be for the right reason. Not because I'm trying to bury my guilt."

"I love you, Quill."

He stared at her as if she were speaking a foreign language. Not because of the words she'd spoken. He knew she loved him, as he loved her. "You never fail to surprise me," he said with a faint grin. "On this night of all nights, I'm not sure I deserve either your love or your trust."

"It wasn't your fault," she said sternly. "If anyone's to blame, it's that Knight. You weren't hurting anyone. He had murder in his heart."

"Ah, Callie," he murmured. "I love you beyond words. Someday I hope to show you how much."

Someday. She smiled inwardly as she thought of the

sexy nightgown tucked in her suitcase and wondered if she would ever have the nerve to wear it.

In the morning, Callie ate breakfast, then spent the rest of the day cleaning the house from top to bottom so it would be spotless when Vivian arrived. She watered the plants, changed the sheets on the bed, went through the refrigerator and dumped her leftovers, emptied the dishwasher.

By the time she'd showered and dressed, the sun had set but there was no sign of Quill.

Going to the guest room, she rapped on the door. His was the only room she hadn't dusted or vacuumed. "Quill?"

When there was no answer, she peeked inside. The bed was made. There was no sign of him. Chewing on her thumbnail, she wandered through the house. Where was he? Why had he left without telling her? Had he even stayed the night? And if not, where had he gone?

In the kitchen, she made a cup of hot chocolate and carried it into the living room. Curling up in a corner of the sofa, she sipped her cocoa, then bolted upright. Had he gone hunting? What if that Knight had found him again and been successful this time? Oh, Lord! Putting the cup aside, she went in search of her cell phone.

Her imagination went into overdrive when he didn't answer.

Where could he be?

She paced the floor for several anxious minutes and then called him again.

* * *

Quill stared at the two Knights. They were both young, probably not more than twenty years old, and looked scared half to death. He was leaving town just in time, he thought ruefully. The place seemed to be crawling with the Knights of the Dark Wood, although these two didn't seem to be a problem. They had come upon him while he was looking for prey. Now that they'd found him, neither of them seemed to know what to do next. New initiates, he thought, and almost felt sorry for them.

"Why don't you both just run along," Quill suggested, careful to keep his voice mild.

The Knights glanced at each other, their expressions uncertain.

He could almost hear their thoughts. Should they let him go? Or attack? How would they explain it to the others if they turned tail and ran? Quill shook his head. If these two didn't grow some backbone, the Knights would be looking for two more brothers.

While they were making up their minds, his phone rang again.

Deciding to make the decision for them so he could answer the call, Quill vanished from their sight.

He answered on the second ring. "Callie, is anything wrong?"

"I guess not. I was just wondering where you were. And then I started wondering if you'd tangled with that Knight again."

"No, although I ran into a couple of his brothers. But don't worry. These two were harmless."

"Are you coming home?"

Home. He liked the sound of that. "I'm on my way."

She was waiting for him at the front door. Sweeping her into his arms, he knew that he would always be home as long as Callie was there. "Are you ready to go?" Stepping inside, he dropped a small duffel bag on the floor.

"You never said how we were going to get there."

"I'm taking us the quickest way I know how."

"So, we're flying?"

"In a way."

"What does that mean?"

"I'm going to transport us there."

Callie stared at him. "What? How?"

"Using one of my amazing vampire powers."

"Can't we just drive?"

"This is faster." He tapped the end of her nose with his forefinger. "When you've perfected your magic, you'll be able to do it, too. But for now, we'll do it my way. Where are your suitcases?"

"In the bedroom."

Nodding, he went to get them while Callie walked through the house one last time to make sure she hadn't forgotten anything. When she returned to the living room, Quill was waiting for her.

"Got everything?" he asked.

"I guess so. Oh, wait." Grabbing her handbag, she located her house key, stepped out on the front porch, and slid the key under the potted fern in the corner.

"All set?" he asked when she locked the door behind her.

"Yes."

"Can you carry my duffel?" he asked.

"Sure." Pushing the strap of her handbag over her shoulder, she picked up his bag and held it against her chest.

Quill tucked her smaller suitcase under his arm and picked up the second one by the handle. "Come here," he said, holding out his free hand. When she stood beside him, he wrapped his arm around her waist and held her close. "Trust me. There's nothing to be afraid of," he assured her, "although it might make you a little nauseous the first time. Ready?"

"I don't think so." She looked at him warily, wondering just what "transporting" meant exactly.

He chuckled softly. "Close your eyes, love. We'll be there before you realize we've gone."

Not knowing what to expect, Callie took a deep breath, swallowed hard, and closed her eyes. Her stomach plummeted, the way it did when planes took off, only much worse. She felt as if she was falling through darkness at the speed of light, and just when she was sure destruction lay ahead, it was over.

Blowing out a shaky breath, she opened her eyes to find they were at the edge of a small town surrounded by mountains thick with pine and juniper. The air was cold, the sky dark with the promise of rain.

"That wasn't so bad, was it?" Quill asked.

"I'll let you know when my stomach settles and my head stops spinning."

He laughed softly. "Come on, let's find a place to stay."

"Don't we need reservations or something?"

"No. My people own most of the houses on the west side. We'll just find a vacant one." He shifted the smaller suitcase to his free hand and set off down the street.

Callie followed him. The town was divided in half, with houses on one side and businesses on the other. Most of the houses had lights showing in the windows.

Near the far end of the road, Quill stopped in front of a single-story house that was dark. He opened his senses, searching for signs of life, and when he found none, he climbed the two stairs to the narrow porch and opened the door. Glancing over his shoulder, he said, "Welcome home, love."

Feeling like a cat burglar, Callie followed Quill into the house, then set his duffel bag on the floor. "Are you sure this is all right?"

He nodded as he turned on the lights, revealing a large, square room. A stone fireplace took up most of the wall to the left of the entrance. A watercolor painting depicting a herd of wild horses running across a starlit meadow hung above the mantel. The furniture was made of heavy dark wood. A sofa and love seat, both covered in a flowered print, stood on either side of the hearth with a coffee table between them. A half-wall divided the room. The other side held another sofa, a couple of easy chairs arranged in a semi-circle around a large TV set.

Quill dropped her suitcases, then locked and bolted the door.

Callie glanced around. An open archway led into a kitchen. A second arch opened onto a hallway. She assumed the bedrooms and bath were down the hall.

"What do you think?" Quill asked.

"It's lovely."

Taking her hand, he said, "Let's take a look around."

The kitchen held all the latest appliances—stove, microwave, refrigerator, dishwasher. A rectangular table and six chairs stood in front of the room's single window. Three bedrooms opened off the hallway. The larger one had its own bathroom, and the two smaller rooms shared a bath.

"The larger one is yours," Quill said. "I'll go get our bags."

"Okay." Callie looked around the room. The queen-sized bed was flanked by a pair of cherrywood nightstands. A matching four-drawer dresser stood across from the bed. A dainty, padded rocker stood in one corner beside a window. There was a small walk-in closet and a large bathroom with both a tub and a shower.

"So, what do you think?" Quill asked, dropping her suitcases on the foot of the bed.

"I love it."

"I thought you would. If you get bored tomorrow, you can go into town and pick up some groceries and whatever you want. Just charge everything to me."

"I can't let you do that."

"You're here as my guest. It's only fitting that I pay the bills."

Callie nodded reluctantly, though she wasn't sure she felt comfortable with that arrangement. She was used to paying her own way.

"What's wrong?"

She shook her head. "Nothing."

He took her hands in his. "I know something's

bothering you. What is it?" he asked, and then he knew. "You just realized you're in a town populated mostly by my kind and you're wondering if coming here with me was a good idea."

Her gaze slid away from his, telling him that was exactly what she'd been thinking. "I won't let anything happen to you," he said, pulling her into his arms. "I know most of the vampires who live here. They're all married. Most of them have children. No need to feel like a lone lamb in a den of wolves."

Callie laughed because that was exactly how she felt—like a little lost lamb among predators.

"It's a beautiful night," Quill remarked. "Why don't we go for a walk?"

"Sounds great. Just let me get my jacket."

Bundled up in jeans, a jacket, and boots against the chill of the night, Callie walked beside Quill, her hand tucked in his. A cool breeze rustled the leaves on the trees; a bright moon peeked through a break in the clouds as they walked along what she thought might be a deer path that wound its way behind the house.

"Where does this lead?" she asked.

"Down to the lake."

"Awesome."

Quill grinned at her. "Feel like taking a dip?"

She shook her head. "Are you kidding? It's way too cold for that."

"I can heat the water for you, if you like."

"Really?"

He nodded.

"Is that another of your amazing vampire powers?"

"Yes, ma'am."

"Darn. Too bad I didn't bring a bathing suit."

"You don't need one."

"No? Don't tell me you can make one magically appear."

He laughed softly. "No, but bathing suits these days look more like underwear, anyway, so . . ." He shrugged as if it was no big deal.

Callie stared at him. Was he serious? Go swimming in her underwear? In front of him?

"If you don't like that idea, we could go skinny-dipping."

Callie's mouth went dry at the thought of seeing Quill in the buff. She'd seen him naked from the waist up and the view had been spectacular, but . . . She shook her head. "I really don't think *that's* a good idea."

"Probably not," he agreed with a rueful smile. There were limits to his restraint, after all. And he was pretty sure seeing Callie as the Good Lord made her would shatter even his prodigious self-control.

Callie gasped when they reached the lake. It stretched in front of them like a mirror of black glass, flat and smooth as it reflected the moon's pale light. "It looks magical," she murmured.

Quill nodded, then pointed at the far shore. "Look."

Lifting her gaze, Callie saw a deer and a half-grown fawn make their dainty way down to the edge of the lake. The doe stood there, poised for flight, ears flicking back and forth while the fawn drank. She sighed, thinking what a rare and beautiful sight it was. Suddenly, the doe darted away, white tail flashing in the moonlight, the fawn at her heels.

Quill felt his heart swell as he watched the play of emotions on Callie's face. Being there beside her was like looking at the world through her eyes. He had lived so long, he'd become almost indifferent to the world around him. No matter how things changed, for him everything remained basically the same.

"It's getting late," he said. "We should head back so you can get some sleep."

Callie nodded. She was a little tired. Traveling vampire-style had taken a bit of a toll on her.

When they reached the house, Quill drew her into his arms and kissed her. "Thanks, love."

"For what?"

"I owe you big time for putting up with me. For not letting what I am scare you away."

Smiling, she said, "No charge."

"Rest well, love."

"You, too."

"Always," he said, dryly. "I'll see you tomorrow evening." He kissed her again. "I'm going out for a while."

"Okay. Be careful."

"Worried about me?"

"I can't help it. People want to kill you."

He winked at her. "They've been trying for centuries. Get some sleep, Callie." He kissed the tip of her nose. "Dream of me."

She stood outside for several minutes after he left before going into the house. Her life had changed drastically in a remarkably short time, she thought as she closed the door. Yawning, she turned off the lights then went to her room to get ready for bed.

Slipping under the covers, she closed her eyes and fell asleep with Quill's name on her lips.

Chapter 17

Trey 95 prowled the night, one hand clutching his medallion, but it remained stubbornly quiet. He had been tasked with locating a vampire known as Dougal, but he had no interest in tracking that one down. Let the Brotherhood hunt the rest. He wanted Quill and only Quill. The best place to find him was with the woman, and with that in mind, he headed for the residential area.

The house was dark, the curtains drawn.

Slipping from shadow to shadow, he moved closer, every sense alert as he circled the house.

He swore under his breath as his sharply honed senses told him the vampire wasn't there.

But the woman was. He could sense a human presence in one of the bedrooms. Sooner or later, the vampire would return.

He glanced over his shoulder, every muscle taut, knowing that if he was caught here, the punishment he had received before would be doubled.

But it didn't matter. He wouldn't rest until Quill was dead.

Or he was.

Chapter 18

Callie woke slowly, reluctantly. Last night, Quill had asked her to dream of him, and boy, had she! Smiling, she stretched her arms over her head. Then, remembering where she was, she bounded out of bed and pulled back the curtains. It had rained in the night and the world looked fresh and new. Raindrops glistened like diamonds on the leaves of the trees; the air was fragrant with the scent of rain-washed earth and pine.

Pulling on her robe, she headed for the kitchen, only then remembering there was no food in the house. Changing direction, she went back to the bedroom with its adjoining bath, where she took a quick shower, then pulled on her jeans, a sweater, and her new boots. She paused at the front door. If she locked it, she had no way to get back in. Well, there was no help for it, she'd just have to leave it unlocked. She was too hungry to wait for Quill to wake up.

Settling her handbag on her shoulder, she struck out for town.

It wasn't the best day for a walk. Dark clouds hovered in the west, threatening more rain to come, but the sky above was clear and blue. As she neared the town, Callie saw several women out and about. They eyed her speculatively as she passed by. Were they ordinary people, vampires, or women married to vampires? There was no way for her to tell, since the Hungarian vamps could be out during the day.

As she walked along, Callie realized none of the houses had mailboxes. Odd, she thought, unless people picked up their mail at the post office.

For a small town, it supported a variety of shops, as well as a bank, a gas station, a small drugstore, a movie theater, and a medical building.

The grocery store was located at the end of the block. Finding a cart, Callie walked the aisles, plucking basic items from the shelf. In the produce aisle, she bought a variety of fruits and vegetables, wondering, as she did so, what Quill liked to eat, and how often he ate regular food. In the meat department, she bought chicken and steaks and Italian meatballs.

She was leaving the frozen food aisle when she saw a woman pushing a cart coming toward her. Callie pulled over to let her pass, but the woman stopped, a friendly smile on her face. She was quite pretty, perhaps in her mid-thirties, with short, curly dark hair and brown eyes.

"You're new in town, aren't you?" the woman said.

Callie nodded. "Yes, I am."

"I thought so. I'm Wendy Yates."

"Callie Hathaway."

"Are you staying long?"

"I don't know."

Wendy nodded. "I guess we never know how long we're going to stay in any one place, do we?"

"Excuse me?"

"You know," Wendy said with an airy wave of her hand. And then she frowned. "Or maybe you don't."

"I'm sorry, I don't understand."

Wendy took a step back, her smile fading. "I'm sorry, I thought you were one of us. Have a nice day."

Callie frowned at her. "We are here to stay. At least for a while. My friend's people live here."

"So, you are one of us."

Callie stared at her, momentarily perplexed by the whole conversation, and then she understood. "I'm new at all this," she admitted, "and I still have a lot to learn about vampires."

Wendy's smile returned. "Welcome to town. I'm sure you'll like it here. It's nice, not having to be careful about what you say all the time. The majority of people you see during the day will be mortal, since most of the vampires prefer the night. But everyone who lives here is either a vampire or married to one."

Callie nodded, deciding not to mention that she and Quill weren't married.

"You may have noticed we don't have mailboxes and there's no post office, so if you're expecting any bills or correspondence, you'll have to go to Wendover, which is about ten miles east of here."

"How do the people who run the shops get supplies?"

"They order them in Wendover and pick them up. Some of our older kids go to school there, although most of them are home-schooled. As far as the rest of the country knows, this place doesn't exist."

Callie frowned, wondering how that was even possible in this day and age, what with drones and Google Earth. Had the vampires who lived here warded this place and somehow managed to block modern-day technology?

"Well, I've got to go," Wendy said. "I think you'll find most of the town's residents friendly enough once they get to know you. Well, all except Chloe. She . . ." Wendy glanced at her watch. "Oh! I've *really* got to go! It was nice meeting you."

"Thanks. It was nice meeting you, too."

"I'm sure we'll run into each other again," Wendy called over her shoulder as she hurried down the aisle. "It's a small town, after all."

Feeling as though she had stepped into an episode of *The Twilight Zone*, Callie stared after her. A town inhabited solely by vampires and their human companions. Who would ever believe it?

A rumble of thunder followed Callie home. She had no sooner stepped inside and closed the door than the rain came, a gentle patter against the windows.

She put the groceries away, ate breakfast, and then went into her room and unpacked her clothes. A glance at her phone showed it was only 11 AM. The day stretched before her and she found herself again wondering what she was going to do here while Quill was at rest. There wasn't much to see in town. She didn't have a car, so she couldn't go far.

She glanced at the TV and shook her head. How did they even get TV here? And lights and heat if the mortal world didn't know the town existed? She puzzled over it for a moment, then snapped her fingers. She knew just how to spend the day.

Grabbing the suitcase and the box that held her

grandmother's magical accoutrements, she went into the kitchen and spread the contents on the table. Opening the grimoire, she flipped through the pages. There were instructions for making talismans and amulets to heal the sick or win someone's affections, and other information on how to cast spells—some of which hinted at dark magic. Ceremonial magic was used to summon spirits. White magic summoned angels. Dark magic summoned demons to do a witch's bidding. A note in the margin in Ava's hand warned of the danger in experimenting with black magic.

Callie frowned. Why on earth would anyone in their right mind want to summon a demon? She shook her head as she perused spells that would cause someone's crops to fail, make their cows go dry and their chickens refuse to lay. It seemed unlikely that those spells were much in demand in this day and age. She grinned as she wondered if modern-day witches were responsible for computer viruses and other technological glitches.

She turned a couple of pages. Surely there was some innocuous spell she could try her hand at that wouldn't burn down someone's house or summon a demon from the underworld.

Closing the grimoire, Callie put on her grandmother's pentacle, then opened the notebook of handwritten spells for beginners and turned to the first incantation. Concentrating on gathering her power, she flicked her hand at a candle on the windowsill and spoke the words to summon fire.

She gasped with surprise when the candle sprang to life. Unable to believe the small flame was real, she took a few steps toward the window for a closer look, then held her finger over the flame. "I did it, Grandma," she murmured as she felt the heat. "I really did it!"

A whisper of magic roused Quill from his rest. He bolted upright; then, when he realized the spell had been cast by Callie, the tension drained out of him. Curious, he got out of bed, pulled on a pair of pants, and padded into the kitchen.

He found her bent over a notebook, muttering to herself.

She looked up when he entered the room, a broad smile spreading over her face. "I made magic!"

"I know. I felt it."

"Really?"

He nodded. "It was strong enough to wake me."

"Oh. I'm sorry."

"It's okay." He joined her at the table, his gaze moving over the handwritten text. "What are you going to try next?"

"I don't know. Got any ideas?"

"You could try summoning an object to you."

Frowning, she thumbed through the pages. "Here's one." Brow furrowed, she read the ritual for summoning. Glancing around the kitchen, she focused on one of the apples in the bowl on the sink. She took several deep breaths, spoke the required words, and watched in amazement as one of the apples lifted from the bowl and came to her hand.

Stunned, Callie dropped into one of the kitchen chairs. "I really *am* a witch."

"So it would appear. How do you feel?"

"I don't know. Kind of . . . I don't know, sort of elated

and drained at the same time, as if I'd been working really hard to accomplish a goal and I finally attained it."

"It will get easier with practice, and you'll be able to manipulate heavier objects. And summon items you can't see."

Callie stared up at him. For a vampire, he seemed to know a great deal about witchcraft. And an awful lot about her grandmother's magic. She recalled the dream she'd had about Quill and Ava. If she hadn't known it was impossible, she would have sworn Quill and Ava had known each other.

And then she frowned. Why was it impossible? Her grandmother had lived a good long life. And Quill had lived even longer. They could have met decades ago, way back before she was born, although it seemed unlikely that their paths would have crossed. With a shake of her head, Callie thrust the disconcerting thought away.

"You went out earlier," he said.

"I went shopping and I met a lady named Wendy. She seemed very friendly. She told me this place doesn't show up on maps and very few people even know it exists. How is that possible? Did the vampires do something?"

"Three hundred years ago, a very powerful witch and an equally powerful vampire got together and concocted a spell that shields the town from anyone who intends to do us harm." Anyone except the Knights, he thought ruefully. Their medallions gave them a kind of supernatural power of their own. Thus far, they hadn't been able to locate the town, though they knew of its existence.

Placing his hand on her shoulder, Quill said, "Why don't you rest a bit? I need to go out for a while."

"In the rain?"

"I'm not like the Wicked Witch of the West. I won't melt if I get wet," he said with a grin. "You, however, better be careful."

"Very funny. Will you be gone long?"

"No." Bending down, he cupped her cheek in his palm and kissed her. "Don't burn the house down."

Quill left the kitchen through the back door, then lingered beside the window, out of sight. He had seen the growing suspicion in Callie's eyes. Curious to know the reason behind it, he let his mind brush hers. As he'd feared, she was beginning to wonder if he had known Ava and if so, how and when.

He frowned as he transported himself to the next town.

Perhaps it was time to tell her the truth.

Callie was sitting at the table, eating a ham and cheese sandwich, when a bolt of lightning lit up the sky, followed by a drumroll of thunder that shook the house. She had always loved storms. Rising, she put her sandwich aside and went to the window, hoping to see another flash of lightning.

She let out a startled shriek when a black cat, its fur plastered against its body, jumped up on the ledge outside the window. "What on earth are you doing out there?" Callie exclaimed, and then grinned. "I guess sometimes it really does rain cats and dogs."

The wet feline stared back at her through unblinking yellow-gold eyes.

With a shake of her head, Callie opened the back door. She'd no sooner done so than the cat streaked into the house.

"Well, come on in, why don't you?" she muttered.

The cat looked up at her, as though waiting for something.

Callie frowned, then pulled a dish towel from a drawer and began drying the cat's fur. A deep, rumbling purr was her thanks.

When the cat was dry, Callie opened a can of tuna fish, scooped a little onto a small plate and offered it to her guest. The cat nodded at her—nodded at her!—then crouched down and devoured the tuna. When it was done, the cat padded into the living room, curled up in front of the fireplace and went to sleep.

"That's okay, just make yourself at home," Callie said, a note of sarcasm creeping into her tone as, with a wave of her hand and a few muttered words, she called forth fire in the hearth.

Quill returned an hour later, bringing with him the scent of damp wool and rain. He came to an abrupt halt when he saw Callie sitting on the sofa and the cat sleeping in front of the fireplace. "Where did *that* come from?"

"I don't know. She was on the window ledge outside the kitchen, and when I opened the door . . ." Callie shrugged. "She's been here ever since."

"Well, every witch should have a familiar. Ava had one. . . ." *Damn!* He'd let the proverbial cat out of the bag this time!

Callie stared at him. "I knew it!" she exclaimed. "You *did* know each other."

"Yeah."

She shook her head. Hadn't she somehow known it all

the time? She took a deep, calming breath. "How did you meet her?"

Quill looked at her, one brow raised.

"You *fed* on my grandmother!"

"Eventually. It was over a hundred years ago."

Callie stared at him in horror. "You fed on her when she was a child?"

"Of course not! Ava was right around fifty when I knew her and that was a century ago."

"That's impossible! She would have been well over a hundred when she passed away."

"It's not impossible for witches. Some live for two, three hundred years."

"But . . . she told me she was in her early seventies, even though she never looked more than forty. She said it was just good genes."

"Very few witches ever look their real age."

Callie blinked at him in astonishment. Was it possible *she* could live that long?

"It took me a while to recognize the resemblance between the two of you," Quill said. "You look a lot like her, you know. Not only that, but your blood tastes the same. When I put two and two together, I knew you and Ava were related, though I had no idea she was your grandmother when we met."

Quill had fed off Grandma Ava over a hundred years ago. Ava had known vampires existed and warned Callie against them. How had she put it? *One kind would steal her blood and the other would steal her heart.* How could Ava have known Callie was destined to meet one? Had she known it would be Quill? The very idea was mind boggling. "I don't know what to say."

He could understand that, he thought, sitting on the chair across from her.

Callie frowned as she remembered the dreams she'd had of Quill and Ava. Had they really been lovers? "How do you suppose she knew you and I would meet?"

"She had the Sight. I'm not sure she knew you would meet me, but she must have feared you'd meet a vampire of one kind or another someday. Hence, the spell she wove around you."

"Where did you meet?"

"At a bar in San Diego." Quill smiled at the memory. "She'd been dancing with a Marine, laughing and flirting for all she was worth. I took one look at her and I wanted her."

Much as he had wanted Callie the first time he'd seen her. "I cut in on the Marine, and when he objected, we got into a hell of a brawl." He grinned at her. "I won, of course."

"Of course," she said dryly. "Go on."

"Well, I bought her a drink and we danced and drank some more and . . ." He paused.

Callie chewed on the corner of her lower lip. She had a terrible feeling that she knew what was coming next. "And?"

"There was no denying the attraction between us. One thing led to another and we drove to the nearest motel."

Callie stared at him. Ava had met Quill and slept with him the same night. She tried to summon a sense of shock at her grandmother's behavior, or outrage at Quill for what had happened between them, but all she could think was that the two of them seemed made for each other.

"It was just the one night," he said. "At the time, I

thought she wouldn't make love to me again because I'd been such a rotten lover. But looking back, I think that having the Sight, she knew you and I would fall in love. I hung around with her and her friends for a few months. We had some good times."

"Did you love her?"

"I could have, if she'd let me. It wasn't long after I moved on that she fell in love with one of the Knights of the Dark Wood."

"Did you ever see her again?"

"No. But I never forgot her." Quill's gaze searched hers. "Is this going to change things between us?" he asked, his voice strangely devoid of emotion.

Did it? Callie worried her lower lip as she thought it over. She couldn't help feeling jealous that Ava and Quill had been lovers even though it had happened over a hundred years ago. Still, it had been just one night. After all this time, did it really matter?

Looking away, she shook her head. "I don't know." She felt his gaze resting on her as she remembered the kisses they had shared, the way he always made her feel safe, how he had encouraged her to pursue her magic. She had cared for him, tended his wounds, nourished him with her life's blood. Was she going to let something that had happened long before she was born come between them?

She slid a glance at him. He was tall and dark, strong, and a bit arrogant. A powerful being. And yet he needed her.

But, more than that, he loved her.

And she loved him. "No," she said at last. "It doesn't make any difference."

"Callie!" He was reaching for her when, with a hiss,

the black cat sprang between them, her claws raking Quill's cheek as she twisted in midair and landed in Callie's lap, back arched and tail straight up in the air.

"Bad cat!" Callie exclaimed. "Quill, I'm so sorry."

He wiped the blood from his face with the back of his hand. "I guess I should have told you—cats and vampires don't mix."

Chapter 19

Trey 95 stood outside the woman's house again. His medallion told him the vampire wasn't in residence at the moment. But the woman was there. He could see her shadow moving from room to room behind the curtains.

Frowning, he glanced at his watch. It was only ten. Perhaps the vampire was hunting. He checked his weapons—silver-bladed knife, vial of holy water, wooden stake honed to a fine point.

Satisfied, he returned his attention to the house. He had taken an oath to do no harm to mortals, but he reasoned within himself that holding the woman captive to get his hands on the vampire wouldn't cause her any harm. A little mental distress, perhaps, but no lasting physical damage.

He thrust aside the consequences he would face if he was caught here. Another lashing was worth the risk.

Besides, if he took Quill's head, he would be a hero.

He closed his eyes a moment, imagining what it would be like to be hailed as the Knight who had destroyed one of the oldest Hungarian vampires in existence. He would be crowned with honor, his previous shame and embarrassment forgotten.

Trey 95 smiled inwardly. He would make his move later tonight, when he was less apt to be seen by her neighbors.

And if the vampire came home in the meantime, so much the better.

Fading into the shadows, Trey 95 shoved his hands into his pockets. He was a predator of sorts, and like all predators, he had learned the infinite value of patience.

Clearing his mind, he settled down to wait.

Vivian switched off the TV, made sure all the doors and windows were locked, and readied herself for bed. She wondered how Callie and her mystery man were getting along. There was something not quite right about him. She shook her head, unable to put her finger on why she felt that way. But it worried her. Callie didn't have a lot of experience with men—especially older men—and Vivian didn't want to see her best friend get hurt. Maybe she'd give her a call tomorrow.

Deciding to read for a while before going to sleep, Viv grabbed a book from the shelf and padded into the guest room. Settling on the bed, she propped the pillow behind her back and flipped to page one. By page ten, she had lost herself in the story, imagining herself as the damsel in distress being rescued from certain death by the fair-haired hero.

* * *

From his place in the shadows, Trey 95 watched the house grow dark. He waited another half an hour, giving the woman time to settle down for the night, and then he ghosted across the street.

On the porch, he reached into his pocket and withdrew a small set of tools. Selecting one, he slid it into the lock, turned it just so, and the door opened with a quiet *snick*. A safety chain slowed him for only a moment.

Slipping the lockpick back in his pocket, he stepped inside. In the faint glow of a penlight, he made his way through the house.

The master bedroom was empty.

Continuing down the hall, he peered into the next bedroom. It was also empty.

Brow furrowed, he opened the door to the next room. The woman lay with her back toward him, her breathing slow and regular. Why was she sleeping in here?

Shrugging, he crept into the room. He drew a small brown bottle from his pocket, splashed a few drops from the container on a rag and placed it carefully over her nose and mouth.

She let out a startled gasp, took a few breaths, and went limp.

With a grunt of satisfaction, Trey 95 draped the woman over his shoulder and carried her across the dark street to where his car waited.

Vivian woke with a terrible headache and a horrible taste in her mouth. When a man opened the curtains, she squinted against the early morning sunlight.

The first rush of fear congealed in her stomach when he turned around. She was in a strange place with a strange man and had no idea of how she'd gotten there.

"I'm not going to hurt you," the man said.

Somehow, his words of reassurance only scared her more. "What do you want?"

"The vampire."

"Vampire?" Vivian shook her head. "What are you talking about?"

"The vampire! Don't play dumb with me. He's been living in your house. I want to know where he takes his rest."

"In *my* house?" Vivian shook her head, and then her eyes widened. He had mistaken her for Callie. "It's not *my* house. I don't live there. I'm just staying there as a favor to a friend while she's away."

"Are you trying to protect him? Has he threatened you? Just tell me where he is and he'll never hurt you again."

"It isn't my house! I don't even have a house!" Vivian exclaimed and burst into tears. "I live in an apartment with a roommate. And I don't know anything about vampires!"

Trey 95 studied her through narrowed eyes. "If you're lying to me—"

"It's the truth! I swear it!"

He came to stand beside the bed. Arms crossed at his chest, he hovered over her, his whole demeanor menacing. "So, where is she, this friend of yours?"

"I . . . I don't know. She went away with her boyfriend."

"The vampire." He nodded.

Vivian felt a bubble of hysterical laughter rise in her

throat. It was obvious she was in the hands of a madman. "I don't know anything about vampires," she sobbed, "except that they don't exist."

"Where did they go?"

"I told you, I don't know."

The man pulled a cell phone from his pocket and thrust it into her hand. "Call her and ask."

Chapter 20

Callie stood in the kitchen, trying to decide what to have for breakfast, when her cell phone rang. Picking it up, she glanced at the number. Not recognizing it or the area code, she didn't bother to answer, figuring it was either a wrong number or another telemarketer.

She looked down at the cat, who was twining around her ankles. "Do you have a name?" she mused out loud. Not that she'd ever had a cat who actually came when it was called by anything but "Kitty." And not always then.

She would have to go to the store later, she thought, and pick up some cat food and a litter box, but for now, she dumped the leftover tuna in a dish, filled a bowl with water, and placed both on the floor.

With a flick of its tail, the cat took a dainty bite of fish.

"You're welcome," Callie said as she poured herself a cup of coffee. A look out the window showed the rain had stopped, though the sky remained gray.

Carrying her cup to the table, Callie sat down and

watched the cat eat. "Are you here to stay?" she wondered. "Or are we just a port in the storm?"

Callie was still engrossed in watching her four-footed visitor when the phone rang again. She frowned when she saw the caller was the same one who had called earlier. "Persistent," she muttered, and was about to disconnect the call when something prompted her to answer. "Hello?"

"Callie."

Alarm skittered down her spine at the note of distress in Vivian's voice. "What is it? What's happened, Viv? Are you all right?"

There was a moment of silence, and then a deep male voice said, "Who is this?"

"Who is *this*?"

"You don't need to know. I want the vampire. Bring him to me at your house no later than tomorrow night or your friend dies."

Stalling for time, Callie said, "How do you expect me to do that?"

"That's your problem," the man retorted, and the line went dead.

Callie stared at her phone a moment. Other than the Knights, she couldn't think of anyone who wanted to hurt Quill. But what was a Knight doing at her house? The answer was obvious—he had come looking for Quill and found Vivian instead. Quill had told her the Knights didn't hurt people and she wanted to believe that. But the man on the phone had sounded deadly serious when he'd threatened Vivian's life. And Viv had sounded scared to death. Was her life really in danger?

Heart pounding, Callie ran down the hall and into the bedroom where Quill took his rest.

He sat up when she entered the room. "What's wrong?"

"I had a phone call from Vivian, but it didn't come from her cell." Too nervous to sit still, Callie paced the floor beside the bed. "When I said hello, I heard Viv's voice say my name and then a man came on the phone and said if I didn't bring you to him by tomorrow night, he would kill Vivian. What are we going to do?"

Quill swore under his breath. With a shake of his head, he muttered, "You never should have answered that call."

She stared at him a moment in confusion. And then she broke out in a cold sweat. In this day and age, it was all to easy to track someone's whereabouts using their cell phone. And then she frowned. "Whoever it is, he can't find us, can he? I mean, isn't the town warded against intruders?"

"It is, but only against those seeking to do us harm."

"Doesn't that include the Knights?"

"Unfortunately, no. The Knights all possess a degree of power in the medallions they wear. It allows them to penetrate wards and spells that repel ordinary mortals."

"So, who do you think was on the phone?"

He swung his legs over the edge of the mattress, then scrubbed a hand across his jaw, his expression thoughtful. "It had to be one of the Knights."

Callie felt the color drain from her face. She had unwittingly put her best friend's life in danger when she'd asked Vivian to house-sit. Dropping the phone on the bed, she gripped Quill's arm. "He wouldn't really kill her, would he?"

"I don't know. The Knights take a solemn oath to protect humanity from my kind. I'm not sure how far they're willing to go to find us. To find me."

Quill raked his fingers through his hair. How far *would* the Knights go? He was one of the oldest of his kind. Whoever destroyed him would be seen as a hero, his name forever enshrined on the Wall of Memory as the Knight who had destroyed Quill. The Brotherhood would sing his praises, stories would be told of his bravery. Dammit!

"Quill?"

"We have to warn the others to get out of here."

Callie pulled a chair away from the desk in the corner and sank down on it. She felt terrible. Quill had said she shouldn't have answered the phone. And yet, there was no telling what might have happened to Viv if she hadn't. "What are we going to do?"

"Call the Knight back. Tell him we'll come to the house tonight on the condition that he frees Vivian when we get there."

"But . . . is that a good idea?"

"Do you have a better one?"

She shook her head.

Quill laid his hand on her shoulder. "Cheer up. We're not helpless. Remember, we have a lot of power between us."

But was it enough? Callie wondered.

Quill slid his arm around her waist and gave her a reassuring squeeze. "Make the call while I go warn the town."

* * *

Callie had just finished making arrangements to meet with the Knight when Quill returned.

"Are you ready?" he asked.

"Almost." She slipped her grandmother's pentacle over her head and tucked Ava's wand in her jacket pocket. "Were you able to warn everyone?"

"Yeah." He shook his head. "Some of the vampires are refusing to leave."

"What? Why?"

"Just stubborn, I guess. I think most of them will send their human companions and kids away."

"What about the ordinary people who are just passing through?"

"There were only three. I compelled them to get out of town and to forget the place existed." He wrapped his arm around her waist and pulled her body close to his. "Here we go."

Callie was trembling from a sudden onset of nerves when they reached her house. It was after midnight. The neighborhood was quiet. All the lights in her house were on, all the curtains drawn.

Standing across the street, Quill opened his vampire senses. "As far as I can tell, the only people inside are Vivian and the Knight." Unfortunately, there could be a dozen more hiding under one of their invisibility cloaks, which not only masked their presence, but their scent, as well.

"What do we do now?"

"You stay here. I'll call you if I need you."

"But . . ."

He silenced her with a kiss. "Let me go in and look

around. If he upholds his end of the bargain, he'll send Vivian out when I go in. If he does, you take her and get the hell out of here. Go to her place. The two of you should be safe enough there."

Callie stared up at him, her expression mutinous.

Quill placed his hands on her shoulders. "I don't want you near him," Quill said. "I don't want him to try to use you against me. Do you understand?"

She nodded unhappily.

"That's my girl," he murmured. Drawing her into his arms, he kissed her hard and long, and then he was striding across the street, climbing the porch stairs.

Callie's heart was in her throat when he opened the front door and crossed the threshold.

Quill stopped just inside the entryway. A thought closed the door behind him.

Vivian sat in a kitchen chair in the middle of the living room, her whole body rigid, her face fish-belly white, eyes wide and frightened. It was obvious she was under a spell of one kind or another.

The Knight stood behind her, a dagger at her throat.

"I'm here," Quill said. "Let the woman go."

"All in good time." With his free hand, the Knight pulled a pair of heavy silver manacles from his coat pocket and dropped them in Vivian's lap. "She's going to bind you first. Put your hands behind your back."

Quill eyed the manacles. All vampires, Hungarian or Transylvanian, were weakened by silver if it was pure. He had little doubt about these. Even from a distance, he could feel their power. Jaw clenched, he did as he'd been told.

The Knight nudged Vivian's shoulder. "Bind him."

Pushing to her feet, Vivian took one stiff-legged step after another until she stood in front of him.

The Knight jerked his chin at Quill. "Turn around."

He did so reluctantly. His flesh burned as soon as she locked the manacles in place. Turning to face the Knight, he said, "Now let her go."

"Very well. Vivian, go home."

She didn't hesitate. Flinging open the door, she ran out into the night.

The door hit the wall with such force that it flew back and slammed shut.

"Over here!" Callie hollered when Vivian ran outside.

Vivian darted across the street toward her, tears streaming down her face. "Callie! Oh, Callie!"

"It's all right," she said, throwing her arms around Viv. "It's over now. What's going on in there?"

"That man . . . he made me handcuff Quill. I think he's going to kill him!"

"I know. Listen, I want you to go home and lock your door and don't open it for anyone. Can you do that?"

Vivian shook her head. "What's going on, Callie? Who was that man? Why does he want Quill?"

"I don't have time to explain it all now. Just go home. Or, better yet, go stay with your parents or your sister. I'll call you as soon as I can. Now, go!"

With a nod, Vivian hurried down the sidewalk.

Callie waited until Viv was out of sight, then she ran across the street. Keeping to the shadows, she crept around the side of the house. A whispered word parted the living room curtains just enough so she could see inside.

"What now?" Quill asked.

"You die." Trey 95 tapped the point of the dagger against his chin. "But how? Something slow and painful. Perhaps I'll take you back to the Dark Wood and let the Brotherhood watch." He grunted thoughtfully. "Or maybe I'll just avenge my brother's death and kill you now." He nodded. "Your head will be enough to prove that I destroyed you."

"Looking for a little glory, are you?"

Trey 95 grinned. "Why not? I'll be famous! They'll write songs about me long after we're both gone."

Quill stared at the Knight, his mind racing. It was useless trying to manipulate the Knight's mind while he was wearing that damn medallion. He couldn't break the shackles that bound him. His powers were virtually useless. All preternatural creatures had at least one weakness and silver was his. *Damn!*

"Now or later," Trey 95 muttered. Eyes narrowed, he looked at his prisoner. And then he nodded. "I think now is better, after all. A head is so much easier to carry than a body."

Quill watched as the Knight sheathed his dagger and then bent down, reaching for something out of sight. When the Knight straightened, he held a long, silver-bladed sword in his hand.

"Say your prayers, bloodsucker." Tightening his grip on the weapon, Trey 95 rounded the chair and walked slowly toward Quill.

Quill took a step back. Closing his eyes, he summoned Callie's image, wanting it to be the last thing he remembered.

There was a loud *thunk* as the heavy shackles that bound him hit the floor. Startled, Quill opened his eyes to see the sword arcing toward him. He ducked out of the way as the blade sliced through the air where his head had been. Darting forward, he locked his hands around the Knight's throat. For a moment, their gazes met, and then Quill gave a quick, clean twist. The sword fell from the Knight's hands as the life went out of his eyes.

Quill let the body fall to the floor as the front door flew open and Callie ran inside. She didn't say anything, just threw her arms around him and held on tight.

"I thought I told you to get out of here," Quill murmured, thinking he'd never been happier to see anyone in his life.

Leaning back, she looked up at him. "Did you really think I'd leave you here alone?"

He smiled down at her. "No. In fact, I was counting on a little outside magical help. That's the second time you've saved my life."

She grinned at him. "But who's counting?" Then, cupping his face in her hands, she went up on her tiptoes and kissed him.

After a few moments, Quill lifted his head. "Where's Vivian?"

"I told her to go home or go stay with relatives."

He nodded. "We need to get back to town right away.

Something tells me that this guy sent the town's location to all the Knights. I just hope we aren't too late."

Callie closed her eyes as his arm wrapped around her waist, a silent prayer in her heart. He wasn't the only one who had a bad feeling about what they might find when they got there.

Chapter 21

Callie's stomach churned as she stared at the charred bodies sprawled in the street. The vampires—nine in number—had all been shot numerous times—with silver bullets, Quill told her. Too weak to fight back, they had been decapitated, their hearts cut from their chests, their remains burned. A single human female lay among the vampire remains, a gun at her side, a bullet hole in the side of her head.

"I thought the Knights were sworn to protect humanity," Callie said, her voice bitter.

Quill glanced at the spent cartridges near the woman. They told the tale. "She tried to defend her husband and when that failed, she took her own life."

Callie turned away. There was no sign of Wendy. Hopefully she and her husband had heeded Quill's warning and fled before it was too late.

An eerie silence hung over the town, as if the wind and the trees were in mourning.

"How?" she asked in a voice choked with tears. "How did the Knights come and go so quickly?"

"I'm sure the Knight I killed notified his Brothers as soon as he talked to you." Quill told himself it wasn't his fault that not all of the vampires had left town. He had warned them in time. The ones who hadn't left had paid the ultimate price.

Callie glanced around, her gaze probing the shadows. Any number of men could be hiding in the forest that surrounded the town. "Are you sure all the Knights are gone?"

"As sure as I can be."

Looking up at him, Callie felt an icy chill run through her. She had never seen him look so fierce, so angry.

"I need to bury them," he said, his voice raw with emotion.

Trying not to look at the bodies, she followed Quill to a partially burned store in town. Inside, he found a shovel and a large wheelbarrow that had escaped the flames.

Handing her the shovel, he pushed the cart back to the scene of the carnage.

Callie trailed behind him, pausing each time he stopped to load a blackened body into the wheelbarrow. When it wouldn't hold any more, he pushed it deep into the forest. Taking the shovel from her hand, he quickly dug a large hole.

She stood quietly watching as he gently lifted each body and lowered it carefully into the grave. When the conveyance was empty, he dropped the shovel and went back to gather the rest.

When the last corpse had been laid to rest, he filled in the grave, then stood there, jaw rock hard, fists clenched at his sides.

Moving to stand next to him, Callie took his hand in hers, her lips moving in a silent prayer for the dead.

"If you're going to pray for anyone," Quill said, "pray

for the Knights of the Dark Wood. Because when I find them, what happened here will look mild by comparison."

With Trey 95 dead, the vampires scattered and most of the town destroyed, Quill and Callie packed their belongings. Quill made two separate trips to Callie's house to transport their luggage, leaving Callie to go through the house and make sure they hadn't forgotten anything.

On her final walk-through, she found the cat sleeping on the floor in one of the closets.

Hunkering down, Callie stroked the cat's head. "What are we going to do with you?" She glanced over her shoulder, one brow raised in question when Quill entered the room. "Do we take her with us?"

"If she wants to go."

Callie looked at the cat. "I guess it's up to you."

Purring loudly, the animal jumped nimbly into her arms.

Callie smiled up at Quill. "I guess she's ours."

"Yours. Not mine. She doesn't like me."

It was near dawn when they arrived at Callie's house. When she would have opened the door, Quill shook his head.

She looked at him askance, and then remembered that there was a dead body on her living room floor.

"Wait out here," he said. "I'll dispose of it."

Nodding, she sat on the porch's top step with the cat curled up in her lap. What was he going to do with the Knight's body at this time of the morning? Drop it off at the mortuary? Dump it on the side of the road?

Quill returned five minutes later. The front door opened at his touch. He stood aside so she could enter, then followed her into the living room.

"I'm going to bed," Callie said, smothering a yawn. "I'm exhausted."

Quill nodded. She looked beat.

"Are you going to spend the night here?"

"Yes." Unless she threw him out, he intended to spend all his nights here from now on.

"How are you going to find the Knights?"

"We'll talk about it tomorrow." She needed sleep. And he needed to feed.

Callie was too tired to argue. Careful not to look at the place where the Knight's body had been, she shuffled down the hall to her room.

Quill locked up the house and reinforced the wards around it, wondering, as he did so, if there was any way to ward it against the Knights. Perhaps Callie's magic could find a way. A witch had infused the medallions the Knights wore with supernatural power. Perhaps another witch could nullify it.

He waited until the soft, steady sound of Callie's breathing told him she was asleep, then willed himself to the next town.

Prey was scarce at this time of the night—or morning— and he mesmerized the first woman he found. She smelled of cheap whisky and sex, and he wrinkled his nose as he sank his fangs into her throat. He drank quickly, released her from his thrall, and returned to Callie's house.

She was sleeping soundly, the cat at her side, Ava's wand within easy reach on the nightstand. She had left a light burning.

The cat stared at him through slitted yellow eyes, hissed at him as he moved closer to the bed.

With a wave of his hand, Quill said, "Get out of here."

The cat growled at him, then jumped off the mattress and onto the dresser, where it sat staring at him.

Turning his back on the feline, Quill brushed a kiss across Callie's cheek and then, not wanting to leave her, he removed his shirt and boots and stretched out beside her on the top of the covers.

When he closed his eyes, the darkness carried him away.

Callie frowned when she tried to turn over. Wondering what was weighing down the blankets and preventing her from doing so, she turned her head to the side, let out a startled gasp when she saw Quill lying beside her on top of the covers.

Her gaze ran over him. He had removed his shirt. Apparently, he didn't wear an undershirt, since she didn't see one on the chair. But she couldn't be sorry. He had broad shoulders and a magnificent chest, scarred though it might be. She bit down on her lower lip. If she ran her fingertips over his chest, would he wake up?

She whispered his name, but he didn't stir.

Unable to resist, she placed her fingertips on his chest. His skin was cool. When he still didn't move, she walked her fingers toward his six-pack abs, a little thrill of excitement bubbling up inside her as she did so.

"Careful there, woman. You're treading on dangerous ground."

She jerked her hand away at the sound of his voice.

Without opening his eyes, he reached for her hand, placed it on his chest, and covered it with his own. He took a deep breath. Another. And then he rolled onto his side, his face only inches from hers.

Anticipation thrummed through Callie as her gaze met his. Desire rippled through her from head to heel when he reached for her, one hand sliding beneath her neck, the other drawing her closer. His breath was hot against her skin, his tongue like fire as it laved the sensitive place beneath her ear.

When he groaned her name, she closed her eyes, a whispered "yes" sliding past her lips.

His bite was gentle, innocently erotic and yet sensual as he drank from her. She sighed with regret when he lifted his head.

"Kiss me, Quill," she whispered.

"Still playing with fire?" he asked, his voice a low growl.

Murmuring, "Stop talking," she pressed her lips to his.

A low rumble rose in his throat as, with a wave of his hand, he sent the covers flying across the room, leaving nothing between them but her pajamas and his jeans, and then he was showering her with kisses, his mouth hot on hers, his erection hard against her thigh.

She ran her hands restlessly up and down his back, reveling in the way his muscles flexed at her touch. Feeling bold, she ran her hands over his shoulders, his chest, his flat belly. Her fingers stilled at the waistband of his jeans.

Quill drew back, his gaze searching hers, his breathing rapid, eyes blazing with a fierce hunger.

Callie's breath caught in her throat. Had she gone

too far? Would he expect her to go all the way? Was she ready?

She felt his mind brush hers. And then he was gone.

Sighing with mingled regret and relief, Callie rolled onto her back, her arms flung out to the sides. Next time she might not be able to stop him in time, she thought.

And then she smiled.

Next time, she might not want to.

It was almost noon when Callie woke. For a moment, she lay there with her eyes closed, replaying the events of the last two days. She had seen death in its most hideous form, feared for the life of her best friend, used her magic to save Quill from a vengeful Knight, been sorely tempted to surrender her heart and soul to the vampire she loved.

Rolling onto her side, she found herself staring into the cat's golden-yellow eyes. "Hey, kitty," she said, scratching its ears. "We really need to give you a name. How about Blackie? Pepper? Storm?"

The cat shook its head with each suggestion.

"Ebony?"

When the cat purred, Callie took that as approval. "Okay, Ebony it is."

As though agreeing, the cat jumped off the bed and padded into the living room.

After dressing, Callie went to the store for cat food, a couple of pet dishes—one for food, one for water— a self-cleaning litter box, and a bag of kitty litter. She also picked up a loaf of bread and a quart of milk and a rotisserie chicken for dinner.

When she returned home, she found Ebony waiting for her on the front porch. "How did you get out here?" Callie wondered as she unlocked the front door. "I'm sure I left you sleeping on the sofa."

Inside, Callie set up the litter box in a corner of the laundry room. On her way to the kitchen, she peeked into the guest room, smiled when she saw Quill sleeping peacefully.

She fed the cat and then fixed her own breakfast. Sitting at the table, she found herself again thinking about Quill and how, since meeting him, her whole world had turned upside down.

Deciding to practice her craft, she concentrated on her dirty plate and cup, uttered a magical incantation, and smiled as the dishes floated into the sink. Tomorrow, she would try magicking them into the dishwasher.

With the black cat trailing at her heels, Callie gathered her spell books and other items and spent the rest of the morning at the kitchen table studying protection spells while the cat looked on.

Once, when she'd been about to add a dash of rosemary to a spell, Ebony jumped on the table and knocked her hand aside.

"What are you doing, you crazy cat?" Callie exclaimed. Irritated, she reread the spell's ingredients. "Looks like I owe you an apology. I was supposed to use rose *hips*, not rose*mary*. And how did you know that, anyway?" she asked. And then shook her head. It wasn't like the cat could answer.

The sun was setting when Quill sauntered into the

kitchen. With a hiss, Ebony leaped to the top of the refrigerator, golden eyes narrowed.

Quill grunted softly. "I don't like you, either," he muttered.

Callie looked up, frowning. "What?"

"I was talking to the cat." Drawing her into his arms, he said, "You, I'm crazy about. How's the magic coming along?"

"I found a spell for warding the house. If it works, no one will be able to enter except you, me, and Ebony."

"Ebony?"

"Our cat."

"*Your* cat."

"Whatever. How will we know if the spell's working?"

"Invite Vivian over tomorrow, leave the door unlocked, and see if she can get in."

"Good idea. I need to call her anyway and see how she's doing." She glanced at the timer on the oven. "I'm having chicken for dinner. It'll be ready in a few minutes. Do you want to share it with me?"

He cocked one brow. "Do I have to have chicken?"

"What else . . . Oh." She lifted a hand to her neck.

He grinned at her, then kissed her cheek. "I'd love to have dinner with you, sweet Callie, if you'll be dessert."

She smiled up at him. "All you have to do is ask."

"You're spoiling me. You know that, don't you?"

"I love you. You know *that*, don't you?"

His gaze burned into hers, so hot she thought she might melt on the spot.

She flinched when the timer went off. Saved by the bell. Slipping out of his arms, she went to take dinner out of the oven.

* * *

Later, sitting side by side on the sofa, with Quill's arm draped around her shoulders, Callie asked, "How will you find the Knights?"

"That's a good question. No one knows where they are. I have a feeling their witch cast a spell over the Dark Wood to keep strangers out."

"Even if you find them, we can't fight twelve Knights all by ourselves."

"Wait a minute! There is no 'we,' not where the Knights are concerned."

"What do you mean?"

"You heard me. These aren't your regular run-of-the-mill vampires hunters, you know. They've got those damn medallions, for one thing. And an on-site witch. Rumor has it, she's as powerful as your grandmother ever was."

Callie glared at him. "Listen to me, mister, if you go after those Knights, I'm going with you." She held up a hand when he started to object. "If it wasn't for me, you'd be dead and buried now. And don't you forget it!"

"All right, Wonder Woman, we'll fight them side by side. Assuming we can find them," he added. Eyes narrowed thoughtfully, he dragged his hand over his jaw. "The sword."

"What?"

"The sword. The one the Knight tried to decapitate me with. Where is it?"

"I don't know. Last time I saw it, it was on the living room floor. I thought you took it with you when you buried the body."

"No." Quill swore under his breath. "One of the Knights must have retrieved it while we were gone."

"Why didn't they take the body, too?"

"Beats the hell out of me. Maybe something scared

them off. Dammit, if we had that sword, you might have been able to concoct a spell that would lead us to the Dark Wood."

"Really?"

"Theoretically." He frowned. "He had a dagger, too. That would work just as well."

"Where is it?"

"I buried it with him. His blood would work even better than the sword."

Callie grimaced. "You're not thinking of digging him up, are you?"

"Have you got a better idea?"

She shook her head. "Do you remember where you buried him?"

"'Fraid so." He brushed a kiss across her cheek. "I'll be right back."

Callie shuddered at the thought of exhuming the Knight. True, the body hadn't been in the ground long, but . . .

Yuck!

Quill returned in a remarkably short time, bringing with him the scent of cool air and freshly turned earth.

Looking up from the sofa, she asked, "Where's the dagger?"

"The body's gone and the dagger with it."

"Gone?"

Brow furrowed, he dropped onto the sofa beside her. "I guess when one of them dies, the Brotherhood doesn't leave anything behind."

"So, we're back to square one."

"For now."

"I called Vivian while you were gone. She's coming over tomorrow. I don't think she's recovered from her ordeal yet. What am I going to tell her?"

A muscle worked in Quill's jaw. "I'm afraid to mess with her mind again, considering the state she's in. I think in this case you should tell her the truth. If she can't handle it, then . . ." He shrugged. "Let's see how it goes."

Chapter 22

The Knights of the Dark Wood stood in a loose circle around the coffin that held the remains of Trey 95. A white sheet covered him from neck to heel; his sword lay at his side.

The Elder Knight, clad in red robes, stood at the head of the bier. "We are gathered here tonight to honor our fallen Brother, slain by the hand of our enemy." Drawing a knife from his belt, he made a shallow cut across his palm, then held his hand over the body, letting his blood drip onto the white sheet. "By my blood, I swear to avenge his death," he intoned, and passed the blade to his left.

One after another, the remaining twelve members of the Brotherhood made a similar oath. When they finished, the sheet was splattered with crimson.

The four oldest members lifted the coffin and carried it into the woods, followed by the others.

After the coffin was lowered into the ground, each Knight threw a handful of dirt on the casket, then each took a turn filling in the grave.

There was no marker, nor would there be.

When they were done, the Knights stood in a long line at the foot of the grave.

The Elder Knight walked from one end of the line to the other, his gaze piercing each man. "This vampire has now killed another of our Brothers. From this night forward, all of our efforts will be directed at finding the vampire known as Quill and bringing him to justice. I do not want him killed! I want him taken alive. There will be no swift, merciful death for the likes of this creature. Or for anyone who harbors him."

The Elder Knight pivoted at the end of the line and walked back the other way. "Brandon 6, Ricardo 42, Emanuel 51, Edmund 14, I charge you to find the vampire. You will leave tomorrow morning after we initiate Paul 18." He held each man's gaze. "Do not return without the vampire. The rest of you will fortify our compound and instruct Paul 18 in our ways. And each of you must be prepared to immediately go to the aid of those charged with finding the vampire. He is evil and cunning. Our losses may be heavy. But we will prevail!"

Chapter 23

Callie called Tony's and ordered a large ham and pineapple pizza, hot wings, and breadsticks for lunch. She put it all in the oven to keep it warm, quickly made a tossed green salad, and then set the table with Ava's best china. And all the while she wondered what she was going to tell Vivian. How did one explain the existence of a vampire without sounding completely insane?

Everything was on the table and ready when the doorbell rang. Callie crossed her fingers. Now was the time to see if her new protection spell worked. She had left the front door open, knowing Viv would just walk in.

A moment passed. And then Vivian called, "Hey girlfriend, what did you do? Install an invisible screen door?"

Callie's smile stretched from ear to ear as she went to greet her friend. "In a way. Come on in."

"Seriously," Viv said as she followed her into the living room. "What was that?"

"I'll tell you later," Callie said, leading the way into the kitchen. "How are you, Viv?"

"I don't know." Vivian glanced at the table. "This is really nice. You didn't have to go to so much trouble. Paper plates would have been fine."

"I know, but . . . I just wanted to make it special. Help yourself."

"Ham and pineapple," Vivian said, sitting down. "My favorite."

"I know. I never thanked you for looking after the house, although after everything that happened, I'm sorry I asked you."

Vivian nibbled on a breadstick, then put it aside. "Who was that man? Why was he looking for you?"

Callie took a deep breath. "He was a Knight."

"Like a real, sword-wielding Knight of the Round Table?"

"More like a modern one."

"He said he was looking for a vampire."

"I know. That's what they do. They kill vampires."

Vivian shook her head. "If you can't tell me the truth, then let's just talk about something else."

"It is the truth. When I first met Quill, I told you he was a vampire."

"You did not."

"I did, but it's dangerous for you to know they exist, so he wiped the memory from your mind. I know this is hard to believe, Viv, but I swear it's all too true."

"This isn't funny," Vivian said, her voice thick with unshed tears. "I thought we were friends. Friends don't lie to each other."

"She isn't lying."

Vivian jumped, her eyes widening when Quill appeared in the doorway dressed all in black.

He wasn't hiding what he was. Preternatural power emanated from him, so thick Callie was surprised they couldn't see it. A faint hint of red tinged his eyes.

Vivian stared at him, let out a strangled cry when he smiled at her, showing a hint of fang.

"It's all right," Callie said quickly. "He won't hurt you. He's just trying to prove that I'm telling you the truth. Quill, stop it. You're scaring her."

Withdrawing his power, he folded his arms over his chest, listening quietly as Callie answered her friend's numerous questions while they picked at their lunch.

When Vivian finally ran down, Callie said, "You can't tell anyone, Viv. Promise me you won't."

Vivian risked a glance at Quill. "I promise. Who would believe me?" When he left the room, she leaned across the table. "Aren't you afraid of him?"

"No. He's very kind and sweet and . . ."

"Kind?" Vivian exclaimed. "Sweet? Callie, the man's a vampire!"

"But he's not like the ones in movies that go around ripping out hearts and throats. His kind don't kill people. I love him, Viv. He's the most wonderful man I've ever met, and people are trying to kill *him*."

"Does he drink blood?"

Callie hesitated before nodding, afraid of what the next question might be. And she was right.

"Does he drink from you?"

"Yes. And it's wonderful."

Vivian shook her head. "He is very handsome and sexy, but, Callie, he isn't really human."

"He's human enough for me." Callie smiled, wondering what Viv would think if she knew her best friend was a witch. Perhaps, one day, she would tell her.

But not today.

* * *

Vivian left shortly after lunch. She renewed her promise not to tell anyone about Quill, assuring Callie that the mere thought of breaking her promise was enough to ensure her silence.

Brow furrowed, Callie stood at the door, watching her friend drive away. Even if Viv told someone about Quill, it was unlikely that anyone would take her seriously.

Returning to the kitchen, she cleared the table and loaded the dishwasher. It wasn't until she went into the living room that she realized she hadn't seen Ebony since early that morning.

Frowning, she looked in her bedroom, peeked into the guest room where Quill was resting, though she didn't expect to find the cat there. She looked in the bathrooms and the service porch. No Ebony.

In the hallway, she glanced at Ava's room. The door was closed, as always. There was no way the cat could be in there, but she couldn't resist taking a look inside.

Ebony was curled up in the middle of one of the bed pillows. The cat lifted its head when Callie opened the door.

"How on earth did you get in here?" Callie muttered. The windows were both closed, the curtains drawn. The door had been shut tight. There was no other way into the room.

The cat blinked at her, then lowered its head and went back to sleep.

Callie spent the rest of the day cleaning out the small attic her grandmother had used for storage. She hadn't been up there since Ava had passed away, and the first order of business was going through all the cardboard boxes, most of which held Callie's baby clothes, toys, and stuffed animals. One box held old photograph albums; another held an assortment of outdated hats and shoes.

Callie put the boxes holding her baby clothes and toys beside the attic door to carry down and dispose of later. She stacked the box of old photos in a corner, intending to go through them at another time.

A small wooden trunk held her grandmother's wedding dress and veil.

Callie smiled as she ran her hands over the gown, which was silky smooth to the touch. She had played dress-up in it when she was a little girl, yet the dress remained spotlessly clean, as if it had been wrapped in plastic since her grandmother had worn it. No doubt Ava had woven a spell to keep it looking new.

On an impulse, Callie removed her T-shirt and jeans, then slipped the gown over her head. It fell in graceful folds to the floor. She twirled around, smiling as the skirt flared around her ankles, then lifted the gossamer veil from the box and set it in place.

"You're going to make a beautiful bride."

Feeling a blush warm her cheeks, Callie turned to face Quill. "You think so?"

"The proof is right in front of me." The gown fit as if it had been made for her. Rays from the setting sun came through a narrow, tinted window, bathing her in a halo of rosy light. She looked, he thought, like a fairy princess. "You're beautiful, Callie."

"Thank you." Her heart skipped a beat as he took her hands in his and drew her closer. His gaze moved over her. "Callie, would you marry me?"

She blinked up at him, stunned by his proposal. "You want to marry me?"

"More than anything."

"But we hardly know each other."

"You know me," he said quietly. "It doesn't have to be today or next week or even this year. But will you think about it?"

She nodded.

"Can I help you with anything up here?"

"You could carry those boxes downstairs for me."

"All right. Where do you want them?"

"In the garage, for now."

He stacked the cartons one on top of the other, moved to the opening left by the trap door, and floated to the floor below.

Callie stared after him. He wanted to marry her. Any marriage was bound to change her lifestyle, but being married to a vampire would come with a whole different set of adjustments, the main one being that any child she had would be a boy and a future vampire. Was she strong enough to handle that? She had always wanted a daughter, but if she married Quill, that would never happen. Of course, it might never happen no matter who she married, but at least there would have been a fifty-fifty chance.

Sighing, she stepped out of the gown and removed the veil and replaced them in the wooden trunk.

She had a lot to think about.

After stacking the cartons in the garage, Quill went in search of prey. He hadn't been thinking of marriage when he went up to the attic looking for Callie. It had never once entered his mind. But after seeing her in that dress, he had known there would never be another woman for him. Having met her, his biggest fear was that she would leave him to spend the rest of his life without her.

And being an honorable man, the only decent way to keep her with him was as his wife.

Callie was online, updating her Facebook page, when Quill returned home.

Glancing around, he asked, "Where's the cat?"

"Sleeping in my grandmother's room, although I don't know how Ebony got in there since the door was closed."

"Maybe she's a witch, too."

"Very funny."

Standing behind her, he perused her page. He didn't spend a lot of time on the Internet, but her business had a lot of friends.

Leaving her Facebook page, she opened her email. There were three from brides seeking her services.

"Do you miss working?" he asked.

"Sometimes."

He frowned as he read her replies, noting she had declined to accept any of them.

"Callie, don't let me stop you from pursuing your career."

"You aren't. It's really more of a hobby, anyway. And I don't want to make any commitments until this trouble with the Knights is over."

She was shutting down the computer when a shadow passed by the window.

Quill saw it, too. "Stay here," he said, and hurried out of the room.

A moment later, the lights went out.

Rising, Callie drew back the curtain and peered out the window. She heard a crash, followed by a sharp cry of pain.

Hand pressed to her heart, she ran into the living room, but paused at the door when she heard footsteps on the porch. A few muttered words and a wave of her hand brought the lights back on.

She breathed a sigh of relief when Quill called, "It's me," before entering the house.

"Who was it?" she asked, afraid she already knew the answer.

He nodded. "It was another one."

"Is he . . . ?"

"Yeah. I dumped the body behind the old fire station where his buddies will be sure to find it."

Callie shuddered. Another dead body. "Is this insanity ever going to end?"

He grunted softly. "Not as long as I live. Or they do."

"You're not hurting anyone. Why can't they just leave you alone?"

"Destroying my kind is their sole purpose in life."

Suddenly cold, Callie scrubbed her hands up and down her arms. If she married Quill, she would always be a little on edge, always wondering when the next attack would come, wondering if the next time it would be the Knight who walked away.

Chapter 24

"We need to get away from here," Quill said.

"We tried that, remember?"

"I'm not likely to forget." But they couldn't go on like this. There seemed to be no end to the number of Knights of the Dark Wood. Although there were only thirteen active members of the Brotherhood at any given time, they seemed to have an unlimited number of initiates waiting in the wings, eager to shed the blood of his kind. Where to go? Perhaps the safest place was back to Northern California. The Knights wouldn't expect them to return so soon, not after what had happened. On the other hand, maybe that would be the first place they looked.

"I need coffee," Callie said. "Lots of coffee."

Quill followed her into the kitchen. "The Knight couldn't get into the house," he mused aloud. "I know he tried because he stepped in a mud puddle in the backyard and left his footprints on the porch. I think my wards, combined with your magic, has made the house invincible."

"Really?"

"If he could have gotten inside, I've no doubt he would have."

Callie poured herself a cup of coffee, then looked askance at Quill, who shook his head. She leaned back against the counter. "So, where does that leave us? We can't stay locked inside forever."

"True. But if we can ward this house against them, why not a whole town?"

Callie stared at him, wide-eyed. "That would take an amazing amount of power, wouldn't it? Wait a minute, do you mean *this* town?"

"No. I had another one in mind. There's a little community in Montana that doesn't get many visitors since the new freeway made a wide detour around the town. The place is surrounded by cattle ranches. The population is less than a hundred. Eight of my kind were living there the last time I passed through. They're all young vampires with wives about your age. Between us, we should be able to ward their homes the way we did yours."

"You want to move to Montana?"

"Temporarily." He watched the play of emotions on Callie's face as she weighed the pros and cons of what he was suggesting. Did she care for him enough to stay with him? And if she didn't, what then? He didn't want to leave her, yet his presence could be putting her life in danger. The Knights weren't supposed to harm humans, but if they were willing to take Vivian prisoner, there was no telling what else they might do.

"Callie?"

"All right. If you think it's the right thing to do. But no house sitter this time. We'll just lock up the place while we're gone."

* * *

Callie spent the next day packing, emptying the refrigerator, stopping the paper and the mail. She did her banking and paid her bills online, so her mail was mostly junk.

She packed two suitcases with clothes and a third with the grimoire and the other things her grandmother had left her. A wooden crate held the cat box, litter, dishes, and a bag of food. She made a quick run to the pet store for a pet carrier and she was ready to go.

Quill rose with the setting sun. Glancing at the covered furniture and suitcases, he said, "You've been busy."

She nodded. "Are you packed?"

"I'll get my stuff later. Are you ready to go?"

She lifted one shoulder. "I guess so. Wait! Where are we going to live?"

"I rented a house. And a car."

The cat hissed at him from inside the carrier when Callie picked it up.

"All right, let's go." He picked up the largest suitcase, then wrapped his other arm around Callie's waist. "I'll come back for the rest of your stuff later."

She nodded, then closed her eyes as his power washed over her. Ebony yowled as they were transported through time and space at blinding speed.

When Callie opened her eyes, they were in the middle of a large, rectangular living room.

Quill set her suitcase on the floor. "What do you think?"

"It's lovely." She did a slow turn. The walls were a pale gray, the furniture covered in a gray and blue plaid, the tables a gleaming cherry. A white brick fireplace took up the wall across from the front door. An arched doorway to the left led to the kitchen, a second arch to the right showed a wide hallway.

Setting the carrier on the floor, Callie lifted the latch and let the cat out. With a hiss, Ebony darted under the sofa.

"I guess she doesn't like flying," Callie said.

"I guess not," Quill agreed. Grabbing her bag, he headed for the hallway. "The bedrooms are this way."

Callie followed him, her gaze darting right and left. Two good-sized bedrooms, each with its own bath, faced each other across the hall. The master bedroom was located at the end of the corridor behind a pair of elegant double doors.

"For milady," he said, opening one.

Callie let out a soft gasp. The room was beautiful, with its own TV, bathroom, and fireplace. The walls were a warm, pale yellow. Cream-colored curtains graced the windows, and a matching quilted spread covered a king-sized bed. A large painting of a waterfall hung over the fireplace. A tall shelf held DVDs and books.

Quill smiled. "I think you'll be comfortable here."

"This must be costing a fortune."

"Only a small one," he said, setting her suitcase on the bed. "Why don't you get settled in while I go back and get the rest of our things?"

"Okay."

When Quill left the room, Ebony padded through the door, let out a long meow, and jumped up on the bed.

"I should have named you Cleopatra," Callie remarked as the cat yawned, stretched, and made herself comfortable on one of the pillows. "You certainly act like the queen of the castle."

Deciding unpacking could wait, Callie went into the bathroom, thinking that a nice long, hot bath was just what she needed. She rummaged in her suitcase for her nightgown and robe and laid them on the bed, then dug around until she found a bottle of bubble bath. She added a generous amount to the water, undressed, and slid into the tub.

Quill returned to Callie's house to pick up the rest of her things. While he was there, he double-checked to make sure all the doors and windows were securely locked. He parked her VW next to the Jag in the garage, then warded the house and yard again before going to his lair to pick up his clothes.

In the living room, he did a slow turn. He had spent the last ten years here and it meant nothing to him but a place to rest. Callie's house had been the first home he'd had since leaving his parents' residence decades ago.

He rarely thought of those days in Hungary. As a boy, he hadn't thought there was anything strange about having a father who slept during the day. Lots of men worked nights and slept days. It wasn't until he'd hit puberty that his parents had told him the truth—his father was a vampire and in the next year or so, Quill would undergo a gradual change.

It hadn't been easy. There had been times when he couldn't think of anything but his desire for blood. In the beginning, the more he drank, the more he wanted. It had been hell. He hadn't been allowed outside at night alone. Until he learned to control his lust, his father had been his constant companion, teaching him how to find prey, how to feed without taking too much. His kind boasted that they didn't kill their prey, but that wasn't always true with the young ones. There were fatal accidents now and then, though they were rare.

Quill had come close on one or two occasions, but his father had always been there to stop him, to teach him how to listen to the rhythm of his prey's heartbeat for the warning that his prey's life was in danger. He learned that going without regular food for long periods of time increased his desire for blood, and so he made it a point to eat dinner with his mother a couple of times a week.

He smiled at the memory. His mother was a remarkable woman, wise beyond her years, devoted to her husband and son, and yet she managed to live a full life as a schoolteacher. She was still teaching.

Perhaps one day he would take Callie to Australia to meet his parents.

It took only moments to return to Montana. The lights were on, the house quiet. Had Callie gone to bed? He left their luggage by the door, put the crate holding the cat box on the floor, set the carton holding her grandmother's things next to it, then padded down the hallway to the master bedroom.

Curled up on a pillow, Ebony lifted her head and hissed at him when he entered the room.

Grimacing at the cat, he rounded the bed and glanced in the bathroom.

His breath caught in his throat when he saw Callie reclining in the tub, her shoulders and a tantalizing view of her cleavage visible above a froth of bubbles.

Sensing his presence, Callie turned toward the door,

felt her cheeks flood with heat when she saw him standing in the doorway.

Stifling a grin, he said, "Mind if I join you?"

She stared at him, wide-eyed and speechless.

Quill shrugged. "No harm in asking," he said, with a wicked grin. "If you don't want to share the tub, I'd be glad to wash your back."

Scooping up a handful of bubbles, Callie murmured an incantation and let the suds fly. They multiplied and thickened as they flew through the air and hit him squarely in the face.

She burst out laughing at his surprised expression, but the laughter died in her throat when he advanced toward the tub, bubbles dripping from his chin.

She watched warily as he dropped to his knees beside her.

"Not funny," he growled. And then he cupped her nape in one large hand and kissed her until she was breathless. "Next time," he warned, a glint of humor in his eyes. "I'll yank you out of that tub, bubbles and all."

He kissed the tip of her nose, took one long, last look, and sauntered out the door, whistling softly.

As soon as he was gone, Ebony padded into the bathroom and jumped up on the toilet lid.

Callie grinned at the cat. "I love him," she said, not a doubt in her mind. "So if you plan to hang around, you'd better get used to the idea."

Chapter 25

Later that night, after Callie had eaten dinner and Quill had gone hunting, they sat side by side on the sofa in front of the fireplace. Callie was toasty warm in a long nightgown, slipper-sox, and a velour robe. Quill wore a pair of sweatpants and a black T-shirt.

"Aren't you cold?" Callie asked. It had started raining earlier, a constant steady downpour.

"No."

She lifted one brow.

"We don't get cold."

"But you have coats and jackets."

He shrugged. "People look at me oddly if it's storming outside and I'm running around in a T-shirt and jeans."

Callie laughed. "I guess that makes sense. Does the heat bother you?"

"Not much, but more than the rain."

"How do you stand it, being hunted all the time? Isn't there anywhere you can go and be safe?"

"Being hunted was troubling when I was a young vampire. But you get used it. The only really safe place to go is back to Hungary."

"Are there Knights of the Dark Wood all over the world?"

"Just here in the States as far as I know. But there are hunters of one kind or another no matter where you go."

In bed later that night, Callie thought about what Quill had said. If she married him, they would never really be safe. Unless they moved to Hungary, and while she liked the idea of traveling to a foreign country, she didn't want to live anywhere but here, in the good ol' USA.

Unbidden came the thought that Quill had slept with Ava. She told herself it didn't matter. It had happened over a hundred years before she was born and only the one time. When he had first told her about it, she hadn't given it too much thought. It had happened so long ago—what did it matter? Now, she couldn't get it out of her mind. Could she really make love to Quill knowing that he had made love to her grandmother first? It seemed almost incestuous somehow. Would he compare the two of them?

She tossed and turned for an hour, unable to stop thinking about it, imagining Quill and Ava together. She had to admit, they made a striking couple—Quill, so dark and handsome, Ava so beautiful and fair.

And then a new thought brought her upright. Was Quill staying with her because she reminded him of Ava? Was he trying to relive the past?

She groaned low in her throat, wishing he had never told her.

"Callie?"

Feeling a flush rise in her cheeks, her gaze darted to

the door. Oh, Lord! Had he read her thoughts? She'd forgotten he could do that.

He rapped on the door. "Callie, I know you're awake."

"Come in." She didn't turn on the light.

Neither did he. "Do you want to talk about it?"

"About what?" she asked, her voice little more than a squeak.

"Don't play games with me. I know what's bothering you." He sat on the edge of the mattress. "Is a one-night stand that happened over a hundred years ago going to cause a problem between us?"

"I don't know. I keep telling myself it doesn't matter, but . . ."

"It does."

Grateful for the dark, she said, "When you look at me, do you see her? When we kiss . . . ?"

Quill swore under his breath. "Is that what you think?"

She let her silence answer for her.

Pulling back the covers, he drew her into his arms. "I love *you*, Callie. I never loved Ava. We spent one night together. We remained friends after that. We had a few laughs. She practiced her brand of magic on me, and I practiced mine on her and her friends. We were always trying to outdo each other. But we were never in a serious relationship. Yes, you look alike, but that's where the resemblance ends. I've never been in love with anyone else. Only you, sweet Callie. Hey," he admonished softly, "don't cry."

Sniffling, she said, "I can't help it."

Using a corner of the sheet, he wiped her eyes. "Can you sleep now?"

"I guess so." When he moved to rise, she grabbed his

hand. "Don't go." She could feel his gaze moving over her face.

"Callie?"

She had never heard him sound quite so uncertain "Stay the night with me."

"Are you sure?" he asked, a hint of wry amusement in his voice. "You know where that's going to lead, don't you?"

She nodded, grateful again for the dark that hid her burning cheeks.

He removed his T-shirt but not his sweatpants. He slid under the covers, then drew her into his arms. For a moment, he simply held her, giving her time to change her mind. Turning onto his side, he began to caress her, his hands moving lightly over her back, along the length of her thigh, then back up, sliding under her nightgown to stroke her bare skin.

She shivered at his touch, her breath catching in her throat as she laid her hand on his chest. Her fingers traced the raised scars that marred his skin, tentatively sliding lower until she reached the waistband of his sweats, where her courage deserted her.

Catching her hand in his, he lifted it to his lips and kissed her fingertips. "Relax, love. I'm just going to hold you."

"But . . ."

"There's no hurry. We have lots of time."

She sighed with relief. "You're not angry?"

"No, my sweet girl. I can wait until you're ready. There's only one first time. I don't want to rush you."

"Will you still stay with me?"

"If you like."

She nodded, then yawned. Pillowing her head on his

shoulder, she closed her eyes. A moment later, she was asleep.

Quill held her all through the night, content to lie beside her and inhale the warm, womanly scent that was hers and hers alone, to feel the silk of her hair against his check, the length of her thigh alongside his.

As dawn approached, the slow, steady beat of her heart lulled him to sleep.

Callie woke with her breasts pressed against Quill's back, one arm draped over his waist, her legs entwined with his. It was a nice feeling, having him so close, waking up next to him. If they married, she would meet every morning with him at her side.

Last night, she had been sorely tempted to give in to the attraction between them. She'd thought she was ready, but Quill had sensed her hesitation. Ava had once told her to hang on to her virginity because, once gone, there was no getting it back. And a smart girl waited until she knew in her heart that she was giving her greatest treasure to the right man, the only man who deserved it.

Callie sighed. She wasn't sure why she'd hesitated. She loved Quill with every fiber of her being. Was it possible she harbored reservations about their future because he was a vampire? Well, who could blame her? It was a little more complicated than marrying a man from a different religion or one who was a vegetarian. They would both have to make adjustments, but she was willing to do whatever was necessary to make it work. She just needed a little time.

Easing away from Quill, she swung her legs over the

side of the bed and grabbed her robe. When she opened the door, Ebony meowed a loud protest at having been shut out.

"Sorry. I guess our vampire must have closed the door last night. Funny," Callie muttered, heading toward the kitchen, "I didn't think a closed door could keep you out."

Ebony trailed at her heels, making guttural sounds of complaint low in her throat.

"This will make you feel better," Callie said, filling the cat's bowl with food. "A little tuna chow for you, toast and coffee for me."

After breakfast, Callie crept into the bedroom, pulled a pair of jeans and a sweater out of her suitcase, along with a change of underwear and a pair of socks and boots, and went into the hallway bathroom to change.

Running her fingers through her hair, Callie went out the front door. A deep blue Range Rover was parked in the driveway.

The day was cool and cloudy, the ground damp from last night's rain. The house sat in a clearing surrounded by tall trees and boulders. Through the trees, she spied a chimney. Neighbors, she thought, though they were a good, long walk away.

Callie stood there a moment, her breath making little white puffs in the cold air. She thought of taking the car and seeing if she could find a town, then decided to take a walk instead. She struck out on a narrow trail that led into the woods.

The quiet closed in around her as she strolled along,

broken only by the faint drip-drip of raindrops from the pines and the scuff of her boots.

She rounded a bend in the trail, came to an abrupt halt when she saw a beautiful four-point buck walking toward her. The stag froze in its tracks, liquid brown eyes wary, ears flicking nervously back and forth.

Callie felt something ethereal and mystical pass between herself and the deer as they stared at each other. Hardly aware of what she was doing, Callie held out her hand, palm up. *Come to me.*

The buck took a tentative step forward. And then another. And another. It huffed a breath, then nosed her palm. Smiling with excitement, Callie stroked the animal's neck.

She let out a cry when a splotch of bright red appeared on the deer's shoulder, followed by the sharp report of a rifle shot. The deer took a couple of wobbly steps, then dropped to the ground, legs twitching.

Whirling around, Callie saw a hunter emerge from the cover of the trees. "Are you out of your mind?" she shouted. "You could have killed me!"

"I'm . . . I'm so sorry," the young man stammered. "I didn't see you."

Callie glared at him, her nerves humming as she gathered her power. Murmuring under her breath, she held out her hand, then clenched her fist until her knuckles were white.

The hunter let out a yelp as his rifle, now red hot, the barrel bent in a U-shape, singed his fingers. He dropped the gun, sent a frightened glance in her direction, then turned and ran away.

Callie knelt beside the deer, who lay quiet, its beautiful brown eyes staring up at her. Whispering "It's okay," she placed her hands over the bloody wound and again summoned her magic. She didn't know where the words came from, but as they fell from her lips, her palms grew warm and she felt power pour from her hands into the deer.

Time seemed to stand still. And then the stag lifted its head and scrambled to its feet.

Feeling suddenly weak, Callie stared up at the deer. The bullet wound was completely healed, leaving only a faint scar behind.

The deer lowered its head, as if to say thank you, then bounded into the trees and out of sight.

Rising, Callie shook her head, thinking Quill would never believe this. When she turned back toward the house, she saw Ebony sitting in the middle of the trail.

Callie blinked at the cat. "How did you get here? I left you in the house."

With a flick of its tail, the cat turned and trotted down the path.

Callie stared after Ebony. What had just happened here? she wondered as she followed the cat back to the house. Just what manner of feline had they taken in?

Chapter 26

Ricardo 42 stood in front of the Elder Knight, his head bowed.

"Speak," the Elder said, tersely.

"I went to the woman's house. It was empty. No sign of the woman or the vampire."

"Where have they gone?"

Head still bowed, Ricardo 42 admitted, "I don't know."

"Did you try to follow their trail?"

"There was none. I believe the vampire employed his powers to transport them to another location."

In a fit of rage, the Elder Knight struck Ricardo 42 across the face with the back of his hand. "You incompetent fool!"

Ricardo pressed his hand to his throbbing cheek. "I have more information, if I may speak?"

The Elder grunted his permission.

"I believe the woman practices witchcraft."

"What proof have you?"

"As you know, magic always leaves a signature behind."

"This could complicate matters," the Elder remarked,

his voice thoughtful. "Go back to the house and see if you can find any substantial proof."

"Yes, Elder."

"Ricardo?"

"Yes, Elder?"

"My apologies for striking you. Dismissed."

Chapter 27

"What are you saying?" Quill asked, glancing at Ebony, who sat on the mantel glaring at him. "You think the cat had something to do with your healing the deer?"

"Yes. No. I don't know! It was just so surreal. I've never studied any kind of healing magic, and yet I knew exactly what to do, what words to say, even though they were in another language. How is that possible? And how did Ebony get into Ava's room when the door was closed? And how did she get out of the house and follow me this morning?"

"I don't know." Opening his preternatural senses, Quill looked at the cat again. But as far as he could tell, it was just a cat. "Ava was a powerful witch. Perhaps she bequeathed her magic to you in the same way she wrapped you in her protective spell."

Callie nodded, but looked doubtful. She had told Quill about her adventure in the woods as soon as he rose that evening. She'd thought saying it out loud would somehow make it seem less bizarre. Instead, she was more confused than ever. Was it possible to transfer magic from one witch to another?

Mouth set in a determined line, she went into the

vacant bedroom. After her walk, she had taken the suitcase carrying her grandmother's books and things into the extra room. Humming softly, she unpacked the suitcase, then set up Ava's cauldron, candles, and wand on the long sofa table she had dragged in from the living room.

Opening her grandmother's grimoire, she perused the pages, looking for a spell that transferred magic from witch to witch.

She was dimly aware of Quill coming to stand behind her, of the cat making itself at home on the bed.

"Find anything?" Quill asked after several minutes.

"No." She slammed the book shut, then turned to face him. "I guess I'm just being . . . I don't know what."

Resting his hands on her hips, he backed up, tugging her along. When his legs hit the mattress, he fell back, carrying Callie with him, so that she landed on top of him.

Ebony let out a screech, jumped off the bed, and bolted from the room.

"Stop worrying, love," Quill said, sliding his hands up and down Callie's back. "Your grandmother was an incredibly powerful witch. It stands to reason that you would have inherited at least some of her power." He cupped her face in his palms, his eyes hot. "You've certainly worked your magic on me." And so saying, he claimed her lips with his.

Callie surrendered to the thrill of his mouth on hers, the crush of his arms holding her close, the feel of his chest beneath her breasts. His tongue stroked hers, igniting little fires of desire in the pit of her stomach. She ground her hips against his, felt his immediate response, and knew she'd gone too far. "Quill. . . . "

He groaned deep in his throat. "Don't move."

She stilled instantly, remembering that his desire and his thirst were closely entwined. At this moment, she didn't want to arouse either one.

His eyes were closed, his breathing rapid, his whole body rigid beneath hers.

He took a ragged breath. And then another. And then he rolled onto his side, carrying her with him. Needing some time alone to tamp down his desire and his hunger, he said "Why don't you go start dinner? I'll be there in a few minutes."

A quick nod and she swung her legs over the edge of the bed and left the room, careful not to run. He was a predator, she reminded herself. And she was prey.

In the kitchen, Callie stared out the window into the darkness beyond. There was no doubt she was playing with fire, she thought. The attraction between them seemed to burn hotter and stronger with every passing day. It might be in her best interest to ease that desire before it got out of hand.

Her grandmother's admonition not to surrender her chastity until she was certain she was giving it to the right man whispered in the back of Callie's mind.

She blew out a sigh. She thought Quill was the right man. But how was she to know for sure? Fifty percent of marriages ended in divorce.

Quill shared a meal with her from time to time, but not tonight. She had been setting the table when she heard the front door open and close and knew, without being told, that he had gone in search of prey.

She felt a little guilty for being relieved, but she

couldn't help it. She loved Quill desperately. She wanted to spend the rest of her life with him . . . didn't she?

Yes, of course. He'd asked her to marry him.

Perhaps that was the answer.

"Life's a gamble," she told Ebony. "I guess marriage is, too. You make your choice and hope it pays off. What do you think?"

The cat stared at her. Then, with a disdainful flick of its tail, padded out of the room.

Callie huffed a sigh. It was time to make a decision, probably the most important one of her life.

Callie was curled up on the sofa in front of the fireplace, the cat asleep at her feet, when Quill returned.

He frowned at Callie. "What is it?"

"What do you mean?"

"You're nervous about something."

"Am I?"

"I can scent it on you, Callie. Your heart's beating a mile a minute."

She frowned at him. Like it or not, he would always know when something was bothering her. But she could live with that. Smiling, she said, "I made a decision tonight."

"Oh?"

"You asked me to marry you a while back."

He nodded.

"Well, I thought it over and . . ."

He clenched his hands at his sides as he waited for her to go on.

"My answer is yes."

"Callie!" Sweeping her off the sofa and into his arms,

he hugged her close. "I'll do everything in my power to make you happy, love. I swear it."

"You already make me happy," she said, breathlessly.

"Anything you want," he said, "anything you need, it's yours."

"I just want you."

Setting her on her feet, he wrapped his arms around her and kissed her, a long, slow kiss that was filled with hope and the promise of forever. "When?" he asked.

"As soon as we can, I guess."

Taking her by the hand, Quill sank down on the sofa, then settled her on his lap. "What kind of wedding would you like?"

She shrugged. "I don't have any family. My only close friend is Viv. What about you? You'll want your parents here, I guess."

He nodded. "My mother would never forgive me if she wasn't front row center."

Callie grinned, suddenly nervous at the thought of meeting his mom and dad.

"They'll love you," he assured her with a smile. "My mother has resigned herself to the fact that she's never going to have grandchildren."

"Do you have any brothers?"

Something dark passed behind Quill's eyes. "I had a younger brother. He was killed by the Knights."

Cupping his cheek in her hand, she said, "I'm so sorry."

"It was a long time ago." He took a deep breath and let it out in a long, slow sigh. "Why don't you spend a few days looking for a wedding dress? I'll get in touch with my folks and give them the good news."

"Okay. Hey, what's your last name, anyway?"

"Falconer. My ancestors raised hunting birds."

"Missus Callie Falconer," she murmured. "I like the sound of that."

In the morning, Callie called Vivian to tell her the good news.

Viv's reply was less than enthusiastic. "Are you sure about this? I know you think you love him, but aren't you rushing things just a little?"

"It's complicated, Viv."

"What do you mean?"

"I don't know how to explain it, but I know it's the right thing to do. I can't just sleep with him to make things easier."

"Easier? What are you talking about?"

"He's a vampire, Viv. He's very passionate by nature and driven by a need for blood, and the two get all mixed up when we're together."

"Well, if you want my advice, which I know you don't, you'll leave him while you still can."

"It's too late for that. I'd like you to be my maid of honor. Will you?"

"Of course."

"I'll let you know where and when. And don't worry about airfare or anything. We'll take care of that."

It was happening, Callie thought after disconnecting the call. For better or worse, she was going to follow her heart and marry Quill.

Smiling, she went online to search for the nearest bridal shop.

Chapter 28

Ricardo 42 smiled. Before leaving the Dark Wood, he had gone through all the reports ever written on the Hungarian vampire known as Quill. Most of the information, which stretched over hundreds of years, hadn't told him very much about the elusive bloodsucker. But the last few pages, written by Trey 95, had included a name—Vivian Brown.

Shortly before his death, Trey 95 had taken the woman prisoner in hopes of using her as bait to trap the vampire. In so doing, he had jotted down the woman's name and address. With no other leads, Ricardo 42 had spent the last few days tailing the woman's every move, following her to work, secreting himself outside her apartment.

And listening to her phone calls, which had provided another name—Callie.

This morning, his vigilance had paid off.

Sometime in the next few days or weeks, Vivian Brown would meet with the vampire's woman.

And he would be there when it happened.

Chapter 29

Callie had just finished breakfast when there was a knock at the door. She knew a moment of apprehension as she went to answer it. She didn't know anyone here. Who could it be?

She peeked through the narrow, leaded window alongside the front door, surprised to see a tall, slender brunette clad in hip-hugger jeans and a bright pink sweater standing on the porch. The visitor held a covered dish in her hands.

Curious, Callie opened the door.

"Good morning," the woman said brightly. "I'm your nearest neighbor, Brooke Jeffries. I just came by to welcome you to the neighborhood."

"Hi. I'm Callie. Come in, won't you?"

"Thanks. I hope you like apple pie," Brooke said, offering her the dish. "I made it this morning."

"It's my favorite! Have a seat, won't you, while I put this in the refrigerator? Oh, would you like a slice?"

"No, thank you. I have another one at home."

After putting the pie in the fridge, Callie ran a hand through her hair, then went back into the living room.

Brooke sat perched on the edge of the easy chair across

from the sofa. "We noticed the smoke from your fireplace the other night," Brooke remarked. "My husband told me Quill was here with a young lady. We don't get many new people, so I thought I'd come by and see if you needed anything."

"Nothing I can think of. You say your husband knows Quill?"

"Yes. I guess they met some years ago."

Callie nodded. Quill hadn't said anything about knowing anyone here.

"Nolan and I have been married just over three years," Brooke said. "I'm still adjusting. Are you and Quill . . . ?"

"Married? Not yet. But soon." Callie leaned forward. "Do you have any children?"

Brooke shook her head. "No, but we're trying."

"What's it like, being married to one of them? Is it so different from being married to an ordinary man?"

"Yes," Brooke said slowly. "And no. Nolan told me that Quill has been a vampire for hundreds of years. He's well-known among their kind. My Nolan has only been a vampire for fourteen years, so he's not nearly as powerful."

"Oh?"

"They grow stronger as they age," Brooke said. "Didn't Quill tell you that?"

"Not that I recall. But it makes sense, I guess. Are you . . . ?" Callie bit down on her lower lip.

"Am I what?"

"Are you happy with your husband?"

Brooke's smile lit up her face. "Oh, yes."

"No regrets?"

"None so far. He treats me like a queen. Can I ask *you* something?"

"Of course."

"Nolan told me he sensed witchcraft coming from this direction. Is it you?"

"He sensed it?" Callie asked incredulously.

"Witchcraft leaves a signature. Didn't you know that?"

"No."

"Well, I didn't, either, until I married Nolan. So, it's true? You're a witch?"

There didn't seem to be any point in denying it. "Yes, but I've only recently discovered it."

"Do you think . . . never mind."

"What is it?"

Brooke made a vague gesture with her hand. "I shouldn't ask. I mean, we just met and . . ."

Callie frowned, wondering what was so awful that the woman didn't have the nerve to ask. Curious, she said, "Please, just tell me what it is. If I can help, I will."

After taking a deep breath, Brooke blurted, "Is there any chance you could find my lost puppy?"

Callie stifled a grin. That was what she'd been afraid to ask? "How long has it been missing?"

"Since last night. Nolan left the back door open. Neither of us realized Lady was missing until early this morning."

"I've never tried to locate anything missing before, but I'll certainly try. Do you have anything that belongs to her?"

Brooke reached into her pocket and withdrew a small dog brush. Several short brown hairs were caught in the bristles. "Will this help?"

Callie nodded. "I'll see what I can do. You'll understand if I need to be alone when I try?" That wasn't entirely true, but she'd just met Brooke and didn't feel comfortable practicing her magic in front of a stranger.

"Yes, of course," Brooke said, pushing to her feet. "It was nice meeting you, Callie."

"You, too." Callie held up the brush. "I'll let you know if I have any luck with this."

They exchanged cell phone numbers, and then Brooke Jeffries took her leave.

Callie stared after her, brow furrowed. What kind of signature did magic leave behind? And was there any way to mask it?

Curious, she went into the spare room and opened Ava's grimoire.

"You had company today," Quill remarked. They were sitting at the dinner table, the remains of a spaghetti dinner between them.

"How did you know?"

He lifted one brow.

"Oh. Right. Our neighbor came calling. Her name's Brooke Jeffries. She said you know her husband, Nolan."

Quill nodded.

"She asked me if I could find her lost dog."

"Did you?"

"I haven't tried yet. I did some reading on location spells. I'm going to attempt one in a little while. Brooke said something about magic leaving a signature. I looked in Ava's grimoire, but it didn't say anything about that."

"Every witch's magic leaves a trace—or signature—

behind. And every one is different. Although yours and Ava's are much alike."

"Hmm . . ."

"What's that mean?"

"Nothing. Just hmm." She took a deep breath and blew it out. "Okay, I'm going to see if I can find Brooke's dog."

"Mind if I watch?"

Callie shrugged. "I guess not."

Quill followed her down the hall to the spare bedroom, stood in the doorway while she plucked the hairs from the dog brush and dropped them into the cauldron. Picking up her grandmother's athame, she pricked her finger and added a drop of blood to the bowl. Then, chanting softly, she lit the hair on fire. A plume of blue-gray smoke rose from the bowl and drifted through the open doorway.

"I'm supposed to follow it," Callie said.

Quill grunted. "Not without me, you don't."

Callie opened the front door as the smoke wafted through the crack at the bottom.

The blue-gray plume led her into the woods, down a rocky path to a craggy bluff, where it hovered in midair.

Moving carefully, Callie peered over the edge. Three feet down, a flat rock jutted from the side of the bluff. A small brown puppy huddled there, whining softly.

"I'll get it," Quill said. Moving to the edge of the bluff, he slowly floated down to the ledge and picked up the dog.

A moment later, he placed the pup in Callie's arms. "Mission accomplished."

Callie grinned at him. "It worked. It really worked."

"Come on, witch woman. Let's return the missing pooch to his grieving mistress."

* * *

Brooke Jeffries let out a squeal of excitement when she saw her lost puppy. Scooping the furry little thing into her arms, she exclaimed, "Callie, how can I ever thank you?"

"That look on your face is thanks enough."

"You must be Quill," Brooke said, laughing softly as the puppy licked her face. "Come in, won't you? Nolan's in the living room watching a football game."

Callie looked up at Quill, a question in her eyes.

He shrugged. "It's up to you."

"I guess we can stay for a few minutes," Callie said.

Brooke led the way into the living room, where she made the introductions. Nolan Jeffries was of medium height and stocky, with short brown hair and deep-set brown eyes. Quill looked like a vampire. Nolan Jeffries looked like a bank clerk in a white button-down shirt and brown slacks.

Tension lifted the hair on Callie's arms as the two vampires shook hands. She felt Quill's power move over Nolan, a silent show of strength. Callie glanced at Brooke, but all of her attention was focused on the puppy in her lap. She seemed oblivious to everything else.

Callie listened quietly as the two men reminisced about places they'd been, people they'd known, and then Nolan said, "Have you run into any of the Knights lately?"

Quill nodded. "They wiped out our settlement in Northern California a few days ago."

All the color drained from Brooke's face. "Did they kill everyone?"

"All of our people who didn't heed my warning were killed."

Brooke looked at her husband. "You don't think . . . ?" When he held out his arms, she went into them, sobbing. The puppy squeezed out from between the two of them and jumped to the floor.

Callie looked at Quill. "We should go."

Rising, he took her hand. "I'm sorry to be the bearer of bad news," he told Nolan.

Jeffries nodded, his expression somber as he patted his wife's back. "Let's get together later."

Quill met Nolan Jeffries in the woods at 4 AM. "I take it Brooke knew someone in California?"

"A good friend of ours lived there with his mortal wife and their teenage son. She tried calling him after you left, but there was no answer."

"We only found one dead female. She took her own life."

"We need to do something about those damn Knights," Jeffries said. "But what?"

"They're getting stronger. Even though they only have thirteen active members at any given time, it's rumored that they have members in training in just about every big city. I'm afraid they're planning some kind of coup in hopes of wiping out every one of our kind here in the States."

"Are they strong enough to do that?"

"Perhaps."

"You're one of the oldest of our kind," Jeffries said. "What can we do?"

"This confrontation has been a long time coming.

We're few in number." Quill stared into the forest, his brow furrowed. "There are some Transylvanian vampires living in Louisiana."

"You're not suggesting we unite with those blood-sucking monsters!" Nolan exclaimed.

"Only as a last resort."

Jeffries shook his head. "We can't trust them." And then he frowned. "Do you know any?"

"No."

"Our feud with them is even older than our war with the Brotherhood of the Knights. Even if you could get in touch with any of the other vampires, they'd never agree to join us."

"Maybe, maybe not. At the moment, it's a moot point. Go console your woman. She needs you."

Nolan stared at him. Then, with a nod, he vanished into the night.

Quill stared after Jeffries. He didn't know any Transylvanian vampires personally, but he knew where to find one.

When Quill returned home, he paused inside the door, then made his way to Callie's room. "I thought you'd be asleep," he remarked, switching on the bedside light.

She shrugged. "I tried." Sitting up, she propped a pillow behind her head. "What did you and Jeffries talk about?"

"He asked me what we were going to do about the Knights."

"What did you say?"

Quill sat on the edge of the mattress, hands resting on

his knees. "It's late. Are you sure you want to talk about this now?"

She nodded.

"I've heard the Knights are growing in number. I think they might be planning a nationwide attack on my people."

Callie's eyes grew wide. "Do they have enough men to do that?"

"From what I've heard, they already outnumber us."

"What are we going to do?"

He smiled at her use of the word *we*. "I'm not sure. I think that our best chance of winning is to unite with the Transylvanian vampires."

"Are you serious?"

"Once the fight begins, the Knights will kill every vampire they find, Hungarian and Transylvanian alike. But it's not my decision. My father is the oldest of our kind. His decision will be final."

War, Callie thought. *He's talking about going to war.* "Brooke said they're trying to get pregnant."

Taken aback by the abrupt change of topic, Quill lifted one brow. "If she wanted to be pregnant, she'd be pregnant. It's up to her."

"I don't understand."

"The man plants the seed. The woman decides when it grows."

"What do you mean?"

"I mean it's up to her when she gets pregnant."

Callie stared at him in disbelief. "I've never heard of such a thing."

"It's the way of my people."

"That's just plain weird."

Quill smiled wryly. "Don't ask me to how it works.

All I know is, human females can reject our sperm. I suspect it's some kind of protection against bearing a child if a woman is attacked by one of us, something that's punishable by death." Leaning forward, he kissed her lightly. "This is a heavy conversation for so early in the morning. Let's get some sleep."

"Stay with me?"

Nodding, he removed his boots, socks, pants, and shirt, then stretched out on top of the blankets, naked save for a pair of navy-blue briefs.

Callie snuggled under the covers, then pillowed her head on Quill's shoulder. Soon, she thought, soon they'd be married and he wouldn't have to sleep on top of the blankets anymore.

Chapter 30

In the morning, Callie ate a quick breakfast, then drove fifteen miles to the bridal shop she had located online. She had considered wearing her grandmother's gown but rejected the idea. She wanted something new, something that was hers and hers alone.

She spent the next hour and a half trying on a dozen dresses—long ones, short ones, tea-length, sleeveless, strapless, plain and fancy, sexy and modest. None of them seemed quite right. Discouraged, she decided to try on one more.

And fell in love. It was perfect. A sweetheart bodice. Long, fitted sleeves made of delicate lace. And a beautiful floor-length skirt. Callie bought the dress on the spot and arranged for alterations, which would take two weeks. She picked out a shoulder-length veil and a pair of white heels and left the store, smiling.

Filled with excitement, she didn't pay any attention to the black SUV that pulled in behind her.

At home, she put the veil and the shoe box on the shelf in the bedroom closet and closed the door. When she turned around, Ebony was at her heels.

"I'm going to be a bride," she said, bending down to stroke the cat's head. "What do you think about that?"

The cat hissed and arched her back.

Callie huffed a sigh. "Why don't you like Quill? He's never done anything to you."

Ebony stared at her through unblinking yellow-gold eyes.

"You're impossible," Callie muttered. "Just remember, if I ever have to chose between the two of you, you're outta here."

Tail twitching, the cat padded out of the room.

With a shake of her head, Callie went into the kitchen to fix a sandwich. She ate it at the table, then decided to take a walk in spite of the clouds gathering overhead. She grabbed a jacket, just in case, and headed out the back door.

She followed a meandering path that wound between tall trees. The air was fragrant with the scent of pine and damp earth. When she reached a fork in the road, she paused, then turned left. The trail led her to a narrow stream and there, standing in the shade on the other side of the water, she saw the buck she had healed the day before, easily identified by the faint scar on its shoulder.

The deer stared at her, ears twitching, nostrils flared, and then it picked its dainty way across the stream and nosed her hand. Callie stroked the buck's coat, thinking what a rare and special moment it was, standing there in the middle of a forest petting a wild animal.

A faint noise sounded behind her.

In a flash, the deer was gone.

Callie whirled around, her heart pounding as her gaze darted left and right. Seeing nothing, she ducked behind a tree, then peered around the trunk. There! A flash of black moving through the shadows. Wishing she had Ava's wand to focus her power, she concentrated on the man slinking through the underbrush as she tried to conjure a spell that would render him immobile.

She gathered her power and whispered the spell, but she must have done something wrong. She saw it hit the man, but it didn't immobilize him. Instead, he let out a startled cry, then bolted away from her and disappeared into the forest.

Callie waited where she was for ten minutes before venturing into the open. She darted warily from tree to tree, but whoever had been stalking her was gone.

Quill paced the floor in front of the sofa that evening as he tried to tamp down the fear that had been churning in his gut ever since Callie had told him what had happened in the woods. "You didn't see who it was?"

"Just someone dressed in black." She shrugged. "I might have overreacted. Maybe it was just a hiker."

"Maybe." But he didn't think so. "And your magic didn't work?"

"I'm not sure I cast the right spell."

He grunted softly. Took a deep breath. Callie was here. She was safe. But he couldn't stop worrying. "I'm going to go out and have a look around." When she started to rise from the sofa, he shook his head. "You stay here."

"But . . ."

"Stay here."

Callie glared at him, mutely defiant.

"Please, Callie."

"Oh, all right."

"I won't be gone long." Quill caressed her cheek with his knuckles, then went out the back door.

With his preternatural senses, it was easy to follow her tracks. And just as easy to pick up the trail of the Knight who had been following her. A quick inhale carried the faint signature of Callie's magic. He paused, frowning, when he detected a second signature. He recognized it, too. It belonged to the black witch employed by the Knights of the Dark Wood. He'd never seen her face but she'd come to the rescue of a Knight who had attacked him.

He grunted softly. No wonder Callie's incantation hadn't worked. The black witch had cast some sort of counter-spell on the Knight to protect him. No doubt the dark witch had enchanted every Knight's medallion with the same magical protection.

Damn!

He had little doubt that the confrontation between the Hungarian vampires and the Knights was well on its way to all-out warfare.

Callie was waiting for him at the front door when he returned to the house. "Did you find anything?" she asked anxiously.

"Yeah."

She locked the door, then followed him into the living room. "Well? Tell me."

He dropped down on the sofa, hands dangling between his knees. "It was one of the Knights, all right."

Callie sat beside him, trying not to look worried. "You're sure?"

He nodded. "If I'm right, there was nothing wrong with your spell."

"What do you mean? It didn't work."

"The Knights have a witch of their own. I once met a vampire who'd crossed her path. I don't know what she did to him, but his mind was never the same afterwards. I almost tangled with her once a long time ago." He shook his head at the memory. "I think she's been busy conjuring a spell to protect the Knights from any and all enchantments cast by others."

"So, her magic is stronger than mine."

Quill shrugged. "Maybe."

"There's no maybe about it. I cast a spell, and either it didn't work or my magic wasn't strong enough to overpower hers."

"Or maybe you just cast the wrong kind of spell."

Callie frowned. That was always possible. After all, she was new to all this. She had only practiced a few of the hundreds of enchantments, hexes, and charms in her grandmother's grimoire. So far, she had mastered only a handful of the less complicated ones. "What do we do now?"

"I don't know. But it's time to end this, one way or another." Hopefully before it escalated into all-out war. And the best way to win was to carry the fight to the stronghold in the Dark Wood. Unfortunately, he had no idea where it was located.

As he usually did, Quill stayed up long after Callie had gone to bed. He had traveled every state in the USA at one time or another, visited just about every town and city in the last two hundred years, but the location of the

Dark Wood remained a mystery. The only explanation was that the Knight's dark witch had worked her magic to make the place invisible to outsiders.

He wondered if any of the Transylvanian vampires had any idea of its location. Perhaps it was time to visit New Orleans. He'd heard that one of the more powerful of the Transylvanian vamps had moved there a few years ago. Quill scrubbed a hand across his jaw. He was reluctant to leave Callie here, alone. But he wouldn't be gone long. A few hours at the most. He could always ask Jeffries to look after her.

Relieved to have a plan of action, he went to bed. He would discuss it with Callie when he woke tomorrow evening and see what she thought.

Callie frowned at Quill. "You want to go to New Orleans? To see a vampire?"

He shrugged. "She might know something I don't, like the location of the Dark Wood. Or who's behind the spells protecting the Knights."

"She?" Callie stared at him over the rim of her wineglass. They were sitting on the swing in the backyard. Earlier, Quill had grilled a couple of steaks for dinner.

Quill grinned. "Do I detect a note of jealousy in your voice?"

"Of course not. Well, maybe a little. I'm aware of your effect on mortal women and witches. Does it work on vampires, too?"

"I don't know. If you don't want me to go, I won't."

"No, we need all the help we can get. I'll be all right."

"I'll ask Jeffries to keep an eye on things here."

"I don't need a sitter!" she retorted.

"It's for my peace of mind."

"Humph. Just how well do you know this Transylvanian vampire?"

"Only by reputation."

"When were you thinking of leaving?"

"Late tomorrow afternoon."

"I'll miss you."

Quill put his glass on the table beside the swing. After setting Callie's beside it, he took her in his arms. "I won't be gone long enough for you to miss me."

"An hour is long enough."

"Ah, Callie. Do you know how much I love you? How much I need you? How empty my life was before you came along?" Sliding a finger under her chin, he tilted her head up and kissed her, a slow sweet kiss that made her toes curl with pleasure.

Tears stung Callie's eyes as she wrapped her arms around him. "I love you more."

"Impossible," he said, smiling down at her. "Promise me you'll stay close to the house while I'm gone."

She nodded, willing, at that moment, to promise him anything he desired.

"Anything?" he teased.

"Stop reading my mind. It's not fair."

"Right now I'll bet *you* can read mine."

She poked him in the side with her elbow. "I don't have to read it. I can *see* what you're thinking."

Quill burst out laughing, and then he hugged her tight. "Sometimes a man just can't keep a secret."

Callie glared at him and then joined in the laughter, wondering if she could put a rush on the alterations to her wedding gown.

* * *

Quill left at four o'clock the next afternoon. He kissed Callie long and hard, wanting to imprint the taste and the feel of her lips on his.

She clung to him, then forced a smile. "Promise me you'll be careful, Quill," she said, cupping his cheek. "And hurry back."

"Be safe, love. Dream of me."

Blinking rapidly, she nodded.

Quill took a deep breath, and then, before he changed his mind about going, he willed himself to New Orleans.

It had been fifty years since he had been to the Big Easy. Not much had changed, he thought as he strolled down St. Charles Avenue, famous for its large, antebellum homes and mansions in a variety of styles—American Colonial, Greek Revival, Victorian, and Queen Anne.

He loved the French Quarter. Houses sporting large courtyards and intricate wrought-iron balconies lined the streets. The vampire he was looking for was supposed to reside in one of them.

As darkness descended, he headed for Bourbon Street, which was located in the heart of the Quarter, world renowned for its bars, restaurants, and strip clubs. The place was quiet during the day, but it came alive after dark. It was also renowned for the number of Transylvanian vampires that hunted here, though that was a fact known only to the supernatural community.

It was easy to find prey in the back streets and dark alleys.

Quill glided through the crowded streets, his preternatural senses probing the night for the unique scent of vampire. He passed by several male bloodsuckers. Each time he locked eyes with one of them, they quickly looked away and hurried on. Quill grinned inwardly, aware that they sensed his ancient power and knew instinctively that it was far stronger than theirs.

He continued down another block, pausing to glance in the windows of several voodoo shops as he passed by, intrigued by the dolls and *gris gris*, the masks and amulets and talismans. Voodoo had an interesting history in the city. In the 1700s, African slaves had brought voodoo to New Orleans, where it became infused into the city's predominant religion, Catholicism, and became known as Voodoo Catholicism. In the 1900s, Marie Laveau, born a free woman of color, had reigned in the city as the voodoo queen. She had been a beautiful woman, rumored to possess mystical powers. Having met her once, he had little doubt those rumors were true.

He was turning away from one of the shops when he caught the scent of a female vampire. Was she the one he was looking for? Eyes narrowed, he glanced around, his gaze settling on the tall, red-haired, tawny-skinned woman gliding toward him. She wore a blood-red dress that clung to her voluptuous figure like a second skin. He knew without doubt that she was the mistress of the city. Her power was unmistakable.

Feeling his gaze, she looked up. Her eyes narrowed as she recognized what he was.

"What are you doing here?" she hissed. "Your kind is not allowed within the city."

"I'm looking for you. We need to talk."

"I think not."

"I only want a moment of your time and then I'll be gone."

Her gaze burned into his. "Follow me." Pivoting on her heel, she strode across the street and continued down a narrow, pitch-black alley that ended in a hotel parking lot. Coming to a halt, she whirled around to face him. "What do you want?"

"I've heard rumors that your people know the location of the Dark Wood."

"Even if I knew, why would I tell you?"

"The Knights wiped out one of our towns and killed several of our people."

She lifted one shoulder in an elegant shrug. "What is that to me?"

"If the Knights go to war against us, they'll destroy every vampire they can find. Including you and your kind."

"We can take care of our own."

"I'm not asking you to help us fight them," he said. "I just need to know where the hell they are. Dammit!"

She laughed, a deep, throaty sound. "I have heard about you. Quill, isn't it? Ancient. Arrogant. Needing no one, yet here you are, seeking my help. Why?"

"My woman. She's in danger because of me. My people are being slaughtered. I'm tired of constantly looking over my shoulder. It's time to take the battle to the Knights and end it once and for all."

"You love her, this woman?"

"More than you can imagine."

"What is it like?"

Quill frowned. "What do you mean?"

"Being in love with a mortal. What is it like?"

"Surely you've been in love with a mortal man once or twice."

She shook her head. "No."

"She's the best thing that ever happened to me," he said quietly. "I can't lose her."

Dark eyes narrowed, she regarded him for several moments. "The Knights' stronghold is located deep in the woods near the Canadian border."

"That covers a hell of a lot of territory."

"It is rumored that the stronghold is located near Saskatchewan."

"Do you know anything about their witch?"

"Only that she is very old and very powerful."

"Does she live up there, in the Dark Wood?"

"I think not. It seems odd, does it not, that they employ a witch, when they used to hunt them."

Quill grunted. "How are your people doing?"

She made a vague gesture. "The hunters come through here from time to time. When they do, we lie low and make sure there are no bodies left lying around."

Quill grinned, liking her in spite of himself. "How are you called?"

"Claret."

He lifted one brow. "Like the wine?"

She nodded, a wry grin playing over her lips.

It suited her, he thought. "Be careful," he warned. "Good wine is hard to find."

"You, too." Her gaze met his and then she darted forward, kissed him full on the mouth, and vanished from sight.

Staring after her, Quill licked his lips. And tasted fresh blood.

His blood. She'd bit him and he hadn't felt a damn thing.

It was late when Quill returned to their mountain retreat. He had expected Callie to be in bed. Instead, he found her asleep on the sofa in front of the fire, the black cat curled up at her feet.

With a hiss, Ebony lifted her head, angry yellow eyes glaring at him.

"You damn nuisance," he muttered. "I ought to boot your butt out of here."

Callie stirred at the sound of his voice. "Quill?"

"Why are you sleeping out here?"

"I was waiting for you, of course." Sitting up, she reached for him.

When Quill sat down, Ebony jumped off the couch and left the room. "I think that cat hates me," he remarked, drawing Callie into his arms.

"That's okay," she said, kissing his cheek. "One of us loves you."

"I'm glad it's you and not that damn cat."

Callie laughed softly. "I missed you."

"No more than I missed you, love."

"Did you find the vampire you were looking for?"

He nodded.

"How did you know she was the right one if you've never met?"

"I just looked for a strong female."

"Is there only one?"

"In New Orleans, there is. The other vampires all answer to her. Her name's Claret. Like the wine."

"Did she have any information about the location of the Dark Wood?"

"Nothing concrete. Her best guess is that it's up near the border between Saskatchewan and Montana."

"She touched you, didn't she?" Callie wrinkled her nose. "I can smell her on you."

Quill shrugged. "It was nothing."

Callie lifted one brow. "Define nothing."

"She kissed me." Seeing the flash of anger in her eyes, he pressed his fingertips to her lips. "Before you say anything, it wasn't a sign of affection. Damn vampire bit my lip and tasted my blood."

Callie's eyes grew wide. Pulling his hand away from her mouth, she said, "I don't like the sound of that! Ava said blood has power."

"It does, indeed."

"So, what does it mean, exactly? Her biting you and tasting your blood?"

"It means she'll be able to find me any time she has a mind to."

"Oh, I *really* don't like that."

"I'm not crazy about it, either, but it's done. Anyway, she thinks the Dark Wood is up by the Canadian border." His gaze searched hers. "Are we okay?"

"Do you trust her?"

"No reason not to. Our covens tend to avoid each other, but we've united in times past when it was beneficial to both sides."

"Is she pretty?"

"Callie."

"Is she?"

He shrugged. "I guess so. She only agreed to help me after I told her I was worried about you."

"Yeah, right."

"I mean it."

"She doesn't even know me. Why would that make her change her mind?"

"I have no idea. She asked me what it was like to be in love with a mortal. Turns out she's never been in love with anybody."

"Well, she can't have you!"

Quill's laughter filled the room. "No chance, Callie, my sweet. So, was everything quiet here while I was gone?"

"Yes. Except Ebony's been acting really strange."

"Really? How can you tell?"

Callie poked him in the ribs. "She wouldn't let me out of her sight. I was practically tripping over her every time I turned around. She followed me everywhere, even into the bathroom."

Quill frowned, a disconcerting idea forming in the back of his mind.

Later that night, after Callie had gone to bed, Quill sent a text to every Hungarian vampire he knew, advising them about the slaughter in Northern California and warning them to be vigilant. He also advised them that it might it necessary to take the fight to the Knights of the Dark Wood.

He had no sooner sent the texts than Nolan Jeffries sent a reply, asking Quill to meet him outside.

"What's up?" Quill asked.

"I killed one of the Knights while you were gone."

Quill frowned, wondering if it was the same man

Callie had seen lurking in the forest. "What did you do with the body?"

"I burned it. I hope that was the right to do."

"Did you notice anything else unusual?"

"No."

"Thanks for keeping an eye on Callie."

"Happy to help." Jeffries shoved his hands into his back pockets. "It sounds like we're going to war."

"Maybe. It's been a few centuries since the last one."

"My parents told me about that. Lots of killing on both sides."

"We prevailed in the end."

Jeffries grunted softly. "And yet here we are, on the brink again. How many Knights do you suppose there are?"

"I've no idea. They've had a long time to train new ones."

"And yet our numbers remain few," Jeffries lamented. "And they have a powerful witch."

"So do we," Quill said, glancing back at the house. "So do we."

And maybe more than one.

Chapter 31

Except for taking time to eat, Callie spent a good part of the next day making a wand of her own. Walking around the cabin, she found a broken branch that was reasonably straight and not too fat. Following the instructions in the grimoire to leave an offering, she sprinkled water at the base of the tree where she had found the branch.

Taking her find back to the cabin, she read the next steps, which involved consecrating the wood and then smudging the wand to purify it of negative energy.

When that was done, she peeled the bark from the wood, then carved it into the shape she desired. Next, she sanded the wand until it was smooth, then painted it a dark blue with silver stars.

She spent the rest of the day practicing her craft—mostly protection spells of one kind or another. She also read up on how to block her thoughts and how to launch various projectiles at targets. When she felt confident of her ability, she went into the backyard and practiced mentally hurling sticks, rocks, and bricks at one of the trees. Once she felt she had that spell mastered, she found an ax in the shed and for the next half hour she concentrated on launching the weapon at a target. The ax was large and heavy, and it took an extraordinary amount of concentration just to get it off the ground. By late afternoon, she was mentally exhausted and ready for a nap.

Ebony, who had been lying in a patch of sunlight watching her, rose and stretched and followed her inside.

That evening, Quill called a meeting of all the vampires who lived in the area. He was the oldest out of the eight present, Cory Bridger the youngest. Callie was the only woman in the room. Quill related his conversation with the vampire in New Orleans, though he neglected to mention that Claret had bitten him. "Thoughts?" he asked, when he was finished.

"So, this vampire thinks the Dark Wood is up by the Canadian border," Nolan Jeffries remarked, his brow furrowed. "It makes sense, I guess. There's a lot of unexplored territory up there. Lots of places to hide. The thing is, the sanctuary is bound to be invisible to outsiders." He glanced at Callie. "Do you think you can undo whatever spell their witch has constructed?"

"I won't know until I try."

"I'm not sure this is a good idea."

Quill glanced at the speaker. Like the others, Kels Johansson was a young vampire, no more than thirty-five years old.

"There are less than fifty of us in the States," Johansson said. "We don't know how many Knights are up there. What we *do* know is that their witch is powerful.

Unfortunately, our witch is young and has never been tested."

Several of the other men nodded in agreement.

"Johansson is right," Quill agreed. "Callie's never been to war. But neither have most of you. All I know is, I'm damn tired of being hunted. So, if any of you have a better idea than carrying the fight to them, I'm open to suggestions."

"I say wait awhile," Jeffries said. "We haven't heard of any attacks recently."

"You're forgetting about the one in California," Quill said, his voice sharp. He glanced around the room. "So, what do you want to do, Jeffries, wait until they've killed more of us before we take action?"

"I'm saying at least wait until you talk it over with the rest of our people. And with your father. This isn't something we can decide on our own."

Quill grunted softly. Like it or not, Jeffries was right. "In the meantime, with your permission, Callie and I want to ward your houses against anyone who's not of our blood."

"Can you do that?" Bridger asked.

"We managed it on Callie's home. Her magic combined with the threshold and my wards repelled one of the Knights. If it worked on her place, it should work on all of yours, as well."

"Hell, I'm willing to give it a try," Jeffries said. "Thresholds only repel vampires. Not Knights." He smiled at Callie. "Or witches."

All six of the other men agreed.

Quill nodded. "We'll erect the wards tonight."

* * *

"I hope this works," Callie remarked. She and Quill had just finished working their respective magic on the Jeffries' house and were headed for Cory Bridger's place.

"I'm ninety-nine percent sure it will."

"Only ninety-nine percent?"

"Few things in life are perfect," he muttered. And then smiled. "Except you."

She flushed at the compliment. Hand in hand, they made their way to the next house. "Are you upset because they seem reluctant to fight?"

"No. It's not something I want, either. But if we don't start fighting back, the Knights are going to get more and more aggressive. So far, we've been lucky that more humans haven't been caught in the cross fire," he said, thinking of the woman that Trey 95 had accidentally killed.

At the last house, Callie heard a baby's cry. She pressed a hand over her stomach, imagining herself pregnant with Quill's child. Was she up to the task of raising a baby vampire? Was it like nurturing a human infant?

She put the question to Quill as they walked home.

"Nothing to worry about," he assured her. "Our son will be like any other boy until he reaches puberty."

"Is there any chance at all of having a girl?"

"I've never known it to happen." Then, seeing her crestfallen expression, he said, "but I guess anything's possible." Although he had never heard of any females born to their kind.

Callie nodded. She had always hoped to have a daughter. Of course, even if she married a mortal man, there was no guarantee she would be blessed with a little girl. But at least she'd have a fifty-fifty chance.

"Is that a game-changer?" Quill asked quietly.

"No." She smiled up at him. "I believe in miracles."

"So do I." Quill pulled her into his arms and kissed her, long and hard. He had never believed in miracles until Callie had come into his life.

Quill went hunting when they returned to the house. In his absence, Callie started a fire in the hearth, then went into her room and changed into her pajamas. In the living room, she settled down on the sofa with a paperback she had found in the nightstand.

Purring softly, Ebony curled up beside her.

Callie had just dozed off when the cat sprang to its feet. Back arched, tail straight up, it stared at the door, hissing.

Fighting down a rush of uneasiness, Callie gathered her power around her. Easing to her feet, she glanced at Ebony. The cat was growling now.

Callie's mouth went dry when the door opened. Lifting one hand, she was prepared to launch a spell that would have sent the intruder to the other side of town when Quill crossed the threshold. Pausing, he glanced over his shoulder and said, "Come in."

Power shimmered in the air as a red-headed woman followed Quill inside.

Callie stared at her. The woman was almost as tall as Quill, with a voluptuous figure and eyes so dark they were almost black. She wore a long, jade green dress stained with dark spots that Callie realized were blood. Even without being told, Callie knew that the woman was a vampire. The Transylvanian kind that killed their prey. Preternatural power radiated from her, similar to Quill's and yet different.

Callie looked at Quill, one brow raised.

"This is Claret," he said. "Claret, this is Callie."

The woman nodded at her. "I'm sorry for the intrusion. I had nowhere else to go."

"I found her outside," Quill explained. "Her coven was attacked by hunters tonight. She's the only one who got away."

"I'm . . . I'm sorry," Callie said. "Would you like to get out of that dress?"

"Yes, thank you."

"My room is down the hall. You can wash up in there. I'm afraid none of my clothes will fit you, but . . ."

"I'll take her to my room," Quill said. "I've got a pair of sweatpants and a T-shirt she can wear."

Callie stared after them a moment, then dropped down on the sofa. Was he crazy, inviting that woman into their house?

Meowing softly, Ebony jumped up beside her. Callie stroked the cat's fur, feeling the tension drain out of her. Until Quill returned.

"How could you bring that woman into our house?" she demanded, keeping her voice low.

"She says she's in danger."

"And now so are we. I don't want her here."

"Calm down, love." He sat on her other side. "Transylvanian vampires can't be awake during the day, and she'll be gone tomorrow night."

"How did she find you?" Callie asked. Then, remembering, she lifted her hand to silence him before he could answer. "Your blood. You said she could follow it. Did you know she was going to do it so soon?"

"She didn't come here for me, but because she had nowhere else to go." Even as he said it, he had his doubts.

Still, it was better to have her here, where he could keep an eye on her.

"If you believe that, you're a fool. I'm going to bed."

"Callie . . ."

"I'll see you tomorrow." She stalked toward her room with Ebony at her heels.

Quill stared after her. *Dammit.* He looked up when Claret glided into the room. Although she was tall for a woman, she managed to look petite in his sweatpants and one of his T-shirts. Her hair flowed over her shoulder like a river of red silk.

"I didn't mean to cause you any trouble."

"Why did you come here? And don't give me that story about having nowhere else to go."

"I wanted to see the woman who captured your heart."

Quill snorted. "What's the real reason you're here?"

Her gaze moved to his throat. "I'm thirsty."

"Are you telling me there's no blood left in New Orleans?"

Laughing softly, she padded toward him, lithe as a tiger on the prowl. "I've wanted more of your blood since the moment I tasted it."

Quill shook his head. "That's your misfortune."

She paused, her gaze narrowing, and then she took another step forward.

He watched her eyes, knew the exact moment when she'd made her decision. She sprang toward him, eyes blazing, fangs extended, her hands like claws as she reached for him.

He caught her around the throat and held her at arm's length. "I don't know why the hell you're really here, but you've got two choices. Either you get the hell out of my house and stay out, or I'll kill you."

She glared at him, her eyes red with hunger and fury. "Which will it be?"

"I'll go."

"Your invitation is forever revoked. Be gone."

When he loosened his hold, she vanished from sight.

"Well, that was something to see," Callie remarked from the doorway. "I knew she was up to no good."

"Spying on me, were you?"

"Why did she want your blood so badly?"

"It's old and rare and like catnip to her kind."

"Is that why she really came here? To feed on you?"

"I'm not sure. She could have been telling the truth about her coven being attacked. But I have my doubts. The blood on her dress wasn't vampire or human."

"You could tell that just by looking at it?"

"No. From the smell."

"So, she made the whole thing up about having nowhere else to go?"

"I think so, but I could be wrong. The minds of Transylvanian vampires are difficult to read."

Callie glanced at the front door. "Do you think she's really gone?"

"She'd better be if she values her neck. Come here, love."

She went into his arms gladly. Laying her head against his chest, she closed her eyes. One thing about living with Quill, she thought as his lips moved in her hair, life was never dull.

Callie was surprised to find Quill waiting for her in the kitchen when she got up the next morning. Glancing at the clock on the stove, she said, "A little early for you, isn't it?"

"Yeah." Drawing her into his arms, he kissed her. "I wanted to make sure Claret didn't hang around last night. It gave me time to do some thinking."

"About what?"

"I can't make up my mind if she told me the truth about the location of the Dark Wood, or not. I'm thinking I might just go up there and scout around, see what I can find."

"Oh?"

Pulling out a chair, he sat down and drew Callie onto his lap. "There's a lot of speculation about how many Knights there are. We know for certain that there are only thirteen active at any one time. And we know there are always more in training, but there's no way to know how many, although a good number of my people think there are hundreds of future Knights in reserve, just waiting to be called. But if they had an army that big, they could have wiped us out long ago."

"So, what does any of that have to do with Claret?"

"I'm not sure. Maybe her coven *was* attacked. Maybe she just wanted my blood. Or maybe . . ." He shook his head.

"Go on."

He stroked her back absently. "Maybe sending us up to Canada to look for the Dark Wood is a trap."

"A trap? I don't understand."

"Maybe her coven is located somewhere up in the North Woods near Canada. Maybe the Transylvanian vampires have had scouts in various cities throughout the States just lying in wait for one of my people to show up."

"Whatever for?"

"They've taken my people prisoner before. They have human slaves bind them with silver and keep them locked up to feed on. Like I told you, our blood is like catnip to some of them. They're like addicts. They drink a little, and from then on, they crave more and more. Occasionally, one of them will take too much and they go mad, but it doesn't deter the others."

Callie's eyes widened. "Do you really think that's what this is all about?"

"I don't know. It sounds pretty far-fetched when I say it out loud."

"Maybe. Maybe not."

"There's only one way to find out if she's telling the truth about the location of the Dark Wood."

Callie shook her head. "Oh, no you don't. You are *not* going up there. You just said it could be a trap and now you just want to walk into it?"

"I'm tired of sitting around waiting for the Knights' next attack. Besides, we need to know if Claret was telling the truth. You don't want me to send someone else up there, do you?"

"No, but . . ."

"I'm the oldest vampire here. It's my duty to go. Besides, it's safer to go alone. The more men I take with me, the more likely we are to be discovered."

"I agree."

"You do?" He had expected an argument.

"What you say makes perfect sense. I don't think you should take anyone with you. Except me."

"Dammit, woman, if it's a trap, I don't want you anywhere near the place!"

She glared at him, eyes narrowed. "I can take care of myself, Quill Falconer, and if you sneak off without me, I'll just concoct a spell and follow you."

"Witches," he muttered. "Damned, unreasonable creatures."

"I still don't think going in blind is a good idea," she insisted.

"I'm not going in looking for a fight," he said. "I'm just going up to have a look around. I need to know if Claret's telling the truth."

"And what if *she's* there?"

"Don't worry. I can handle her."

"That's what I'm afraid of," she said sweetly. "And that's why I'm going with you."

Chapter 32

They left after sunset. Quill transported them to within a mile of the Canadian border. The distance was a little over a thousand miles. He had never transported her that far and Callie was feeling more than a little nauseous when they arrived.

Quill held her in his arms and massaged her back and shoulders until the queasiness passed.

"Now what?" she asked.

"I want you to concentrate and see if you can detect any kind of magical enchantments or anomalies in the area."

"All right." Reaching into the large bag she had brought with her, Callie rummaged in the bottom for her wand, let out a shriek when something alive moved beneath her hand.

"What's wrong?" Quill asked.

"This," she said, and lifted Ebony out of the bag.

"What the hell! How'd that blasted cat get in there?"

"I don't know." Callie was about to ask what they were going to do with her when Ebony jumped out of her arms and ran into the forest. "Ebony! Come back here!"

"Let her go," Quill said. "We've got more important things to worry about than that damn cat."

Biting down on her lower lip, Callie nodded. She fished her wand out of the bag; then, holding it in one hand, pointed straight up, she closed her eyes. She spent several moments clearing her mind of everything but the need to find the signature of another witch.

Two minutes passed. Three. Five. And then she felt it, a subtle ripple of magical energy coming from the woods. It rippled down the wand into her hand. Callie opened her eyes as her wand pulled slowly to the left, then to the right and then steadied and pointed straight ahead.

"There," she whispered. "It's coming from in there. He's very powerful, Quill. I'm afraid he's far more adept than I am."

Placing his hand on her shoulder, Quill gave it a squeeze. "Let's hope that your power combined with mine will be enough."

Following the direction of Callie's wand, they made their way along a narrow deer path. There was no designated border crossing and no guards here, in the deep woods. A full moon hung low in a cloudless sky, casting faint, silver shadows on the path and the leaves of the trees.

They walked steadily for several miles. Callie glanced right and left, hoping to find Ebony, but there was no sign of the cat. Occasionally, she heard rustling in the underbrush, arousing visions of bears and mountain lions stalking them.

"There's no danger," Quill assured her. "None of the predators will come near me."

Callie hoped he was right. And then she forgot all

about the wildlife as a surge of power made the hair at her nape stand at attention. She came to an abrupt halt, the wand in her hand quivering. "We're close," she whispered.

Quill nodded. "I feel it, too." It crawled over his skin, arousing his urge to fight. His fangs brushed his tongue and he knew that his eyes had gone red. Taking a deep, calming breath, he opened his preternatural senses.

"Now what?" Callie asked tremulously. "We can't fight what we can't see."

"We didn't come here for a fight. We're just reconnoitering," Quill reminded her, and then froze as he caught the scent of vampire and knew he'd been right.

It was a trap and they had walked into the middle of it.

Before he could warn Callie, the witch's spell dissolved and with it, the forest.

Quill swore under his breath. They were in the middle of a large, empty room, trapped inside a cage barely big enough to hold the two of them. Four male vampires stood in a cluster, their eyes hot, nostrils flaring at the scent of a human female.

Quill glanced at Callie, but her attention was focused on the warlock who stood opposite her outside the cage. Tall and thin, he had a crooked nose and beady black eyes. His hair was brown with a slash of white at his left temple.

Smiling faintly, he muttered an incantation and Callie's wand slowly dissolved into a pile of sawdust. A second incantation locked a pair of thick silver manacles around Quill's wrists.

Callie pressed herself against him, her whole body

trembling as the warlock's power threatened to steal the breath from her lungs and the strength from her legs.

Quill tensed when Claret stepped into view, a self-satisfied smirk curving her lips. "Quill," she crooned, "how very nice of you to come."

Callie looked up at him, desperation in her eyes. "Get us out of here."

He shook his head. "I wish I could." He jerked his chin toward the bars. "They're made of solid silver. I can't go through them."

Claret laughed softly. "I got to thinking—the Knights have a witch. *You* have a witch. Why shouldn't I?"

Damn! He hadn't figured on that. "What do you want?" Quill asked, his voice ice-cold.

She smiled, displaying her fangs. "Only what you're willing to give me."

"And if I refuse?" A foolish question when he already knew the answer.

She laughed again. "I'll drain the woman dry. Or perhaps I'll turn her, and we can feed on you together."

Callie clutched Quill's arm, her face pale, her nails digging into his flesh.

"I'll do whatever you want," he said flatly. "Just let her go."

"Quill, no!"

"Be quiet, love."

"You will do exactly what I want, whenever I want and we both know it," Claret remarked, strolling around the cage. "Jasper, escort the woman into the other room. And don't take any chances. I'm not sure how powerful she is."

The warlock cocked his head to the side and the cage door swung open just far enough for him to reach inside, grab Callie's arm and yank her out. The door immediately slammed shut behind her. Tightening his grasp, he dragged her out of the room.

Quill glared at Claret. "If you hurt her . . ."

"Yes, yes, I know. You'll destroy me."

His gaze bored into hers. "Count on it."

She approached the cage, careful not to touch the bars. "Hold your arms out toward me."

Jaw clenched, he carefully slid his bound hands through one of the narrow gaps in the cage.

Smiling with anticipation, she latched onto his arm and buried her fangs in the large vein in his left wrist.

It was all he could do not to grab a handful of her hair and yank her face against the bars. He considered it for a moment, relishing the thought of the silver burning into her flesh. It would leave a nasty scar. But he dared not do anything that might put Callie's life in danger. He could hear the frightened beating of her heart, taste her fear like it was his own. And so he stood there, like a helpless beast of prey, while Claret fed on him.

Callie sat on the edge of the bed, her gaze carefully averted from the wizard's eyes as he bound her hands and feet. She could feel him watching her like a cat at a mousehole. She had to get out of here, had to find a way to free Quill from that horrible creature. But how?

Her stomach churned with revulsion when she thought of Claret feeding on him. But what made her own blood run cold was the thought of the other vampires feeding on *her*, drinking from her until she grew weak, weaker, until they had taken it all.

Or, worse, turned her into one of them.

She tried to summon her magic, but anxiety for Quill's life and her own kept it trapped deep inside. She took several deep breaths in an effort to calm her fears so she could concentrate, but she couldn't think, couldn't remember a single spell or incantation.

Discouraged and desperate to fight off the fear that threatened to paralyze her, she fell back on the mattress and closed her eyes.

Quill breathed a sigh of relief when, finally satisfied, Claret lifted her head. She licked his blood from her lips and smiled a decidedly feline smile. "Just think," she murmured, "I can have as much as I want, any time I want."

"What about us?" one of the other vampires asked. "We'd like a taste now and then."

"He's mine!" she snapped. "Touch him and you're dead."

"Then give us the woman."

Claret frowned and then shrugged. "You can each have a drink once a day."

Heedless of the silver that seared his skin, Quill made a grab for the vampire through the bars.

Laughing, she danced nimbly out of his way.

"Dammit, Claret!" he snarled. "Leave her alone!"

"*I'm* not going to touch her." And so saying, she sashayed into the room where the warlock had taken Callie.

After a moment, the other vampires followed her. The last one closed the door, leaving Quill alone with his tumultuous thoughts and a raging thirst.

Chapter 33

The witch prowled the outskirts of the building. Five Transylvanian vampires inside—one female and four males.

One Hungarian vampire.

A young, fledgling witch.

And one warlock. He had cast a spell that had transformed the outside of the house so that it appeared to be a part of the surrounding forest, but she had been hiding inside the protective circle when he cast it, so it had not affected her. Not that she couldn't have broken it if necessary, she mused with a touch of arrogance.

She blew out a sigh. She had never doubted her powers. Still, it had been a long time since she had practiced her craft. She tapped her finger against her lips. The prisoners didn't seem to be in any imminent danger at the moment. Perhaps she would spend an hour or so brushing up on some of her more difficult spells before she took on a warlock and five vampires.

She smiled inwardly. With any luck, the fledgling witch might be of some help.

Chapter 34

Quill sat on the floor, legs stretched out in front of him, careful not to lean back and touch the bars. His arm throbbed dully where it had touched the silver. Hours had passed since he had last seen Callie. Reaching out with his mind, he breathed a sigh of relief when her slow, steady heartbeat told him she was alone in a room, asleep. And then he frowned with the realization that she wasn't sleeping but under a spell of some kind. But at least she was safe for the moment.

His preternatural senses told him the vampires were at rest—the males in one room, Claret alone in another. He had no sense of the warlock's presence.

He cursed softly. He had to get Callie out of here before her scent drove the vampires wild. If they gave in to their hunger, they would fight each other like wildcats to get at her, and likely tear her to shreds in the process.

He had been a fool to let her come with him. But how did you keep a determined witch at home?

"Witches," he muttered. They were a law unto themselves.

He shook his head. Finding Claret hadn't surprised

him, but the warlock's presence had. The man was incredibly powerful, perhaps as strong as Ava had ever been. If he'd brought Jeffries and the others with him, it was likely they would all be trapped in here with him. He swore softly. It wasn't just the silver bars that held him. He could feel the warlock's magic all around him, draining his power.

Closing his eyes, he surrendered to the Dark Sleep. Rest would strengthen him and he had little doubt that he was going to need every ounce he could summon to face whatever the future held.

He was on the brink of oblivion when he sensed a presence in the room, and with it the scent of lily of the valley.

Ava.

He opened his eyes. He sensed it was morning, but, with no windows, the room was dark. At first, he didn't see anything. Then, glancing over his shoulder, he saw a pair of golden yellow eyes staring at him. "Ebony," he muttered. "How the hell did you get in here?"

He felt the brush of preternatural power slide over his skin, felt his eyes grow wide as the cat shimmered and slowly changed shape until Callie's grandmother stood before him. Wearing a gauzy white blouse over a multi-colored skirt, she looked as young and beautiful as she had the first time he'd seen her.

"Ava." He shook his head. "I don't believe it." And yet, hadn't he known, deep down, that she was still alive? Hadn't he suspected for some time that she and Ebony were one?

"You seem to be in a bit of a pickle," she remarked, bright blue eyes twinkling.

He rose in a single fluid movement. "Why on earth have you been masquerading as a cat?"

"I ran afoul of a wizard a few years back. Rather than risk a confrontation or put Callie's life in danger, I chose to fake my death. Doing so allowed me to keep an eye on my granddaughter with no one the wiser. And then you came along and I thought you'd look after her, but . . ." She loosed a dramatic sigh. "Here you are, locked up like a tiger in a cage."

"I'm aware of that," he said dryly. "How about getting me the hell out of here?"

"That's no way to ask for a favor, Quill."

"Ava Magdalena Morgana Langley, would you please get me out of here?"

Laughing softly, she spoke a few quiet words and Callie's wand—recently a pile of dust—appeared in her hand. Stepping forward, she touched the tip to the lock and the door swung open without a sound. Next, she walked around the cage, chanting softly, and as she did so, the magic that had surrounded him faded and disappeared.

Returning to the front of his prison, she stepped inside and tapped the manacles that bound him and they dissolved.

"I've missed you, Quill," Ava murmured, and rising on her tiptoes, she kissed his cheek.

"I missed you, too."

"Did you?" She cocked her head to the side. "Somehow I doubt it."

He chuckled softly as he followed her out of the cage. "I'm in love with Callie. You know that, don't you?"

"Of course."

"You got a problem with that?"

"No. I knew you would find her. Let's get her and get out of here."

They had only taken a few steps when the front door opened and the wizard stood there, his long, black cape billowing behind him like the wings of a giant bird. "I'm afraid it won't be that easy," he sneered, closing the door behind him.

"Quill, go find Callie," Ava said, never taking her gaze off the warlock. "I'll handle this."

With a nod, Quill vanished from the room.

"You don't have a chance, witch," the warlock said smugly. "You're old and woefully out of practice."

"So certain of that, are you?"

"Foolish woman! I can sense your weakness."

"You're the fool," Ava retorted. "You see only what I want you to see." She raised Callie's wand as he began to chant softly. She knew immediately that although his magic was strong, he lacked her experience. As he summoned his power, intent on destroying her, she began to sing, the high-pitched notes weaving a spell around him, stealing his magic even as he tried—and failed—to steal hers.

The warlock let out a harsh cry of disbelief as his wand disintegrated, screamed in denial as the last of his magic drained away. Broken, defeated, he sank to his knees. "Don't leave me like this," he begged. "You've taken my magic. Take my life as well."

"It's ever so tempting," Ava replied, "but I think not." A flick of her wand and the warlock transformed into a large, black vulture with a slash of white on its head. Opening the door, she said, "Be gone."

With a shriek, the bird took wing and flew out of the house.

"One down," she said, brightly. "Five to go."

Quill looked up when Ava entered the room where Callie was being held, his expression troubled. "I can't rouse her."

With a nod, Ava murmured a few words, then shook Callie's shoulder. "Wake up, child."

Callie's eyelids fluttered open. She stared at her grandmother, certain she was dreaming until Ava leaned forward and kissed her cheek.

"Yes," Ava said, smiling. "It's really me."

Callie sat up, eyes wide with disbelief. "How can you be here? They told me you were dead. I visited your grave."

"I'll explain it all to you at another time, dear. Right now, you and Quill need to get out of here."

"What are you going to do?" Callie asked, frowning.

"Take care of the vampires, of course."

"Leave that to me," Quill said. "You take Callie home."

Callie shook her head. "I'm not leaving you."

"Yes, you are and right now. Ava, get her out of here."

"Come along, dear," Ava said, taking her hand. "Let the man do what has to be done."

Callie stared at him. "Are you going to kill them in cold blood?"

"No. I'll give them a better chance than they would have given us. And then I'll destroy them."

Before Callie could argue further, Ava led her out of the house.

* * *

Quill waited until the women were gone, then strode purposefully into the room where the four male vampires rested. Like all of their kind, they could wake from the Dark Sleep when their lives were in danger.

And they were definitely in danger.

He woke them one at a time by touching their shoulders.

They were all young vampires and as such, no match for his greater strength. But he gave each of them a fighting chance, easily countering their every move. He could have prolonged each battle, but he dispatched each one quickly and mercifully.

The scent of battle and fresh blood had roused Claret. She was waiting for him when he entered her room. She was older than the others, wiser, stronger.

She didn't waste time asking how he had freed himself from the cage or why he had destroyed the others. Fangs bared, hands like claws, eyes red as the fires of an unforgiving hell, she sprang at him, needle-like fangs sinking deep into his left shoulder, ripping through muscle and flesh.

Cursing viciously, he wrapped his hands around her throat and held her at arm's length. Kicking and scratching like a wildcat, she twisted free, pivoted on her heels, and flung herself at him again.

She let out an angry snarl when he ducked out of her way, then threw herself at him a third time, fangs tearing into the flesh of his neck, her tongue darting out to taste his blood even as she tried to destroy him.

He had never killed a woman—human or vampire— and found himself reluctant to kill this one.

Closing his mind to what he was about to do, he captured her head in his hands but before he could break her neck, Claret twisted out of his grasp and disappeared from sight.

Quill swore a vile oath as he pressed a hand to his wounded shoulder. She was even more powerful than he'd thought, he mused, and then he swore again, knowing it was his own blood that had increased her strength.

Heaving a sigh, he left the house. He was about to transport himself home when he hesitated. Unwilling to take a chance that the four vampires he'd killed might rise the next night when the moon came up, he summoned fire and set the place aflame, then stood there, jaw clenched, and watched it burn.

He swore softly, wondering if Claret was going to be a problem in the future. He didn't know if she'd been telling the truth when she said her coven had been attacked. He could only hope it was true, and that the four vampires he had destroyed had been the last of them.

But he couldn't worry about that now. There remained the Knights of the Dark Wood, and they were a far bigger threat than Claret. Trey 95 might be dead, but the others were just as dedicated, just as determined.

And then there was Callie's grandmother, still looking as young and lovely as she had the first time he'd seen her.

As he watched the flames engulf the house, he found himself wondering how Ava's return would affect his relationship with Callie. It was one thing for her to accept the fact that he had made love to her grandmother over a hundred years ago. After all, there was little point in being jealous of someone you thought dead and buried.

But how would Callie feel about it now that Ava was again among the living?

Back in their house in Montana, Callie paced the floor in front of the sofa where Ava sat. "Where have you been all this time?" she asked. "Why didn't you let me know you were alive? Why didn't you tell me you were a witch? Why didn't you—"

"Callie, dear, calm down."

"Calm down? Calm down! You let me believe you were dead and you want me to calm down? I grieved for you! I cried for days, filled with grief and guilt because I thought you'd died alone while I was off in Paris having a good time. I—"

Ava patted the cushion beside her. "Callie, child, come and sit with me."

Shoulders slumped, Callie dropped down on the sofa.

"I explained in my letter why I didn't tell you I was a witch. As for why I faked my death . . ." Ava sighed. "I did it to protect you and to put some much-needed distance between myself and a rather nasty wizard I'd had a disagreement with. I knew if Ranald thought I was dead, he wouldn't bother you and he would stop looking for me. But you had to believe it, too, or he never would."

Callie frowned. Looking back, she dimly recalled seeing a tall, thin man with gray hair and colorless eyes at the cemetery every time she had gone there to put flowers on Ava's grave.

"I never left you alone," Ava went on. "I was frequently nearby in one form or another."

"You were the cat!" Callie exclaimed.

"Yes," Ava said, reaching for her hand. "Once you

found out you were a witch, I wanted to be close to you. I was curious to see if you would pursue your magic and if it was as strong as I suspected it would be."

Callie looked at her grandmother's hand, frowned as an image of that hand caressing Quill's bare skin leaped into her mind. Startled, she jerked her hand away.

"What's wrong?" Ava asked.

"You. And Quill."

"Oh." A faint flush colored Ava's cheeks. "He told you about that, did he?"

"Yes."

"It was such a long time ago."

"Did you love him?"

"I could have."

Callie frowned, thinking Quill had said much the same thing when she'd asked if he'd loved her grandmother.

"I was very vulnerable when we met. And he was very dashing. The attraction I felt for him was mutual and we . . ." Ava made a vague gesture with her hand. "It was only one night. I realized soon after that the two of you were destined for each other, and we never made love again." She paused. "It bothers you, doesn't it?"

"Of course it does!"

"Callie, don't let what happened one night all those years ago ruin what you and Quill have. A love like yours is rare. Cherish it."

Callie nodded. Suddenly needing a few minutes alone, she said, "I'm going to get a soda. Can I get you one?"

"No, thank you, dear."

With a nod, Callie hurried out of the room. In the kitchen, she braced her hands on the counter and stared out the window. It might have been a long time since Ava and Quill were lovers, but Ava was here now, looking as young and vibrant as ever. And Callie didn't know how to handle it. She loved her grandmother and felt guilty for wishing she hadn't come back. Not that she wished her dead. Never that. Just not . . . here.

Callie shook her head. She was supposed to marry Quill in a few days, but how could she? What if he found her wanting when compared to her grandmother? What if he was still attracted to Ava? What if Ava was still attracted to him? How could she not be? He was gorgeous and sexy and . . .

Callie slammed her hands on the counter. She had to stop thinking about it before she drove herself crazy—if she hadn't already.

She jumped when someone knocked at the back door. Peering through the window, she saw Nolan Jeffries staring at her through the glass. Blowing out a sigh, she opened the door. "Hi. What brings you here so early in the morning?"

"Wendy saw your light. She sent me over to make sure everything was all right. Is Quill here?"

"No."

Nolan's brows knit together. "Where is he?"

"Still up north, as far as I know."

"Did he find the Dark Wood?"

"No." She shook her head. "Why don't you come over tonight? He'll probably be here by then."

"Okay, sure." He sent her a troubled look, then turned and jogged back toward his house.

Callie stared after Jeffries, wondering where Quill was and what she would say to him if and when he returned.

* * *

Quill hesitated at the front door. Needing some time alone to sort out his thoughts, and thinking Callie might feel the same, he had gone to his lair, where he'd showered and changed clothes. The wounds he had received from Claret and the others had already healed.

Opening his senses, he located the women in his life. Ava was pacing the floor in one of the bedrooms. Callie was in the living room, her thoughts troubled. Well, that wasn't surprising, all things considered. As he opened the door and crossed the threshold, he couldn't help wondering if Callie would be glad to see him, or if she would ask him to leave.

She looked up when he closed the door behind him.

Quill shoved his hands in his pockets. "Do you want me to go?"

She hesitated for several moments, sighed, and said, "I don't know."

"I understand how you feel."

"Do you? Then tell me, Quill, how *do* I feel? How would *you* feel if you found out that the woman you loved had indulged in a torrid affair with your grandfather? Would you just sweep it under the rug and pretend it never happened?"

Muttering an oath, he dropped into the chair across from the sofa. "I know you're upset. I know it's hard to accept this on top of everything else that's going on, but dammit, Callie, it was only one night! It has nothing to do with you and me."

"Doesn't it? Every time I look at her, I think of the two of you together." She shook her head as tears filled her eyes. "How am I supposed to get past that? She's my grandmother and I . . . I . . ."

She didn't have to put it into words. He knew what

she was thinking, knew she felt guilty as hell for wishing her grandmother hadn't come back—not that she wished her any ill. Never that.

Quill scrubbed a hand over his jaw. Maybe he would never fully understand how she felt. It had all happened over a century ago. She hadn't even been born at the time. It wasn't like he had cheated on her or lied to her. "Callie, honey, I don't know what to say." He shook his head "I can't undo the past."

"I wish you could."

"So do I, love. Believe me, so do I." Raking his fingers through his hair, he asked, "Where do we go from here?"

She exhaled a deep, shuddering sigh, then clasped her hands in her lap. "I'm going home."

"Do you think that's wise?"

"I don't know, but I need some time alone."

"You can stay here. I'll leave."

"No." Mouth set in a stubborn line, she shook her head. "I'm going home."

He nodded slowly. "If that's what you want."

"We're leaving tomorrow afternoon. I've already booked a flight."

"You didn't have to do that. I could have taken you."

She looked at him, mute, her eyes twin pools of pain and sadness.

"If you ever need me," he said, his voice tight, "all you have to do is call my name and I'll be there."

Blinking rapidly, she said, "I know."

Rising, he leaned down to brush a kiss across her cheek. "I'll always love you, my sweet Callie," he murmured.

And then he was gone.

Chapter 35

It felt good to be home again, Callie thought as she went through the house, turning on the lights. Ava hadn't asked any questions on the flight home—not about Callie's sudden decision to leave Montana, not about what had happened between her and Quill. Callie had the distinct feeling Ava didn't have to ask because she already knew the answers.

They had stopped on the way and bought some Chinese takeout for dinner. They had eaten in silence. While Callie cleared the table, Ava disappeared into her bedroom without a word.

In her own room, Callie quickly changed into a pair of jeans and a sweater and ran a comb through her hair. After finding paper and pencil, she hastily scribbled a shopping list. Grabbing her keys, she went out the side door into the garage and came face-to-face with the Jaguar that Quill had given her. No way she could keep it now, she thought. She would have to give it back.

Sliding behind the wheel of her old VW, she turned on the lights and backed out of the driveway.

* * *

Brow furrowed, Ava sat on the edge of the bed. The rift between herself and Callie troubled her deeply. Not that she could blame the girl for being upset at learning the man she loved had been intimate with her grandmother. That wasn't something that happened in a normal family. But then, their family was far from normal. There had been witches in Ava's ancestry as far back as her line went. A few had ignored their gift. Most had embraced it.

What was she going to do about Quill and Callie? The man was just as sexy and good-looking as she remembered, his power even stronger than it had been when she first met him. It had been that power, combined with the instant physical attraction between them, that had sent them to that motel room. But for her vision of Quill and Callie together, their affair might have lasted far longer than one night. Since then, she had married two men and loved them both, but she had never forgotten Quill. He might be a vampire, but she knew him to be an honorable man. A good man. And he was deeply in love with her granddaughter.

How was she going to mend the breech between herself and Callie? Between Callie and Quill? Knowing how the news of his brief interlude with her had upset Callie, Ava couldn't help wondering why Quill hadn't simply erased the knowledge from her mind.

Should she? Perhaps that was the answer. A murmured word summoned her grimoire to her hand. There were several spells to alter one's memories. It wouldn't hurt to brush up on one or two, just in case.

* * *

Callie moved leisurely up and down the grocery store's aisles, slowly filling her cart. She had hoped shopping would divert her thoughts from Quill and Ava, but she couldn't stop thinking about the two of them. She told herself to put it behind her. It was old news. She loved Quill and he loved her.

Callie blew out a sigh. Maybe she would feel less threatened if her grandmother *looked* like a grandmother instead of a beautiful woman in her late thirties. She grinned as she imagined going home and asking Ava to add a few lines and wrinkles to her face, sprinkle a few age spots on her hands, a little gray in her hair. Maybe increase her waistline by a few inches.

She paused in the dairy aisle to pick up a quart of milk and realized that she had filled her cart with an inordinate amount of comfort food—cookies and cupcakes and candy bars. With a rueful shake of her head, she added a half-gallon of chocolate fudge ice cream, a can of whipped cream, and a jar of cherries. If she was going to have a pity party, she might as well go all the way.

Back at home, while putting the groceries away, she caught a subtle whiff of magic. No doubt Ava was concocting a spell, she thought, and wondered what it might be.

Quill lingered in the shadows outside Callie's home, his presence masked from those inside. He had gone through the house before she and her grandmother arrived to make sure it was safe for them to return.

He had watched Callie drive away and debated whether to follow her or go inside and speak with Ava.

In the end, he had decided against both. He knew Callie had a lot on her mind—she was angry about Ava faking her death, upset about his one-night stand with her grandmother. He didn't know what he could say or do to make things right between them. All he could do was hope that her love for him was strong enough to see them through.

Lost in thought, he almost missed the hint of witchcraft coming from inside the house. Curious, he ghosted inside and followed the whisper of magic to Ava's bedroom.

She called, "Come in," before he knocked on the door.

He found her standing over her cauldron, wand in hand. "What are you doing?"

"What you should have done," she retorted. "I'm going to erase the memories that are causing Callie so much distress."

"Do you really think that's a good idea?"

"Have you got a better one?" she snapped. "If I'd known before we made love that our brief affair was going to cause her so much pain, I never would have taken you to my bed."

He grunted softly. "And I never would have gone with you. But that's neither here nor there. What's done is done." Arms crossed at his chest, Quill leaned against the doorjamb. "I tried erasing the truth of what I am from her mind when we first met. It didn't work."

"Are you comparing *your* powers to mine?" Ava asked incredulously.

He shrugged. "Knowing Callie, I don't think she'd be too happy if she knew what you're planning."

"She won't find out if you don't say anything. She's

so unhappy. I'm just trying to help." With a sigh, Ava stared into the depths of the cauldron, then looked up. "We're both to blame for that, aren't we?"

Quill nodded. "Maybe she wouldn't feel so threatened if you looked your age."

Ava scowled at him.

"Hey, I took the thought from Callie's mind."

"She thinks that?"

"It might be worth a try."

Ava waved her hand over the cauldron and the thin plume of blue-gray smoke rising from its depths disappeared. "Maybe I should just leave."

"I'm not sure that's the answer. Maybe we . . ." He paused when he heard the garage door open. "She's home. Don't tell her I was here." And with that, he vanished from the room.

Ava took several deep breaths, then murmured a few words in ancient Greek. She shuddered as she felt the spell gather around her. Then, pasting what she hoped was a smile on her face, she walked purposefully into the kitchen.

Callie looked up, the grocery sack in her hands falling to the floor when her grandmother appeared in the doorway.

"I didn't mean to scare you," Ava said. "Do I look that bad?"

"N . . . no." Stooping, Callie picked up the scattered cans. "You just surprised me, that's all. What . . . why?"

"I thought it was time I looked my age . . . well, part of it. After all, I am over. . . . Well, let's just say I'm much older than you thought."

"I know how old you are," Callie said. "Quill told me." In reality, Ava was well over a hundred. But today she looked more like a youthful seventy. She wore a flowered polyester dress belted in the middle, and sensible black shoes. Her hair, once golden, was faded now and lightly streaked with silver. Her face was lined, her hands spotted with age. Her figure was a little plumper. But for all that, she was still a pretty woman.

Callie frowned. Earlier, she had wondered if accepting what had happened between Quill and her grandmother would be easier to accept if Ava looked her age. Had her grandmother read her mind? She had never known Ava to do that, but she supposed it was possible. Quill had certainly done it often enough.

Quill. She felt an odd catch in her heart when she thought of him. Shoving him out of her mind, she said, "Were you practicing magic earlier?"

"Yes." Turning away, Ava reached into the bag on the counter and removed the milk, butter, and cheese, which she put in the refrigerator. "Why do you ask?"

Callie shrugged as she picked up the sack she had dropped, glad it hadn't held the eggs. "I thought I felt something."

"I was going to do an obliteration spell and erase some of your memories."

Callie stared at her. "Why would you do that?"

"Why do you think? I know what happened between me and Quill is eating you up inside, but he loves *you*, Callie. A blind man could see that. He never loved me. We shared a few hours of passion that didn't mean anything. Had I known you and Quill would fall in love, I never would have looked at him twice." She paused.

"Well," she said, with a lopsided grin, "at least once. He is a remarkably handsome man."

"He is that. I love you, Grandma."

"And I love you, dear. And because I do, I've decided to move out."

"Move? But why? This is *your* house. If anyone moves, it should be me."

"The house is in your name now. I left it to you, re-member?"

"But . . . where will you go?"

"Not to worry, dear. I have a darling little place in Portland. Will and I used to spend our summers there."

"You're not going right away, are you?"

"I think it's for the best. I've packed a few necessary items." Ava smiled. "I'll send for the rest. This will never feel like it's really your home as long as my belongings are still cluttering up the place." She glanced around the kitchen. "I can't believe you kept it all."

"I couldn't bring myself to part with any of it. It was a way of keeping you close."

"You're a witch, Callie. I think, deep down, you've always known I was still alive."

"Maybe." She remembered telling Quill she had sometimes felt that Ava was nearby. Apparently, she'd been right.

"I want you to keep my grimoire, but you need to purchase your own sword and athame and select your own cauldron. Having your own implements will make your magic stronger." Ava patted Callie's arm. "I wrote my address in Portland in the front of the grimoire. I'll text you when I get settled. Now, go call Quill and tell him to come home before some other beautiful witch lures him away."

Callie stood there, her mind reeling as she tried to get the nerve to call Quill. What could she say? *I'm sorry* seemed inadequate. Then again, what did she have to be sorry for? She had told him how she felt, and she didn't see any reason to apologize for that. Maybe for hurting his feelings? Or for . . .

"Callie."

She whirled around at the sound of his voice, her heart leaping at the sight of him standing in the doorway.

"You don't have to apologize for anything, love," he said.

"Oh, Quill," she murmured, "I'm *so* glad you're here."

She didn't know who moved first, but suddenly they were in each other's arms, clinging to one another as if it had been days instead of hours since they had been together. He rained kisses over her brow, her eyelids, her cheeks, finally settling on her lips for a long, long kiss she never wanted to end.

"Say you'll marry me now, tonight," he rasped. "I can't wait any longer."

"How? Where?"

"I don't know. I'll find a place. Just say yes."

She thought briefly of her beautiful wedding dress. And then she looked into Quill's eyes. She didn't need a lovely gown, she thought. She had everything she needed, everything she wanted, right here. "Yes," she said tremulously. "Oh, yes!"

He kissed her again, short and quick. "I won't be long," he promised as he headed for the door.

Smiling, Callie stared after him. She was getting married.

Tonight.

To Quill.

Humming, she hurried into the bathroom, where she took a quick shower and washed her hair. Wrapped in a towel, she used the blow-dryer, applied her makeup, and found a dress she had worn to a friend's wedding—a deep turquoise sheath with a provocative slit up one side. Slipping it over her head, she smoothed her hand over the silky fabric.

When she turned around, Quill was standing in the bedroom doorway. He let out a wolf whistle, his eyes hot as his gaze moved over her.

"Did you find a church?"

"No. But I found a minister. He's waiting in the living room. Are you ready?"

"Just let me get my shoes. Vivian is never going to forgive me for this," Callie remarked. "Neither will Ava."

"We'll get married again and you can wear your wedding gown and invite anyone you want. This one is just for us. I'll go keep the minister company."

Callie laughed softly as she pulled a pair of pumps dyed the same color as her dress from the closet. She frowned when she heard a thump coming from the living room, followed by a curse and a hoarse cry. Dropping the shoes on the bed, she hurried down the hallway, only to come to an abrupt halt at the sight that met her eyes.

Quill stood in the middle of the floor, a dagger buried to the hilt in left shoulder. Blood trickled from a jagged gash in his right arm. Two Knights lay on the floor, obviously dead. A third one cradled his broken arm against his chest. A fourth Knight was on his knees, gasping for air. Blood trickled from his nose and mouth.

There was no sign of the minister.

Callie stared at Quill.

"I underestimated the Knights," he said flatly. "Apparently they've been watching your house ever since we left for Montana, just waiting for us to come back."

"But . . . how did they get in? What about the wards we set in place?"

"I guess the minister thought they were guests and let them in."

"Are you all right?" Her gaze darted to the wound in his right arm. It was no longer bleeding. She flinched when he jerked the blade from his shoulder.

"I will be." His wounds, though painful, were already healing.

"For mercy's sake, lady," the kneeling man pleaded, his voice hoarse. "Help us!"

"Why should I? *We* didn't break into *your* house. *We* didn't attack *you*."

"You're one of us. How can you side with him?"

"I am *not* one of you!" Callie exclaimed, her voice rising. "Quill may be a vampire, but he doesn't go around killing people who've done him no harm!"

Quill grinned at her. "You go, girl."

"What are you going to do with them?" With her first burst of anger spent, she felt an unexpected wave of sympathy for the remaining Knights.

"I haven't decided." Quill wiped the blade on the side of his pant leg, and shoved the knife into his waistband. "What do you think I should do?"

"I don't know."

"I've had enough of this," he said, his voice harsh. "It's time to end it."

Callie bit down on her lower lip. In spite of her earlier outrage, she couldn't stand by and watch while he killed these two men in cold blood.

Quill went to stand in front of the Knight with the broken arm. Taking hold of the medallion around the man's neck, he gave it a sharp yank, breaking the chain. When he glanced at the hearth, a fire sprang to life.

Quill tossed the medallion into the flames. Then, capturing the man's gaze with his own, he said, "You will not move or speak unless I tell you to. Do you understand?"

"Yes," the Knight replied woodenly.

Next, Quill relieved the second man of his medallion and threw it into the fire. Grasping the man's shoulders, he lifted him effortlessly to his feet. The man glared at him, all the color draining from his face when Quill's eyes went red. The Knight let out a startled cry, arms flailing as Quill sank his fangs into the side of his neck.

Callie looked away but then, unable to help herself, she had to watch. She feared Quill was going to kill the Knight, but after a few swallows, he lifted his head. Capturing the Knight's gaze, Quill repeated the words he had spoken to his companion.

"Now what?" Callie asked.

"After I get rid of the bodies, I'm going to get cleaned up. And then one of these idiots is going to tell me where to find the Elder Knight of the Dark Wood."

Lifting a hand to her brow, Callie sighed dramatically. "I guess the wedding is off."

"Sorry, love," he said with a rueful grin. "But it seems the minister ran away."

Chapter 36

After relieving the bodies of their medallions and weapons, Quill buried the two Knights in a single grave in the same empty field where he had buried Trey 95.

Returning to the house, he found Callie perched warily on the edge of a sofa cushion. The surviving Knights were kneeling with their backs to the fireplace. Both looked defiant—and a little afraid, though they hid it pretty well. But the acrid scent of fear clung to their skin and permeated the room.

Standing in front of the Knight with the broken arm, Quill captured the man's gaze. Unleashing his power, he said, "I want the location of the Dark Wood."

The man stared at him, unblinking. "It's situated high in the Black Hills."

Quill grunted softly. The Lakota had long considered the Black Hills sacred. "How many of the Knights are up there?"

"Nine, plus the Elder Knight and his Executioner."

"Where are the rest of them?"

"Scattered around the country, waiting to be called."

"And the witch?"

"She doesn't live with us."

"How many wards surround the place?"

"Just one, to shield our presence."

"That's all?" Quill asked skeptically.

"Yes."

"Where does the witch live?"

"I don't know."

"What's her name?"

"I don't know. Only the Elder Knight is privy to that information."

Quill considered what the Knight had told him. After throwing the medallions and weapons he had taken from the dead Knights into the fireplace, he went to sit beside Callie.

"Is he telling the truth?" she asked.

"Without his medallion, he doesn't have the strength to resist my compulsion."

"So, what are we going to do now?"

"I'm going to South Dakota."

"Not without me, you aren't."

"Yeah, I thought you might want to come along."

Callie jerked her chin toward the Knights. Both stared back at her in mute appeal. "What are we going to do with these two? We can't just leave them here."

"You're going to call the police and have them arrested for breaking and entering."

Forty minutes later, Callie watched as two police officers hustled the Knights into the back seat of a patrol car. Quill had freed them from his control when the patrol car arrived. At first, she had worried that the Knights might try to convince the officers that Quill was a vampire but after thinking it over, she realized they probably kept quiet because such an accusation would make them sound insane.

After they'd gone, Quill told her the Knights were sworn never to reveal the Brotherhood or mention the existence of vampires to mortals.

"So, what's the plan?" Callie asked.

"Tomorrow we're heading for the Black Hills, so find yourself a pair of sturdy boots and some warm clothes. And get a good night's sleep."

Quill woke late in the afternoon. Clad in boots, jeans, and a black T-shirt, he waited while Callie slipped into her warmest jacket, tucked a pair of fur-lined gloves in one pocket and her wand in another. "Are you ready?"

At her nod, he put his arm around her. She closed her eyes as the world fell away into darkness, her stomach churning as they sped through time and space.

When her head stopped spinning, they were standing in the midst of a forest of ponderosa pines. "I've often wondered why they call this place the Black Hills," Callie said. "The trees aren't black."

"No, but they look that way from a distance. Hence, the name."

"Are there bears up here?" she asked, glancing around.

"I don't think so. They're pretty scarce in these parts. You're more likely to see a mountain lion or two."

"That's comforting."

"Like I told you before, predators won't come near me. And probably not you, either, witchy woman."

"So, what do we do now?"

"Concentrate. The witch can shield the place from

view, but one of us should be able to sense any magical residue in the area."

Callie stood with her back to the setting sun, her arms at her sides, her eyes closed as she summoned her power.

Quill stood beside her, thinking that, with the sun still above the horizon, her ability to sense any magical influence was probably stronger than his.

She proved it a moment later. "That way," she said, pointing toward the west. "The signature is faint but steady."

Nodding, he said, "I'll follow you."

It was slow going. The trees were thick, the ground uneven and littered with broken branches and rocks. The air was cool this high up, and she pulled on her gloves as she walked. It was quiet in the heart of the forest, with only the sighing of the wind through the trees and the sound of their footsteps to mar the stillness.

She smiled as a red squirrel darted across her path and scurried up a tree.

As they climbed higher, the magic grew stronger. It raised the hair along her arms, caused her stomach to clench.

She came to an abrupt halt when the spell slammed into her.

"What is it?" Quill asked.

"We're here."

"Can you undo the wards?"

"I think so." Pulling the wand from her pocket, Callie closed her eyes and summoned her own magic. It came at her call, swaddling her in paranormal power. Extending her arm, she began to chant softly. She felt her magic push against that of the other witch, felt the other witch's magic push back.

Raising her voice, she continued to chant, the words coming stronger and faster as she felt the other witch's enchantment weaken and then melt away.

As it did so, a large cavern appeared before them. Tall pines stood on both sides of the cave's mouth.

And standing in front of the entrance was a single Knight clad in a long, gray cloak and armed with a heavy, silver, double-bladed sword and a shield painted red and black.

And sitting at his feet, a black feline with golden-yellow eyes.

Callie stared at the cat, then shook her head. It couldn't be.

Could it?

Chapter 37

Quill swore under his breath as he met Callie's gaze. "What the hell is your grandmother doing here?"

"Are you sure it's her? I know she was secretly married to a Knight once. But she said he died a long time ago. Why would she be here now?"

"I'm an idiot," he muttered. "I should have put two and two together when I read her letter to you. Dammit, she knew where this place was the whole time."

Callie stared at the cat. Was it really Ava? And if so, why hadn't she recognized her grandmother's magic?

Callie felt a moment of shock as she realized that her magic had overpowered Ava's. How was that possible? She was still trying to make sense of it when the Knight in the gray cloak took a step forward.

"He must be the Elder Knight," Quill murmured. "Be careful."

"How dare you violate our Sanctuary!" The Elder Knight's voice, low and deep, rumbled like thunder. "Why have you come?"

"I came seeking a truce," Quill replied, his voice equally powerful.

"A truce?" the Elder Knight scoffed. "Impossible."

"There is no reason for your people to hunt mine. My kind are no threat to humanity, as well you know. The feud between us should have ended centuries ago. It is only your hatred keeping it alive."

"You and your kind are an abomination!"

Quill's eyes narrowed ominously. "Then it will be war. I'm tired of being hunted. I'm tired of killing your Knights, like the two I dispatched earlier tonight. So, let us end it here and now. Just you and me, one on one. If I win, your people will stop hunting us."

"And if I win?"

"You won't."

The Elder Knight snorted. "If you think your witch can defeat me, you are sorely mistaken. I have an enchantress of my own."

Callie stared at the cat. Ava was the black witch of the Dark Wood? How could that be? Ava had never practiced black magic. Had she? Callie shook her head. Was that why she hadn't recognized Ava's magic when they'd approached the cave? And if Ava was the Elder Knight's witch, whose side would she be on if Quill and the Elder Knight decided to fight?

Callie looked up at Quill and knew his thoughts were traveling along the same path as her own. "Do you really think you can defeat him?" she whispered.

"If he plays fair. Which he won't."

"Why do the Knights hate your people?"

"I told you, it's because we can mate with humans. But I suspect the real reason has been lost in antiquity."

"The reason matters not," the Elder Knight exclaimed, his face growing dark with rage. "We have sworn an oath to destroy your kind from the face of the earth, and we will do it or perish in the attempt!"

And so saying, he launched himself at Quill, his double-bladed sword slashing through the air.

Quill pushed Callie out of the way, narrowly ducking aside in time to avoid the Elder Knight's blade.

Callie gasped as a number of other Knights emerged from the bowels of the cave. With a cry, she lifted her wand as she uttered the words of an incantation that, to her surprise, stopped the Knights in their tracks. She stared at them, surprised that the spell had worked since they were all wearing medallions.

Why had it worked?

She glanced at the cat, still sitting quietly at the cave's entrance. Was it really Ava? And if so, had she revoked the protective spell on the medallions? Whether she had or not, it didn't matter now. Nothing mattered but Quill.

She bit down on her lower lip as he effortlessly avoided the Elder Knight's blade, and then, in a move almost too swift to follow, he darted toward one of the other Knights and wrenched the man's sword from his hand.

And suddenly the fight was on even ground.

Callie watched in quiet amazement as vampire and Knight engaged in a lethal battle that was silent save for the ringing of metal against metal as their blades came together time and again. It was a beautiful, deadly dance. Minutes passed, and neither man seemed to tire. Focused solely on each other, they might have been the only two people on the face of the earth.

It seemed as if they had been battling for hours when Quill's blade sliced into the Elder Knight's left arm, even as the Elder Knight's sword drew blood from a wicked slash at Quill's side.

The scent of blood and sweat grew heavy in the air as the fight went on. And on.

Callie wondered why Quill didn't use his preternatural power. And then she frowned. Maybe her power hadn't been strong enough to override whatever magic protected the medallion the Elder Knight wore.

She stole a quick glance at the cat, who remained sitting in front of the cave, yellow-gold eyes darting back and forth as it watched the fight.

Callie let out a cry of alarm as the Elder Knight drove his blade into Quill's chest, only inches from his heart. Quill took several steps back, the sword still embedded in his flesh. And then, grimacing with pain, he drew the blade from his chest. Tossing the weapon aside, he dropped his own sword and sprang forward, his hands locking around the Elder Knight's throat. "Surrender, old man, or I will rip your head from your body."

Eyes filled with hatred, the Elder Knight glared at him. "Surrender."

The Elder Knight shook his head.

"Dammit! Surrender, you old fool."

Callie's gaze moved to the cave's entrance. The cat was gone, and Ava stood there clad in a long, black robe.

"Kill him, witch!" the Elder Knight gasped.

"I fear I cannot," Ava replied with mock regret. "He is betrothed to my granddaughter, and I fear she would never forgive me. Besides," she added, gliding toward the Elder Knight, "the battle has gone on long enough."

Quill eased his hold on the old man's throat, but didn't release him.

"You should have ended this feud years ago," Ava said. "You've only encouraged it this long to avenge the death of your son. But John will never rest in peace until this war is over."

Callie stared at her grandmother. John had been the Elder Knight's son? Ava hadn't mentioned *that* in her journal.

At the mention of his son's name, the fight went out of the Elder Knight. "I surrender," he murmured, his voice little more than a whisper. Then, looking up at Quill, he said, "Kill me and bury me beside my boy."

"Not until you swear on your honor as a Knight that you will stop hunting us. And that you will order the rest of your Knights to cease also. If you want to hunt something that's a threat to humanity, do the world a favor and hunt the Transylvanian vampires."

"I swear the Knights of the Dark Wood will no longer hunt your kind." The Elder Knight closed his eyes, waiting for death—only to open them again when Quill released him. "You said you would kill me! Now, do it!"

"As much as I'd love to, my people don't kill humans unless it's absolutely necessary. Callie, release the Knights from your enchantment."

She murmured the words to recant the spell, watched the Knights gather around their leader.

"Let's go home," Quill said.

Taking Callie by the hand, he willed the two of them back to her house with the Elder Knight's angry cry of betrayal ringing in his ears.

Callie sank down on the sofa and cradled her head in her hands. She had the world's worst headache, partly from traveling through time and space twice in one day and partly from the stress of the last few hours.

She looked up when she felt Quill's hand on her shoulder.

"Why don't you go to bed, sweet Callie?" he suggested. "It's been a long night."

"Will you come with me?"

"After I feed."

"You can drink from me."

He shook his head. He rarely took more than a sip or two when he drank from her. Tonight, he needed more than that. "Not tonight, love." Bending down, he brushed a kiss across her lips. "I won't be gone long."

Callie sat there a few minutes, then went into the bathroom, where she took a long, hot shower before pulling on her PJs and sliding into bed.

She was almost asleep when Quill appeared in the room. He had taken a shower and changed his clothes. Through heavy-lidded eyes, she watched him remove his T-shirt, then sit on the end of the bed and remove his boots and socks. Still wearing his sweatpants, he slid under the covers, his arm sliding around her waist to draw her body against his.

She snuggled closer, her head pillowed on his shoulder. "Will the Elder Knight keep his word?"

"I hope so."

Murmuring, "Me, too," she fell asleep in his arms.

Quill held her close, one hand absently stroking her hair as he thought about finding Ava standing at the Elder Knight's side. To say he'd been surprised to find her there was an understatement. He'd known from reading her letter to Callie that Ava had been married to a Knight decades ago, but he'd had no idea the man had been the Elder Knight's son, or that she was still involved with the Brotherhood. How had that even come about?

Knights were forbidden to marry. Had the Elder Knight been unaware of John's marriage? Or had he turned a blind eye to it rather than lose his son and the Knights' witch?

With a shake of his head, he closed his eyes. Nothing mattered now, he thought, nothing but the woman sleeping peacefully and trustingly beside him. He loved her beyond doubt, beyond reason. Soon, she would be his wife, and he would give her the world if she asked for it.

Callie stirred, wondering what had awakened her. Turning her head to the side, she saw Quill sleeping beside her. For a moment, she was content just to look at him. He was such an incredibly handsome man with his long, dark hair and well-defined features. Even asleep, she could feel the power that clung to him, a constant warning to others to beware.

Moving carefully, she pulled the sheet down, her fingertips lightly tracing the scars on his chest, lingering on the newest one left by the Elder Knight's sword. It amazed her that this man, this supernatural being who could crush her with a thought, was in love with her.

And she with him.

She remembered watching him battle the Elder Knight. He had moved with such confidence, such grace, that had it not been such a deadly conflict, it would have been a beautiful thing to see.

She trailed her fingertips down the narrow line of hair that led to his waist, her hand stilling when she realized he was awake.

Awake and watching her. "Don't stop on my account," he drawled.

Cheeks flaming, Callie met his amused gaze.

For an endless moment, their gazes met. And then he was reaching for her, lifting her body on top of his, his hand cupping her nape, drawing her head down to claim her lips with his own. Desire flamed between them, a need so great it would not be denied.

With a low groan, Quill slipped his hand under her sleep shirt, his fingers sliding restlessly up and down her back as his mouth claimed hers in a long, searing kiss that set her blood on fire and made her whole body throb with longing.

Holding her close, he rolled over and tucked her beneath him. Lifting his head, he looked at her, a question burning in his eyes.

At her nod, his sweatpants and shorts vanished, as did her PJs, and they were locked in each other's arms, mouths fused together, hands caressing, eagerly exploring, until, with one deep thrust, he swept her over the edge into a world of sensual pleasure where nothing mattered but his lips on hers, his voice whispering that he loved her, would always love her, as their bodies moved together in a mating dance as old as time. . . .

Callie drifted back to reality slowly, overcome with a sense of love and contentment unlike anything she had ever imagined. Her body still tingled from his touch. The air was sweet with the scent of their love-making.

When she opened her eyes, she found Quill gazing down at her, a worried look on his face. "What's wrong?" she asked.

"Nothing, love. I just like looking at you." He paused a moment then asked, "No regrets?"

She ran her hands over his chest, loving the feel of his bare skin beneath her palms. "How can you even ask such a thing?"

He shrugged. "I never want to do anything to hurt you."

Tugging his head down, she kissed him. "I guess you'll really have to marry me now."

"I guess so," he said, smiling. "Shall I see if I can get that minister back here again tonight?"

"I don't mind being a fallen woman for another week," she said. "My dress will be ready then."

"Okay, love." His gaze moved to her throat; then he looked at her again, one brow raised.

With a nod, she brushed the hair away from her neck. When he bit her, she sighed as another wave of warm, sensual pleasure washed over her. He was hers now, she thought as she drifted off to sleep, and she would never let him go.

Callie woke an hour later. She lay there a moment, content to do nothing but relive the wonder of making love to Quill. And eager to do it again.

But he was sound asleep, his breathing slow and even.

Slipping out of bed, she took a quick shower, pulled on her robe, then padded barefoot into the kitchen for a cup of coffee. Standing there, looking out the window, she felt the change in the house. Frowning, she carried her coffee to Ava's room. The doors stood open. The bed was neatly made.

Setting her cup on the dresser, she checked the drawers and the closet. Both were empty. Her grandmother's personal belongings were gone, as were all her magical accoutrements. Apparently, Ava had decided to leave nothing behind. It was obvious she had used her magic to transport her things, since there was no way she could have packed everything into a suitcase or two.

Picking up her cup, Callie sat on the edge of the mattress, thinking of all that had happened since she met Quill. She had learned that her grandmother was a witch and still alive. She had discovered that she, too, was a witch. Fallen in love with Quill. Dismantled her grandmother's magic in the Dark Wood.

The thought made her frown. It seemed impossible that her magic could be stronger than Ava's. Had her grandmother simply lowered her guard on purpose? That seemed more likely.

Callie glanced around the room again. It was larger than her own. For a moment, she thought of moving her things into it. And then she changed her mind. After she and Quill were wed, she would ask him how he felt about buying a new house, one with no lingering memories, good or bad.

Callie smiled as she carried her cup into the kitchen. Her future husband was a rich man. Surely he could afford to buy them a new place. Maybe one by the beach. She had always wanted to see the Pacific Ocean, something she'd hoped to do when they went to California.

Picking up her phone, she called Vivian to see if she had found a dress for the occasion. Viv admitted she hadn't found one yet, but promised she would.

Next, Callie sent a text to Ava, advising her of the date of the wedding. She grinned. After all the wedding photos she had taken for others, she was finally going to be a bride.

Humming softly, she went online, looking for romantic places to spend their honeymoon, all the while counting the hours until Quill would wake and she would be in his arms again.

Chapter 38

The Knight shifted restlessly beneath the invisibility cloak, his hand clutching his medallion. He had been here on the Elder Knight's orders ever since the vampire and the woman returned. It was damned uncomfortable under the cloak's hood, the air so thick it was sometimes hard to breathe, but he dared not take it off. He had no desire to confront the vampire face-to-face, not after having witnessed the fight at the cave in the Dark Wood. And no desire to be here, either, but he dared not refuse the Elder Knight's orders.

The man had been in a black rage ever since the confrontation with the vampire. Even the witch couldn't make him see reason. The Elder Knight had been beaten, humiliated, and he wanted revenge, his given word be damned. He had summoned four Knights-in-training to take the place of the two who had been killed and the two who were still in jail, awaiting trial, so that their active number was again thirteen.

Thirteen against two, he thought glumly. It wouldn't be enough.

* * *

Ava stood toe to toe with the Elder Knight, arms akimbo, eyes blazing with anger. "You will not attack Quill! Your word may mean nothing to you, but it does to me. My granddaughter loves him, and I will not see him destroyed. Is that clear?"

"You do not own me!" the Elder Knight retorted. "The ancient vow to destroy Hungarian vampires takes precedence over everything, including my word. We do not need more of his kind."

"You disobeyed part of the Brotherhood's oath when you allowed John to marry me. Or have you forgotten that you looked the other way when your son and I wed? Now, I am asking you to look the other way again, so that my granddaughter can live in peace with the man she loves."

"I've not forgotten! Nor have I forgotten that it was a vampire who killed him! A vampire of the same ilk as that bloodsucker, Quill!"

"If you attack him, it will be the same as attacking me and all that I hold dear. I swear you will live to regret it." Reaching up, she tapped her forefinger to the medallion at his throat. "Without me, you are not as powerful as you believe, Paul 9. I suggest you remember that!"

Chapter 39

Callie spent the next couple of days shopping for her trousseau. She bought everything she thought she might need—dresses for casual outings or a night of dining and dancing, jeans and T-shirts, a couple of warm sweaters. And shoes for every occasion. She also purchased three new sexy nightgowns, as well as several sets of lacy underwear in black, white, and hot pink.

On one of those days, she met Vivian at the bridal shop. Vivian had finally found a dress she liked and wanted Callie's opinion before she bought it.

Callie looked up as her friend stepped out of the changing room.

"What do you think?" Viv asked, twirling around.

"It looks great on you. I love the color." The tea-length dress was pale mauve with a square neckline, short sleeves, and a full skirt.

Smiling, Viv went to change her clothes. After she paid the bill, they went to Tony's for lunch, where they ordered their usual, a large ham and pineapple pizza, salad, and sodas.

"So," Viv said, "how many people are coming to the wedding?"

"Not many," Callie said. "I mean, it's going to be a very small, intimate ceremony. You probably shouldn't haven't spent so much money on a new dress."

"That's okay. I'll be able to wear it again. My cousin's getting married in a couple of weeks. This will be perfect for that. So, who's coming to the wedding?"

"Just you and my grandmother. Oh, and Quill's parents."

"Your grandmother!" Vivian exclaimed. "Isn't she . . . I mean, I thought she passed away a couple of years ago."

"Oh. That was . . . um . . . my other grandmother," Callie said, and quickly changed the subject.

That night, Callie sat on the sofa with Quill while he studied the list of possible honeymoon spots she had come up with.

"Paris. Bali. The Bahamas. Cabo San Lucas. Scotland. Aruba. Thailand. Greece." He whistled softly. "All great places, love."

"I suppose you've been everywhere in the world."

He lifted one shoulder and let it fall. "Not everywhere, but I have done a lot of traveling in my time."

"Is there any place you *haven't* been?"

"A few."

"Name one."

He looked thoughtful a moment, then said, "I never made it to the Maldives."

"Why didn't you go there?"

"Maybe I was waiting until we could go together."

"That's a very romantic thing to say but not very believable. I did see some pictures of it online. It looked beautiful as I recall. I don't know why I didn't write it down." She quickly looked it up on her phone. "Let's see, it says they have white sandy beaches and scuba diving at night. . . ." She glanced at Quill and grinned. "Must be a vampire special."

"Very funny."

"Oh! And an underwater nightclub. How cool would that be!"

"Sounds like we're headed for the Maldives. Should I make reservations?"

"Yes!" Callie said enthusiastically. "Yes, yes, yes!"

Catching her around the waist, Quill drew her closer. "Wherever we go, love, you'll be lucky to get out of bed."

Callie laughed softly. "Is that a threat or a promise, sir?"

"Definitely a promise, madam."

"Quill? What if your parents don't like me?"

"Why wouldn't they? You're pretty and smart, you have nice table manners, you don't gulp your wine. . . ." He grunted when she punched him on the arm. "Ouch! What was that for?"

"I'm being serious."

"So am I. They're going to love you, Callie, if for no other reason than because you've made their son so happy."

With a sigh, she rested her head on his shoulder. What would it be like to have two vampires under her roof? Quill's preternatural energy was a constant, palpable presence. Would his power, combined with that of his father, weigh her down—or worse, weaken her own?

Only time would tell.

* * *

Quill's parents arrived the night before the wedding. Callie was a nervous wreck as she took a last look in the mirror. Closing her eyes, she took several deep breaths, counted to ten, and went out to meet her future in-laws.

Quill's father stood when Callie entered the living room. She would have known without being told that they were related, they looked so much alike. The same dark brown hair, the same deep gray eyes.

"Callie, this is my father, Andras."

When Callie offered him her hand, Andras took it and bowed over it. "I am so pleased to meet you, daughter."

"And my mother, Mirella." His mother was lovely, with curly, russet-colored hair and mild blue eyes. Rising, she gave Callie a smile and a hug. "I'm so glad Quill has found you. I was beginning to think he would never marry. So, tell us," she said, resuming her seat on the sofa, "how did the two of you meet?"

Callie couldn't help feeling relieved when Quill's parents said good-night an hour later. As she'd feared, the combined preternatural strength of two powerful vampires had weighed heavily on her. She had the feeling Andras had suggested they leave early because he was aware of the strain on her.

Quill had invited his parents to stay at his lair. Ever polite, they waited on the porch, giving him a chance to say good-night to Callie in private.

"Do you think I'll ever get used to being surrounded by so much power?" Callie asked.

"In time."

"I hope you're right. I've never felt anything like that. It was like being smothered in blankets."

He laughed softly as he drew her into his arms. "I'd like to smother you with kisses."

Sighing dramatically, she said, "Have your way with me if you must. I'll try to endure it."

Growling low in his throat, he claimed her lips with his. "Get a good night's sleep, love," he said, nipping at her earlobe. "Because tomorrow night I'm going to make love to you until the sun comes up."

Back in his lair, Quill opened a bottle of vintage wine. After pouring drinks for his parents, he poured one for himself, then settled into the love seat across from the sofa. "So, what do you think of her?"

"You neglected to tell us she's a witch," his mother said.

Quill glanced at his father. It was well known that Andras had no love for witches. "You object?"

Andras shook his head. "It's only dark witches I despise. I detected nothing but goodness in your future mate. She seems strong mentally and physically. No doubt she will bear you a healthy son. You have my blessing."

"I found Callie thoroughly delightful," Mirella said. "I doubt any other mortal would have accepted you so readily. I believe the two of you are well-matched. You have my blessing, as well. And my love, as always."

Callie woke early after a restless night. Today was her wedding day! Excitement churned in her stomach, along with an unexpected rush of doubt. She was marrying into a vampire family. If she conceived, she would bear a vampire child.

Quill's child.

That thought chased all her doubts away. She loved him with her whole heart and soul. And tonight, she would be forever his.

She started to peek into the guest room, only then remembering that Quill had taken his parents to his lair to spend the night. She wondered if he would ever trust her enough to tell her where it was.

Too nervous to eat, she decided to go jogging in hopes of burning off her restless energy. She pulled on a pair of well-worn jeans and a sweatshirt, laced up her running shoes, and left the house.

She had gone less than a block when a large, black dog appeared beside her.

Callie slowed a moment, then grinned as she caught the signature of her grandmother's magic. She laughed as she picked up the pace again and jogged to the park. Twice around and she headed back home.

The dog followed her inside, then morphed into her grandmother.

"Why were you following me?" Callie asked. "You should be getting ready for tonight."

"Don't worry about me," Ava said with an airy wave. "I'll be there with bells on."

A shiver of unease slid down Callie's spine. "Is something wrong? No more secrets, Grandma. What's going on? Why were you working for the Dark Knights? And why didn't you tell us?"

"It's complicated, dear. When I married John, I promised him I would never betray him or the Knights or tell anyone of the location of the Dark Wood. I had worked magic for the Elder Knight before I met John, although John didn't know that. I changed my appearance whenever I went to the Dark Wood so that he wouldn't recognize me. I knew you would meet Quill and that there was a chance you would learn about the Knights, but I never dreamed your life would get so entangled with theirs. I was vain enough to think I could prevent that."

"So, what's going on now that has you so worried?"

"Maybe nothing." Ava sighed. "I met with the Elder Knight. I'm afraid he's still out for blood. Quill's blood."

"But . . . he gave his word."

"I'm afraid his oath to the Brotherhood means more to him than his word to Quill."

Brow furrowed, Callie dropped down on the sofa to untie her shoes. Why did she have to hear about this now, just when she thought all of their troubles were behind them, she mused ruefully as she peeled off her socks. Maybe with Quill she would never have a normal life. He was a vampire. Chances were there would always be someone hunting him.

Slapping her hands on her knees, she grinned at her grandmother. "Good thing he's got us to watch his back, isn't it?"

Ava's laughter filled the room. "Callie, dear, you never fail to amaze me! I'll see you at six."

Chapter 40

Callie was a nervous wreck when she arrived at the church. It was a magnificent old place, the walls made of ancient white stone. Light from within shone through the colorful stained-glass windows on either side of the heavy, oak double doors.

"Callie, I can feel you trembling," Ava said, walking up the steps beside her. "Have you changed your mind?"

"No. I just . . . it's nothing. A case of bridal jitters, I guess." She forced a smile. "You look beautiful." Ava wore a long gown of pale blue with a matching flower in her hair.

Vivian was waiting for them in the vestibule. "Oh, Callie, you look lovely!"

"Thanks. I don't think you ever met my grandmother. Ava, this is my best friend, Vivian."

"I'm so pleased to meet you," Viv said.

"And I, you," Ava replied with a smile.

Callie glanced inside the church. Quill's parents were sitting on the front row. The minister, clad in a long, black cassock, stood in front of the altar. Quill stood beside him, looking resplendent in a black Armani suit and tie.

Feeling her gaze, he looked up and winked at her, then signaled to the organist, who began to play the "Wedding March."

"Here we go," Ava said, patting Callie's arm.

Vivian preceded them down the aisle, her steps slow and measured.

When she reached the front, she turned.

"Now," Ava said.

Hand in hand, they walked toward the altar.

Callie's heart was beating a mile a minute when she reached the minister. Taking a calming breath, she handed her bouquet to Viv.

"Who giveth this woman to this man?"

"I do." Ava hugged Callie, then placed her hand in Quill's and took a step back.

The minister's gaze rested on Quill's face and then Callie's, his expression solemn. "We are gathered here this night to join this man and this woman in holy matrimony, which is an honorable estate instituted of God, and not to be entered into lightly. Do you, Quill Falconer, take Callie Hathaway, here present, to be your lawfully wedded wife, to cherish her in sickness and in health, for richer, for poorer, and give yourself only to her for as long as you both shall live?"

Looking deep into Callie's eyes, Quill said, "I do. With all my heart."

"And do you, Callie Hathaway, take Quill Falconer, here present, to be your lawfully wedded husband, to cherish him in sickness and in health, for richer, for poorer, and give yourself only to him for as long as you both shall live?"

Tears of joy welled in her eyes as she murmured, "I do. With all my love."

"Then, by the power vested in me, I now declare that you are husband and wife, legally and lawfully wed. Amen." With a faint smile, the minister said, "You may kiss the bride."

Quill lifted Callie's veil. For a moment, he stood just looking at her, as if he wanted to imprint the way she looked on this night of nights deep in his memory. And then he drew her gently into his arms and kissed her.

Callie leaned into him, her heart swelling with joy and peace and excitement. She was his now. And he was hers. Forever.

She smiled when he lifted his head, thinking that tonight she could kiss and caress him to her heart's content.

Stepping forward, Quill's father put his arm around Callie's shoulders. "Now you're really our daughter," he said. "And I couldn't be happier."

Callie nodded, too choked up to speak.

Quill's mother took both of Callie's hands in hers, then leaned forward and kissed her cheek. "If you ever need anything, you have only to call. I hope Quill makes you as happy as you've made him."

"Oh, he does!" Callie said, smiling through her tears. "He does!"

She had just looked over at Quill, who was speaking to the minister, when she glimpsed the stricken expression on Ava's face. Before she could voice her concern, a dozen armed Knights suddenly dropped their invisibility cloaks.

Quill let out a curse as five Knights wielding silver-bladed swords and daggers surrounded him. Alone, he would have vanished, but Callie was here and he wouldn't leave her.

He glanced around. Ava and Callie stood side by side, swords at their throats.

Vivian had fainted. The minister had ducked out a side door.

Four Knights surrounded his father; his mother was being held captive by another.

Quill met his father's gaze. They could have easily overpowered the Knights, but to do so might put his mother's and Callie's lives at risk. Better to let the stand-off be settled without violence, if possible.

He and his father exchanged knowing smiles as magic built in the air.

With a whispered word from Ava, all the Knights' medallions disintegrated. With their protection gone, Callie murmured a few words. One by one, the Knights dropped their weapons as her enchantment held them frozen in place.

Quill took a step toward his bride, only to let out a startled gasp of pain as the point of a sword sliced across his back. The silver burned into his flesh like acid.

With an incoherent cry of frustration, the Elder Knight dropped his cloak of invisibility. Raising his sword, he lunged at Quill as the vampire turned to face him.

Callie screamed as Quill darted to the side and the blade meant for his heart cut into his left side. The lunge left the Elder Knight off-balance. He let out a harsh cry of denial as Quill's hands curled around his throat.

One quick twist broke the Elder Knight's neck.

The other Knights stared helplessly at their fallen leader.

Callie had eyes only for her husband. Dark red blood poured from the wicked slash across his back, leaked from the wound in his side.

Quill tossed the body of the Elder Knight aside, then dropped to his knees, weakened by the cut inflicted by the silver blade.

With a cry, Callie ran toward him. Kneeling, she removed her veil and pushed her hair aside. "Drink, Quill. Now!"

When he shook his head, she slapped him. "I'm your wife and I'm telling you to drink!"

With a wry grin, he gathered her into his arms. "I guess the minister should have added 'obey' to our vows," he muttered.

"Just do it, my love."

Closing his eyes, he bit her ever so gently while his parents and Ava politely turned their backs.

After Callie released the Knights from her spell and sent them on their way, the wedding party tidied up the church then made a quick visit to Callie's house so Quill could change out of his torn and bloody suit. When that was done, they piled back into the limousine Quill's parents had rented for the ride to the hotel, where they had arranged for a lavish buffet in a private room, complete with a small wedding cake, a bottle of red wine, and iced champagne.

Vivian had recovered while still at the church. With Callie's reluctant approval, Quill had erased all memory of the Knights' attack from Viv's mind.

After dinner and toasts to the bride and groom, Vivian congratulated Quill, hugged Callie, wished them well, and took her leave.

"Well, thanks to some remarkable magic, I guess the Knights of the Dark Wood won't be bothering anyone anymore," Quill's father remarked. "At least not until they've initiated a new leader, which could take some time."

Quill, thoroughly recovered from his wounds, kissed his new bride. "Every vampire should have a witch or two in the family."

Andras nodded. "Good night, son."

Mirella hugged her son and then Callie. "Come visit us soon."

"We will," Callie promised. "Thank you both for everything." She watched her new in-laws leave the room hand in hand, thinking how lucky she was that they had so readily accepted her.

"Ready to go home?" Quill asked.

At her nod, he slipped one arm around her waist and the other around Ava's.

Moments later, they were in Callie's living room.

Yawning, Callie said, "It's been a long day. I'm going to get ready for bed."

"I'll be there in a minute," Quill said.

"Don't be long," she said with an impish grin. "Good night, Grandma."

"Good night, dear."

Quill waited until Callie left the room before saying, "What I don't understand, Ava, is why you didn't put an end to the Knights long ago."

She shrugged one shoulder. And then, between one breath and the next, she changed from a seventy-year-old woman into the beautiful, golden-haired girl he remembered. "I refrained from disbanding them because of a promise I made to John."

"So, you let the Knights slaughter my people because

of some promise made to a man who passed away decades ago?"

Eyes narrowed, Ava glared at him. "The Knights existed long before I was born. Who was I to judge them? When I was young, witches and vampires of whatever stripe were mortal enemies. At the time, I thought I was doing humanity a favor by ridding the world of your kind."

Quill grunted softly. "My people were never a threat to yours, whereas the Knights were."

"I know that now, but it wasn't until much later that I learned all vampires were not the same." She regarded him a moment, her eyes narrowed thoughtfully. "When I married John, I had to choose sides, and I chose his. When he passed away, I remained with the Brotherhood because it made me feel closer to him. I know now it was the wrong decision, but we can't undo the past. You, of all people, should know that."

Quill nodded. He had made more than a few mistakes in his long existence. Some he would regret as long as he lived. "Just one more thing," he said. "Why were you so nasty to me when you were Ebony?" He lifted a hand to the cheek she had scratched. "You knew Callie and I were fated to be together, but you were always hissing at me, or glaring at me."

Ava laughed. "You said it yourself. Vampires and cats don't mix. I needed you to hate me because I was afraid if I let you get too close, you'd know it was me. Even then, it didn't take you long to suspect the truth." She stretched her back and shoulders, then winked at him. "And maybe I was just a little a bit jealous." She grinned at his incredulous expression. "It's late," she said, "and your bride is waiting for you. Be good to her, Quill."

He lifted one brow at the thinly veiled threat in her words. "Thanks for your help tonight, Ava. I trust we won't see too much of you in the future."

"*Touché.* Good night, Quill."

He watched her glide toward the front door, slim hips swaying provocatively, and wondered how he had ever thought Callie was anything like her grandmother.

His bride was sitting up in bed, the covers on his side thrown back in silent invitation. He whistled softly when he saw her. She wore a black negligee that was little more than a whisper of translucent silk and lace. Her hair fell over her shoulders in long, golden waves. She had spritzed herself with perfume, but it was the enticing scent of the woman that teased his nostrils, arousing his thirst and his desire.

A million butterflies danced in Callie's stomach as she watched Quill remove his jacket, his shirt and tie, his belt. He sat on the bed to remove his shoes and socks, stood again to remove his trousers.

"Like what you see?" he asked.

She nodded, her mouth suddenly dry. They had made love once before, but she had never seen him like this, clad in nothing but a pair of black briefs, his gray eyes smoky, his desire for her blatantly evident.

He moved toward the bed, his movements as lithe as a panther stalking its prey. Callie licked her lips as he reached for her, his mouth hot as he rained kisses over the curve of her throat, her bare shoulders, her breasts. He stretched out on his side, drawing her body flush with his, kissing and caressing her all the while.

She whispered a word, and her nightgown and his briefs disappeared.

Quill chuckled deep in his throat. "Like I told my dad," he said, rising over her. "It's good to have a witch in the family."

Epilogue

Two years later

"Push, Callie."

Callie glared at her husband. "Easy . . . for you . . . to say," she panted. "You haven't . . . been in labor . . . for the last . . . five hours."

"Believe me, love, I'd trade places with you if I could. Wait a minute!" he said, rearing back when he saw the speculative gleam in her eyes. "I didn't mean it."

Grimacing, she said, "If I could change places with you right now, I would! Ow!" She clutched his hand as another contraction threatened to tear her in half.

"One more good push," the doctor said, "and you can hold your baby in your arms."

Clinging to Quill's hand, Callie screwed up her face and pushed.

A moment later, Quill watched his son slide into the world.

The doctor clamped the cord and gave the infant a gentle slap on the rump. And smiled when the boy let out a lusty wail of protest. As he handed the baby to the nurse, he glanced back at Callie, and frowned.

"What is it?" Quill asked, alarmed by the doctor's worried expression and the way Callie seemed to still be pushing. "What's wrong?"

With a shake of his head, the doctor did a quick examination and called for the nurse. "There's another one!"

"What?" Quill stared at the doctor. "How is that possible, what with ultrasounds and everything?"

But the doctor was too busy to answer, and Quill could only watch in amazement as Callie delivered a second child.

"This one's a girl," the doctor said, clamping the cord.

"What?" Quill stared at the infant and then at the doctor. "Are you sure?"

"I've been delivering babies for nigh onto thirty years," the doctor said, with a grin. "But if you don't believe me, see for yourself."

Quill shook his head as he stared at the tiny scrap of humanity in the doctor's arms. A girl. It was impossible. His kind only sired males. Yet the proof was right in front of his eyes.

"They're healthy?" Quill asked. "Both of them?"

"Amazingly so, for twins. Congratulations."

"Thanks, Doc."

Bending over the bed, Quill kissed Callie's cheek. "I love you more than my life," he whispered. "You've given me everything I ever wanted. And more."

"Ditto," she murmured just before her eyelids fluttered down and sleep carried her away.

Later, after the babies had been washed and weighed and wrapped in pink and blue blankets, Quill stood beside Callie's bed, one of her hands clasped in both of his.

"A daughter," Callie said, her voice filled with wonder. "How did we get a little girl? You said your kind could only produce male children."

"I don't know, love. I'm as shocked as you are."

"Will she become a vampire, too?"

"I have no idea, but I think not. I guess we'll just have to wait and see." He glanced over his shoulder as Ava and his parents entered the room, their faces wreathed in smiles as they congratulated Quill and hugged Callie.

Ava went straight to the plastic bassinettes that held the infants. Cooing softly, she picked up the baby girl.

Quill hadn't told his parents they had a granddaughter as well as a grandson because he'd wanted to see the looks on their faces when he told them the news.

They glanced at him now with mingled wonder and disbelief, then went to stand on either side of Callie's grandmother, who had resumed her elderly persona.

Quill's gaze narrowed as he looked at Ava. In her family, witchcraft passed only from grandmother to granddaughter. He didn't know how she'd done it, what magical spell she had concocted, but he would have bet every dollar he owned that Ava had found a way to ensure that Callie's magic would pass to their daughter.

Andras placed his fingertips on the tiny pink bundle in Ava's arms as if to prove to himself that the infant was real. "I don't believe it," he said. "A girl child."

"In thousands of years, it's never happened before," Mirella murmured.

Quill felt his heart swell with love for his son and daughter, and for the woman who had freely given him her love and her trust, chasing away centuries of loneliness.

"A girl." Mirella shook her head. "It's a miracle. May I hold her?"

Ava nodded. "Of course."

Mirella blinked back tears of joy as a tiny finger curled around her own. "We've never had a baby girl in the family. I have a feeling she's going to be spoiled rotten."

"I guess she really is a miracle," Quill murmured.

Looking up, he saw Ava watching him, a secret smile curving her lips.

"A miracle," Quill repeated as he bent down to kiss the mother of his son. And his daughter. Truly, she had given him more than he'd ever dreamed of.

*Please read on for a sneak preview
of a brand-new book in Amanda Ashley's bestselling
Children of the Night series.*

Night's Illusion

Prologue

Father Giovanni Lanzoni strolled through the city park's narrow, deserted, twisting paths. A brilliant yellow moon hung low in the sky, illuminating his way, though he needed no light to guide his feet. He was Nosferatu, one of the oldest of his kind. As such, he was blessed—or cursed—with supernatural senses and preternatural strength.

Like all vampires who had survived more than a century or two, he had grown to love and appreciate the beauty of the night. He enjoyed being able to see clearly in the dark, to hear the flutter of a moth's wings, to be able to move from place to place with astonishing speed, to think himself across great distances, to move faster than mortal eyes could follow, to dissolve into mist. So many amazing supernatural powers, all his to command.

He had never expected to survive so long. He had always been a pacifist—given to contemplation rather than conflict. As a child, he had dreamed of dedicating his life to the Church. It had proved to be all he had hoped for and more. He had loved the discipline, the interior silence, the sense of inner peace born of service and self-sacrifice. Hearing confessions. . .

He grinned inwardly. His most recent confession—heard only a few years ago—had come from Nick Desanto. Nick had been born a slave in Egypt and had been turned by the infamous Queen of the Vampires—Mara, herself.

Giovanni had known Mara for centuries. They had met when he was still mortal. He had been a young priest at the time, hoping to render aid and comfort on a battlefield in Tuscany. She had been in search of prey. The only thing that had saved him that night had been her surprising reluctance to harm a man of the cloth – or perhaps it had been some ancient superstition regarding priests.

They had met again when he was a young vampire in the streets of Paris. He had been badly injured and close to death when she found him. She had generously offered him a little of her ancient blood and it had revived him. And then, for reasons unknown, she had tasted his. They had both undergone some amazing changes since that long-ago night.

In the years since then, he had made a few friends and an enemy or two—both mortal and immortal—in countries around the globe. As a priest, he had willingly given up all thought of home and family. But now, having lived like a monk for so long, he thought he would gladly give up immortality to know the simple joys of one mortal lifetime. To experience a woman's love. To father a child. To watch his sons and daughters grow and have children of their own. What good was endless life when you had no one to share it with?

Leaving the park, he ambled down the street toward his lair.

The DeLongpre/Cordova coven was the closest thing

he had to a family. He considered himself blessed indeed to be a part of their lives and to have officiated at their weddings.

His steps slowed as he gazed at the vast expanse of the sky. Worlds without end, he mused. Times changed, the world itself changed, but he remained forever the same. In mortality, he had been an ordained priest. As such, he had made vows of chastity, poverty, and obedience. He had been celibate in mortality.

And in death.

Lately, he had begun to rethink his vow to remain chaste. Though he was, at least in his own eyes, still a priest, he was no longer recognized as such by the Church that doubtless thought him dead long ago. He had no parish, no superior. Why did he cling to a vow that, after so many centuries, was very likely no longer binding? He had broken the other ones long ago.

Why now, after so many centuries, did he suddenly feel so alone? So lonely?

He thought of Mara again. She had spent centuries refusing to be tied down. Yet, she had been married twice—once to a mortal, and now to Logan Blackwood, the man she had loved for centuries. She had been blessed with a son.

Others of his kind had found companions. Roshan DeLongpre. Vince Cordova and his twin sons, Rane and Rafe. Mara's son, Derek. Nick Desanto. Vampires one and all. Yet each had found love. Even feisty ex-vampire hunters Edna Mae Turner and Pearl Jackson—both turned far past their prime—had found life mates.

Why not him?

Perhaps it was time to remember that, in addition to being a priest, he was first and foremost a man.

Connect with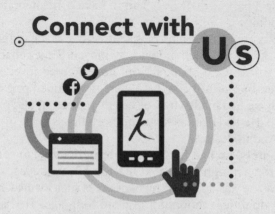